Steel
EVA SIMMONS

Copyright © 2024 by Eva Simmons

All rights reserved.

No portion of this book may be reproduced in any form without written permission from the publisher or author, except as permitted by U.S. copyright law.

No part of this book may be used to create, feed, or refine artificial intelligence models, for any purpose, without written permission from the author.

This novel is entirely a work of fiction. The names, characters and incidents portrayed in it are the work of the author's imagination. Any resemblance to actual persons, living or dead, events or localities is entirely coincidental.

Published by Eva Simmons

Editing by Kat Wyeth (Kat's Literary Services)

Proofreading by Vanessa Esquibel (Kat's Literary Services)

Model Cover Photography by Wander Aguiar

Model Cover Model: Clever

Alternate Cover Artwork by: Atik Sugiwara

Cover Design by Eva Simmons

Model Cover Paperback ISBN: 9798332353932

Alternate Cover Paperback ISBN: 9798332354175

Author's Note

This is a dark MC romance series with **graphic on page violence and explicit open-door scenes**. The characters in this series make morally gray decisions that are not always redeemable. Hard topics will be discussed that may be sensitive for some readers. Trigger warnings (which contain spoilers) can be found on my **website**. Please review before reading.

https://www.evasimmons.com/contentwarnings

For the families that find us and make our hearts whole.

1

Steel

There's nothing like Las Vegas in March.

It's warm without being blistering hot.

A gentle breeze grazes my neck as I ride, and the scent of hibernating sagebrush is thick in the air.

The sun dipped below the horizon over an hour ago, but the earth is still warm from the desert drinking up its rays all day. Heat rises from the pavement as stars become pinpricks of light in the darkness.

It's the perfect temperature to just ride and forget that all I'm doing is jumping from one problem to the next lately. I grip my handlebars and pretend tonight isn't just one more big fucking mess I'm scrambling to clean up.

Every time I think I finally have my club back on track, shit goes sideways.

Turf wars.

Traitors.

There's an endless list of reasons to never let my guard down, and tonight is just one more added onto it.

I should have been halfway down a bottle of whiskey by now. Instead, I'm drained, annoyed, and beaten up from fending off another territorial spat with the Iron Sinners.

Ever since Chaos was put behind bars, the Twisted Kings strip club, Sapphire Rise, has been a breeding ground for trouble. Strip clubs draw enough heat as it is, and without Chaos around to monitor the strippers and patrons on a regular basis, there are nothing but problems lately.

Kansas, the club manager, has only been able to do so much to keep it under control in Chaos's absence. Especially when he doesn't have the Twisted Kings logo on his back, and our rivals know it.

They're taking advantage of all our weak points, and after the upheaval within the Twisted Kings last year, we've got plenty. One wound heals, and we start bleeding from another.

A headache pulses between my temples as I ride.

I took a beer bottle to the head defending a stripper, and it's a reminder as to why I prefer Chaos dealing with Sapphire Rise. Doesn't matter if their tits are out; strippers cause nothing but problems when alcohol and rival clubs are involved.

I'm counting down the days until our club attorney can get Chaos out of prison, but until then, I'm going to have to assign someone besides a prospect to watch over this shit because I'm tired enough without adding the daily oversight of strippers to my list of responsibilities.

By the time I get back to the clubhouse, I'll need a nap or a blow job. Anything to take the edge off today. I'm only thirty years old, but every week feels like a year, and my regular outlets for stress aren't working.

There's no rest for a Twisted Kings president.

I didn't believe my dad when he used to preach that, but now I get it.

The weight.

The responsibility.

At least it's just me and the road for a few more miles.

My bike hums as it eats up the pavement. One mile after another of peace and quiet. In Nevada, the stretches of empty road are endless, and it's paradise for the mind.

The night air is crisp and warm as I ride with my brothers at my sides.

Soul, my VP, is to my right, and Havoc, my sergeant at arms, is to my left. They hung back with me to help clean up some of the mess the Iron Sinners left at the strip club. But now that we're done, we're heading home.

The vibration of our engines fills the desert as we make the ten-mile journey from the outskirts of Vegas to the Twisted Kings compound.

Ten miles of peace.

Ten miles of in-between.

Ten miles where it's just me, my bike, and an empty road.

But ten miles isn't nearly enough when the clubhouse finally comes into view, and it's lit with a party already in full swing.

The guys are celebrating our win tonight, as they should be. A few more Iron Sinners six feet under is always a good thing. They deserve a little downtime after the year we've had. I just wish I was in the mood to share in it.

But I can't shake my endless checklist of responsibilities.

Getting Chaos out of prison.

Repairing the strip club stage.

Doubling security around the perimeter of all our businesses.

It never ends.

Rolling to a stop in front of the clubhouse, I climb off my bike and stretch my legs. Music hammers through the walls—the bass practically shaking the desert. A few people scatter around the front.

Smoking.

Drinking.

Fucking.

At least they know how to take their minds off shit.

Legacy, my treasurer, makes his way down the steps when he spots me, brushing his sandy-blond hair off his forehead. "Hey, Prez. We all good?"

"For now." I pop my knuckles. "I need you to go to the strip club tomorrow and let me know how much the damage is gonna cost us."

If tits and ass didn't bring in so much fucking money, I'd burn the place to the ground myself. But at least the repairs will eventually pay for themselves in lap dances.

"You got it." Legacy nods. "If that's all, I'm gonna hit the sack. But call me if shit pops off again."

I nod, and Legacy heads for his bike, climbing on and taking off down the road that leads to the neighborhood. Most of the guys crash at the clubhouse, but since Legacy has a kid, he spends most of his downtime at his house at the edge of the property.

Families and the club don't mix. It splits your time. Splits your focus. Legacy manages to balance it, but as I watch him ride off, I can't help but wonder when it's going to be a problem. Kids bring nothing but trouble when you're a Twisted King.

Not that Legacy had a choice when one of the patch bunnies dropped Bea off on his doorstep and bailed.

Still, watching him go is a reminder of why I'll never follow in those footsteps.

My club is my life. My brothers are my family. They're all that matters.

Loyalty.

Besides, who needs an old lady when there are patch bunnies hanging from the fucking rafters happy to help me fill the void.

Soul stops at my side, watching Legacy ride off, probably thinking the same thing I am. He's even more vocal about his pledge to lifelong bachelorhood. As bad as my reputation is with women, it's nothing compared to Soul's prolific history of one-night stands.

"He's not even gonna enjoy the fucking party?" Soul watches Legacy's bike disappear. "If anyone could use a lay, it's him."

I look over at Soul. His eye is almost swollen shut from where a Sinner slammed his face into a stripper pole.

"You should have Patch take a look at that."

"It's nothin'." Soul grins. "Besides, black eyes are pussy magnets."

"And what if your vision's too fucked to stare at their tits?" I challenge.

"Who needs to see shit so long as they'll get on their knees to take my pain away?"

"You're a fucking idiot."

Soul shrugs.

He's a compulsive gambler who's reckless with women, so he's not easily offended. He's known for his antics, to the point where some of the guys questioned me putting his name in for VP when my last one stabbed me in the back. But so long as Soul's wild side doesn't impact the club, Soul is Soul. He'd lay down his life for his brothers, and he's sacrificed more for the club than most realize.

When my last VP, Helix, betrayed us, it revealed rot in every corner. We lost half the guys I thought we could trust, and Soul's father was one of them. Soul chose between two families in that battle, and he spilled the blood that earned him his vice president patch.

So if he wants to enjoy the perks, who am I to judge? We all have our vices.

Havoc stops at Soul's side and tips his chin up at the clubhouse. "Let's get fucking wasted."

"Don't have to ask me twice," Soul says, and they make their way up the steps. "You coming, Prez?"

"Yeah."

I'd like to shower and then sleep for a week, but I'll settle for a nice buzz first.

Besides, if my men are celebrating, I need to be there to put on a strong front. Especially after tonight's turf war. They need to see me still standing, unaffected and ready to lead them when this battle inevitably escalates.

The Iron Sinners are getting bolder, and it's only a matter of time before we go to war. As satisfying as that will be, it's also expensive. And the club is still recovering from the internal one we just ended.

I walk into the clubhouse and am met with madness. The building is massive, but most people are in the bar on the left, partying. A few are in a small den on the right, shooting darts and fucking around. Anything beyond that is off-limits to anyone who isn't patched, so it's empty.

Making my way to the bar, I take a seat and look around.

Prospects push through the room, doing anything and everything my brothers ask of them. I watch them fetch drinks and clean up vomit, wondering how many of them are going to pass the vote in a few weeks when the current selection isn't as good as the last.

I need to figure out a way to test them beforehand. I need to know who's really in this for the right reasons and who is here for guns, drugs, and pussy.

I get it; the club offers certain freedoms. But that's not why we're really here, and they need to understand that.

"Drink, darlin'?" Reina stops in front of me on the other side of the bar, tucking her bleach-blonde hair behind her ear.

She leans forward, and her arms push her tits up. I'm tempted to lay her out and fuck them. But she's been getting it in her head that I'm going to make her my old lady, and that shit's not happening. Which is why I had to cut her off a few months ago and haven't gone back since.

"Woodfords."

"Coming right up." She smiles, spinning around to grab the bottle.

Her ass is hanging out of her shorts, and she sticks it out when she reaches for the top shelf to make sure I notice.

"Something on your mind, Steel?" She turns back around with my drink in her hand. "You look a little stressed."

"Nothing more than usual." I drain the glass the second she hands it to me, sliding it back across the bar top for her to pour another.

"Well, if you need help taking your mind off things..." Reina slowly fills the shot glass again before sliding it my way.

"Thanks, but I'm good, sweetheart."

I steal the drink from her hand and spin around before she starts thinking she's my girl. This is why I don't like fucking the same women too often.

The only thing I belong to is the club.

If they want a property patch, they need to find another brother to give it to them.

Scanning the room, I watch a few of the guys playing pool. They're drawing the attention of a group of townies who are hanging out in a corner. It's not unusual for bachelorette parties and groups of girls from out of town to come to our clubhouse in search of a *what happens in Vegas, stays in Vegas* high.

They want a story to tell when they go back home, or they want to test their limits with a biker for the night. They learn quickly that it's fun for an evening, but it's better not to stick around.

At least they offer pretty new faces to look at when Reina's behind the bar plotting how to poke holes in my condoms to have my babies.

Next to the townies, a few of the old timers' old ladies are hanging out by a dart board. They'll bail before shit goes off the rails like it usually does, and that's for the best. Why any of the guys want families or relationships is confusing as fuck, when all it seems to do is stress them out.

It's why I'm content searching the room for less permanent options.

At the back of the bar, a figure catches my attention as she moves through the crowd. She's tiny, slipping around a group of guys as she makes her way across the room. All I see is the top of her sun-streaked honey-brown hair over their shoulders as she weaves through.

When she reaches the bar, she stops beside Havoc and Soul, who notice her immediately. And something about how they both look her over has me gripping my glass.

There's nothing particularly special about her. She isn't dressed up like most of the girls in here, and she's clearly not trying to show off. Her jeans are faded, and her long-sleeved green shirt leaves everything to the imagination. Her hair is down, and she's cried off any makeup she might have been wearing today.

Fuck.

It's a red flag if I've ever seen one.

Just what I need: some girl with a broken heart looking to start trouble with whichever one of my guys fucked her over. If she makes a scene, I'm going to be fucking pissed. I've already had enough drama for one night.

The girl leans against the bar, trying to get Reina's attention, but she'll be waiting for a while. Reina would rather serve anyone with a cock.

It doesn't seem to bother her. She waits patiently, tapping the bar and looking around the room. She's never been here before, I'm sure of it, and from how she scans the crowd, I can't tell who of my guys she's looking for.

Her hazel eyes flit with something edging on indifference as she assesses the scene, and when her gaze pauses on me, her chest expands with the prettiest sharp inhale.

I hold her stare just to see how long it'll take until she gets intimidated. I'm too damn curious about what brings a girl like her to my club. Or better yet—*who*.

When I don't look away, I expect her to break my gaze in embarrassment. Instead, she stares back, ticking an eyebrow up, which highlights a scar that cuts through it. She's no shrinking violet, and I'd be impressed if I didn't sense she's nothing but trouble.

Reina finally reaches the girl, leaning against the bar to say something. Her gaze flits from the girl to me, and a venomous smile climbs the corner of her mouth. They talk briefly before the girl disappears around the corner, and once she's gone, Reina purses her lips in triumph, pulling her blonde hair up into a ponytail.

I thought cutting Reina off would stop the territorial bullshit, but clearly, that's not the case. I told her from the beginning that I wasn't looking for an old lady to ride on the back of my bike, but she took that as a challenge.

I've heard the rumors from the guys. The patch bunnies are all betting on who will be the girl to tie down Jameson Steel.

Good fucking luck.

They don't realize what it really means to be the old lady of a Twisted Kings president. It's not as glamorous as it sounds.

I've seen the proof in other chapters. Their women get lonely and jealous. Or worse, they end up dead.

It's rare for a guy in this life to get a woman to stick around long-term, and even if they do, they're usually not happy about it.

Reina smiles at me before turning her attention to someone ordering a drink.

"Reina causing trouble?" Ghost slides onto the stool beside me.

His eyes are on his phone as usual, but it doesn't mean he doesn't see everything happening around him.

Ghost is somehow everywhere and nowhere. And even when he's physically here, he's never actually *here* at all. He hides behind his electronics and surveillance whenever he can, making him perfect as the club's resident tech genius and hacker, but his people skills are lacking.

He cracks his neck, not taking his eyes off his phone. A couple of townies at the bar stare at him like he's seconds away from killing everyone, and it's not an unusual reaction to him.

Ghost's neck-to-knuckle tattoos and generally cold demeanor make people assume he's more of an asshole than he actually is. In reality, of all my guys, Ghost is the least likely to snap and kill someone pissing him off. Not that he doesn't have other ways to make them hurt.

"Reina's fine for now." I take a sip of my drink. "But give her time."

Ghost hums, still not looking at me or caring.

"I pulled up the footage from tonight. It looks like the Sinners we took down inside weren't the only ones there." He flips his phone around to show me a video of two guys circling through the alleyway on their bikes. "These two went around back before I lost them in a blind spot. The cameras around that side of the building aren't working."

"We need to fix that."

"Already on it." Ghost sets his phone on his lap. "I've got Boone replacing them tomorrow."

"What do you think they were after?"

"Hard to say; the only access point from that part of the alley is a window that leads to the office. It doesn't look like they got in, but they tried."

"You think the fight was just a distraction?"

Ghost nods, his dark hair falling just above his pale-blue eyes. "It would make sense. Iron Sinners are reckless, but they're not dumb enough to show up on

Twisted Kings turf to pick a random fight in our strip club without a reason."

"I don't get it." I shake my head. "Sapphire Rise is one of our more legitimate businesses. Don't know what the fuck they're expecting to find. Or better yet, why they'd care."

The Sinners don't put efforts into legal pussy, given they have no problem exploiting cheaper methods to please men, like trafficking women.

My guys have managed to shut down a few of their operations in the city, but I'm well aware our work isn't done yet.

"Wonderful." I groan. Just when I think one problem is solved, I'm faced with another. "Look into it and keep me updated."

Ghost's phone lights up, and when he looks down at it, his expression changes.

"What is it?"

"We've got another problem." He holds his phone up again to show me a video on the screen, but this time it's a view of inside the clubhouse.

A figure moves down the hallway that leads to our rooms, and when she glances over her shoulder to see if anyone is following her, I get a good look at who she is.

"Looks like someone's lost." Ghost smirks.

I shake my head. "Or looking for something she shouldn't."

Trouble.

I fucking knew it.

2

Tempe

Booze. Drugs. Women.

Every time I say I'm going to get my life together, I find myself in places like this and am reminded what an uphill battle that is.

The Twisted Kings clubhouse reminds me of the bar I work at. Replace drunk frat boys with rowdy bikers, and I might as well be standing inside Dirty Drakes. Except, the Twisted Kings have more of a reputation, so I'm not dumb enough to think they're one and the same.

Motorcycle clubs aren't fun and sexy like they are in books and movies, and the Twisted Kings are the worst of them. They're known throughout Vegas for their ruthlessness. They're unapologetic. Violent. Taking what they want while they battle it out with rival clubs and casino heirs.

Tourists don't see the war zone through their drunken haze, but I live here. I've seen what these men do—what they're capable of.

Up close.

After all, I'm the product of one of them.

Walking through the clubhouse, I'm reminded of everything I hate about bikers. Their arrogance and egos.

Tonight, there's a party raging, and from what I've overheard, they're celebrating a win against a rival club. The guys are getting wasted and taking shots off strippers while a group of girls that might be a bachelorette party huddles in the corner watching the scene unfold.

At least with this much chaos, it's easy to blend in.

I don't want attention.

Get in and get out.

If I'm lucky, it'll be that simple. Although, I know better than to think anything is.

Slipping through the crowd, I make my way toward the bar. The clubhouse is massive, so it hasn't been as easy to find the bathroom as I expected. The building is the size of a warehouse, sitting in the middle of a wide-open compound, and I was lost on my first step inside.

When I reach the bar, I lean against it, waving for the blonde serving someone a drink at the other end. She glances at me long enough that I know she's seen me, but she doesn't seem in a rush to help, so I lean back and look around the room while I wait.

The air is thick and hazy. Every inhale floods my lungs with cigarette smoke and the scent of leather. It rattles around memories of my mom's many boyfriends. Bad boys with pretty faces and broken hearts in the treads of their tires.

Two men are standing at the bar beside me, and from their cuts, they're clearly ranking members of the club. I don't miss their eyes scanning over me, but thankfully, they don't say anything.

My skin itches just being in this place. Nothing but problems follow the Twisted Kings.

Scoping the room, I take it all in, trying to bury my nerves and forget why I'm here in the first place. If I think too much about it, I won't be able to get this done. And that's not an option.

Glancing down the bar, I catch gazes with a man at the opposite end. He's a biker, as evidenced by his leather cut, but there's something different about him. He's not partying like the rest, choosing instead to sit with a drink in hand while watching everyone.

He's confident, not breaking my gaze when I've spent too long staring.

His dark hair is messy on his head, and everything about him screams danger. From the wicked gleam in his eyes to the rough stubble on his face. He's a walking warning sign.

Too good-looking.

Too much blood on his hands.

The man dwarfs the stool he's sitting on, so it's clear he's tall. But even with his broad shoulders, his lean waist makes it clear he's solid muscle.

He doesn't take his eyes off me as he brings his drink to his lips for a sip. The tattoo that stretches his arm winds up over the back of his hand, and I can't help wondering how far his ink goes.

I don't have to know anything about him for his demeanor to tell me everything.

This man is lethal.

And if I'm smart, not worth my time.

"Don't bother, honey." A woman with bright-blonde hair plants her hands on the other side of the bar, pulling my attention.

I glance over, and her cat eyes narrow. She's smiling, but there's nothing friendly about it.

"Don't bother with what?"

"Him." She tilts her head to the left, not taking her gaze off me. "He's taken."

"Don't worry." I breathe out a laugh. "Not interested."

I get the appeal of a man like him—like most of the guys in this room. They're attractive, strong, probably well-versed in the bedroom. But I'm not my parents. I have goals. Dreams. And the second I get out of this mess, I'll never be back here again.

"Whatever you say." The blonde hums, skimming me over. "Can I get you something?"

"The bathroom?" I force a smile, pretending I'm not noticing her territorial irritation.

"Around the corner." She ticks her head to the side. "First door on the right."

"Thanks."

I disappear into the crowd and head toward the hallway behind the bar, pretending to look for the bathroom.

Pulling out my phone, I check the time, and my hands are shaking. I've been gone for a little over an hour, which means I only have one more before things go sideways. All I can do now is hope they keep their word if I get them what they're looking for.

I lock my phone screen and spot a speck of blood on my hand. My fingers shake as I wipe it away, and my eyes burn from the tears I've been holding back.

Don't think about it.

You can do this.

For him, you'll keep it together.

I pass the bathroom and continue down the dim hallway, trying to remember the directions the men gave me. My head is in a fog, and even completely sober, I can barely see straight.

Around the bar.

Past the bathrooms.

Last door on the left.

Was it the left, or was it the right?

I'm pretty sure they said left, so I pause with my hand on the handle.

So long as no one is in here, I'll be fine. The party is enough of a distraction to prevent anyone from noticing. All I have to do is find one little thing. Something they don't even know is there. No one will miss it.

The floor creaks behind me, and I glance over my shoulder, breathing out a sigh of relief to find the hallway still empty.

Get in and get out.

I need to stop wasting time.

Pushing the door open, I'm met with a dark room, and I'm relieved to find it empty.

The curtains are wide open, letting in the moonlight, so there's enough to see around without having to flip on the light switch and risk drawing more attention to myself. Slipping inside, I shut the door behind me.

It's neater than I expected. Besides the unmade bed and a small pile of clothes on the floor, everything seems in its place.

Hanging on the wall behind the bed is a large iron work of art with the Twisted Kings logo branded into it. The dark eyes of the skull watch me as I step deeper into the room.

There's a pack of cigarettes on the dresser and some change sitting beside it. Everything seems too fresh and recently touched. Nothing about this room feels like my father could have once lived here, but there's only one way to find out.

I hurry over to the door that leads to the bathroom and crouch down, feeling for any give in the panel beside the doorframe. They said that all I have to do is push it once to release the latch, and then it will open to reveal my dad's secret hiding place.

I push once. Twice. Nothing moves.

Shit.

I must be in the wrong room.

My hair shifts with a faint breeze, and my skin prickles as the door to the room swings open.

"What do we have here?"

I jump, spinning around as a man closes in on me.

He's too fast, and it's too dark to get a good look at him as my instincts kick into gear. Between six months of self-defense classes and a year working behind a bar, I know how to handle myself. And the same reflexes that help me fend off drunks and perverts serve me well now.

The man reaches for me, and I duck, barely slipping away. I kick him in the shin and then crouch down to avoid his other hand.

"Fuck," he grunts, coming for me again.

I manage to land one more jab to his side before he catches my wrist, stopping the punch I was about to land on his jaw.

In one swift move, he twists my arm, spinning me around so I'm pinned with my chest to the wall and my arm behind my back.

Using the heel of my boot, I try to kick him in the shins again, but it only makes him twist my arm so hard that my shoulder aches. His body presses flush with mine, and I feel every heavy breath from our struggle.

"Let me go."

I try to kick him again, but he widens his stance so I can't.

A chuckle comes from my left, and I turn to see a man standing to the side, watching us. His dark hair falls over his eyes, which are focused on his phone, and his tattoos peek from his hands to his neck.

"Feisty one, Prez." The man smirks.

Prez.

Of all the men in the club I could have run into tonight, I caught the attention of Steel, my father's former president.

I stop struggling because there's no use. If there's two of them in sight, there's probably more on the way.

"You done?" Steel asks, loosening his grip on my arm.

I nod, and he takes a step back, releasing me.

My shoulder aches as I spin around, but he hasn't backed up, so I'm still cornered against the wall.

Craning my neck back, I look up at him.

Steel.

It's a fitting name for a man as cold as his arctic gaze. Stubborn and unmoving as he stands in front of me.

A man whose reputation precedes him.

I wasn't close with my father and didn't spend time at the clubhouse, so I've never met Steel face-to-face. But one look in his eyes and I'm sure he's everything I've heard about him and more. Violent, dangerous, unyielding.

And now that I'm getting a closer look, I see he's the man who was sitting across the bar staring at me.

Except now, there's nothing friendly in his lethal gaze. Any confident flirtation he might have flashed earlier is stripped away. He's strictly business, staring me down, smelling like leather and cinnamon. A blend of scents that I shouldn't like as much as I do.

This close, I get a better look at his square jaw and chiseled features. I get a hit of his body heat closing in around me.

I'm screwed.

"What do you think you're doing in here?" Steel crosses his arms over his chest, not backing up.

I stand up straighter and lift my chin. If he thinks he can scare me, he has another thing coming.

"Looking for the bathroom."

His eyes narrow as he looks me up and down with complete disinterest. I'm not surprised when I'm not much to look at compared to the impressive horde of beautiful women he just left at the bar.

"The bathroom?" He hitches an eyebrow.

"Yes."

Steel plants one hand on the wall behind my head, and his gaze moves to my mouth when I wet my lips.

"Nice try, wildfire. But you see this patch?" He plants his hand over the word "president" stitched on his chest.

I nod, swallowing hard, trying not to breathe in his intoxicating cinnamon scent.

"They call me that for a reason." He reaches up to lift my chin, forcing my gaze on his ocean-gray eyes—the color of the sea at dusk. "Now tell me, what is it you're doing in my club?"

3

Tempe

If my father taught me anything from the few times he came around growing up, it's never to let anyone see your weaknesses—physically or mentally. Staying alert and sharp is the only way to survive in a world where everyone looks out for themselves. And even when an opponent is stronger or in a better position, there's always a way to use it against them to gain the upper hand if you take the time to look for it.

While my father wasn't good for much more than half my DNA, that sentiment settles in this moment.

He was one of them.

A *Twisted King.*

I roll my shoulders back and take the only advice he was good for. I straighten my spine and dust it off, refusing to let Steel sense weakness.

"Are you just going to stand there and stare at me?"

"Yes," he answers without a pause.

Given his position in the club, I doubt he's easily rattled. He's probably rarely challenged. So I'm not surprised he doesn't flinch at my annoyance. I'm probably the least threatening person he's been faced with.

"Hey, Steel." A man walks into the room, glancing between us, and I recognize him as one of the two men who were standing at the bar earlier. "Ghost texted me to say we've got trouble."

The man looks at the one standing beside Steel, who is still typing into his phone, and I assume that must mean he's Ghost.

Eerie name, but strangely fitting.

Ghost doesn't look up from his phone as he types away. He might not seem interested in the standoff between me and his president, but something about him tells me he's still seeing everything.

"Trouble," Steel repeats, not breaking our staring contest, while the intensity of his gaze has the hair on the back of my neck standing on its ends. "That depends."

"On what?"

"Why she's here." Steel lifts off the wall, popping his knuckles and staring down at me.

I narrow my eyes. "If you must know—"

"That's why I asked," he cuts me off.

Impatient asshole.

My fingers clench as I try to keep an even tone. "I'm here to get something."

I'm trying my hardest not to snap. Just because I'm putting up a strong front doesn't mean I want to piss him off. The Twisted Kings aren't known for mercy, and if I don't tread carefully, I'll be carried out of here in a body bag.

"What would that *something* be?" Steel asks, refusing to step back.

I can barely think with him cornering me against the wall.

Much less breathe.

"That's none of your business." I grit my teeth.

"See, that's where you're wrong, wildfire." He ticks his head to the side to assess me. "Anything that happens on *my property* is my business. Don't like it? Then you shouldn't have come here in the first place."

I curl my fingers into fists. My nails dig into my palms, and I bite back a groan as they nearly cut into my skin. Getting angry won't do me any good, no matter how much of a jerk Steel is.

"I can't tell you what it is. It's personal."

"Personal?" Steel huffs with an unamused chuckle. "So is you standing in the middle of my bedroom. I think we've already crossed that line."

"*Your* bedroom?"

He nods, and I glance around again.

Nothing about this room seems fitting for the club president, even with the club brand hanging above the bed. The room is large but mostly empty. There's nothing unique or telling of the man standing in front of me. Nothing personal to hint at who he is.

Once more, I turn to face him. "I'm in the wrong room."

"Clearly." Steel's jaw ticks. "Question is, *who's* room is the right one?"

I close my eyes and exhale.

I can't trust Steel when I don't know what he'll do after he gets the information he's after. But if I keep my mouth shut, this might just get worse. And right now, I can't decide who's more dangerous, the men who sent me here or the one in front of me. All I know is that I'm at Steel's mercy, whether I like it or not, so I have to give him something—anything—if I want to see the other side of this.

Opening my eyes, I take a deep breath and choose my words carefully. "I'm here to get something of my father's."

Steel's eyebrows knit in a silent question.

"Helix," I clarify.

Any hint of kindness wipes from Steel's expression at the mention of Helix's name, and Ghost's attention snaps to me.

A chill runs through the room, but I don't know why.

I didn't speak to my father for a couple of years before he died, but he was the Twisted Kings VP at the time, so I expected his name to soften the blow of me sneaking around the clubhouse. But with the sudden change in energy, I sense I was wrong about that.

"You're Helix's kid?" Steel's expression hardens.

"I'm twenty-two. Not a kid." Not that it matters.

Steel's jaw clicks with his annoyance. "You're Tempe?"

He knows my name, and I can't tell if it's a good or bad thing.

I nod slowly, trying to ignore the tension crackling in the air.

"What the fuck?" Steel glances over at Ghost. "I thought she checked out?"

"She did." Ghost tucks his phone away, crossing his arms over his chest. "Helix hadn't been in contact with her for a couple of years. I couldn't find any ties, so I crossed her off the list."

"Why were you looking for ties?" I hate that they're talking about me like I'm not standing in the room with them, especially when I don't like the sound of whatever they're saying.

Steel's attention snaps to me at my question, and his gaze lands like a cement wrecking ball in the chest. "You have some nerve; I'll give you that. Walking into *my* club, thinking you have the right to ask me questions when you're the daughter of a traitor."

I swallow hard.

A *traitor*?

The change in energy makes sense as that word sinks in. My father betrayed them, and I walked in here with a target on my back, not even knowing it.

"I wasn't close with him," I try to explain. "My mom raised me. We didn't even talk until he came to find me a couple of years ago. And even then, I told him I didn't want anything to do with him or his club."

"Your presence here says otherwise."

I understand why he'd think that, but he's wrong.

"I'm not here because of him."

"You said you were looking for his room."

"To get something of his, that's it."

Steel clicks his tongue on the roof of his mouth, looking me over. "And what would that be?"

"I don't know."

He chuckles again, but there's no hint of amusement on his face. "You *don't know*?"

"They didn't tell me."

"And who are *they*?"

"I—" I drag my fingers through my hair, pulling it off my face and knowing my answer isn't going to make things any better. "I don't know that either."

"Havoc." Steel glances at the man from the bar. "Get her phone."

Havoc steps toward me, and I shift back against the wall. I'm cornered, so I pull my phone from my pocket before he has the chance to search me. The last thing I want is his hands all over me when there's nothing on my phone that I'm trying to hide.

"Here, take it." I hand it over. "There's nothing on there. I already told you I don't know who sent me here."

"You don't seem to know much for a girl who stepped into a shitload of trouble," Steel says while Havoc holds my phone up to my face to unlock it. "Why are you really here, Tempe?"

"I told you I don't—"

"Stop." Steel's voice makes me jump. He shifts forward, planting his hand on the wall. "Lie to me again, and you're not going to like the outcome. Now answer my fucking question."

I close my eyes and take a deep breath, trying to ignore Steel towering over me. Trying not to breathe him in.

I'm out of air.

Out of time.

Blinking my eyes open, I lock onto his gaze and find no empathy.

I don't blame him. My father was a horrible person, and if he was half as bad to his club as he was to his family, I understand why Steel can barely look me in the eyes.

"There's this guy who came into my work a few months ago." I steady my breath and try to level my tone. "At first, I didn't think much of it. Dirty Drakes isn't the nicest place. We get a lot of drifters, people passing through, college students. He was friendly at first... and then, a little too much."

Bile rises in my throat thinking about how handsy he was, and Steel's throat bobs with his swallow at my comment.

"He started coming in more frequently this past week. And that's when he asked about my dad. I told him I hadn't seen him for a couple of years before he died, but the guy didn't seem convinced. Then tonight, he showed up at my house with a few other men. They sent me here."

"How did they know where you live?" Steel's jaw clenches.

"I don't know. When they knocked on the door, I figured it was my mom's boyfriend, but it wasn't."

"Why you?"

"I don't know." I shake my head. "And I know you don't like that answer, but it's the truth. All he said was I'd fit right into the party, so it would be no big deal."

Steel glances at Ghost. "If he knew about the party tonight, he's keeping close tabs."

Ghost nods, and Steel looks back at me.

"What else?"

"He told me how to get in and where to go. He said he needed me to get something from my dad's room and that it was hidden in a panel in the wall by the bathroom. A secret compartment that I just had to push once to release the lock. But he didn't tell me what was in there. He wasn't exactly forthcoming with information."

"And you just went along with it?"

"Yeah." I take a deep breath, my throat burning with my reason. "After they shot my mom, I figured they weren't bullshitting."

I dip my chin and pick at my sleeve, finding another speck of blood staining the green cotton. My throat clogs, and my eyes burn as I fight back tears. I can barely remember what happened. It was all so fast.

The pounding at the door.

The scream.

The blood.

When I look up, I see Steel staring at the proof of my story, not that he seems to care when he looks back up at me.

"Havoc, go check Helix's room for the compartment."

"Got it, Prez." Havoc walks out of the room.

Steel lifts off the wall and finally steps back, making some distance between us. "Ghost, put her in a room until I figure out who the fuck sent her here, then meet Soul—"

"A room? Wait." My hands are shaking. Panic swells in my chest. "I told you everything. You can't keep me here. That's all I know."

"And you expect me to just accept you at your word? You're not going anywhere until I figure out what the fuck is going on."

Steel turns to walk away, and I jump forward and grab his arm, realizing my mistake when he freezes and looks down at me with a glare so cold it has me stepping back.

"Wait. Please." I brush my hands over my arms. "You don't understand. I have to go back. If I don't... they'll... shit."

I clutch my stomach and sink against the wall. The room is spinning, and my heart hammers in my chest. My throat burns, and my eyes are on fire as the tears start falling and bile rises in my throat.

Showing weakness is dangerous, but I can't help it. The walls are closing in, and my insides might as well be splitting open. I wipe the rivers from my cheeks, but the tears won't stop falling.

Steel steps in front of me, tipping my chin up. "Tempe, finish that sentence. They'll what?"

I blink up at him, hating that he's seeing me like this. But I'm out of options, and even if it turns out Steel is the worse of two evils, if I say nothing, he'll keep me here, and that can't happen.

"Please." It's nearly a whisper as I beg mercy from a man who is better known for inflicting punishment. "Do what you have to do to me. But I'm all Austin has now. Please don't let them kill my brother."

4

Steel

"What do you think?" Ghost leans against the wall opposite me in the hallway. "Can we trust anything she's saying?"

"Shouldn't I be asking you that question? You're the one who vetted her and everyone else in Helix's life after shit went down."

My nerves grate at the reminder of my former vice president's betrayal. He thought he was owed something when none of us are. Tried to take out his own club to advance his interests and strip me of my position. He was a liar and a snake. And now his daughter is sneaking into my clubhouse, trying to steal from me.

The second Tempe said Helix's name, a chill ran down my spine. A reminder I'm all too familiar with lately. A constant whisper in my ear telling me the war never really ends, it simply changes.

New enemies.

Evolving threats.

I don't know who sent Tempe here tonight, but if they know she's Helix's daughter, it means choosing her for this task was intentional. My rivals are getting creative, finding new ways to use innocent blood against me.

If that's what she is.

For all I know, Tempe came up with this plan to get vengeance for her father's death. She plays the victim well, but it could be an act.

Tears.

Fear.

Her shaking hand when she grabbed my arm and begged for my help.

It all means nothing when I've seen those tactics used as weapons before.

"She came back clear, Prez. I'm telling you, I checked." Ghost pulls out his phone and types something in before holding it up to show me a picture of her driver's license. "Tempe Evans, twenty-two. She's worked at Dirty Drakes for the past year while putting herself through school for physical therapy. She volunteers at a local clinic on the weekends. There's not one tie to Helix. He didn't even have her number saved in his phone. She checked out."

I can trust Ghost. If anyone is thorough, it's him. But doubt is all I have lately, and Tempe is just another reminder of why.

It's a rot running through me. Making me question my brothers when they've given me no reason to. This isn't their fault—it's mine.

Helix's betrayal and my inability to see it in time are my mistakes to bear.

My family's blood runs through this club. We founded the Twisted Kings. Failing them is a desecration of my bloodline.

"Steel, I'm telling you she's clear." Ghost tucks his phone away.

I rake my hair off my forehead. "I hear you."

"Then you know as well as I do that if she's not involved, she's not safe."

I nod.

"What do you plan to do about it?"

What am I going to do?

I scratch the back of my neck, wishing I could go back to the point in the night where my biggest problem was a couple of Iron Sinners and pissed off strippers. "I don't fucking know yet. But she's not leaving the compound until I figure it out."

If Tempe were anyone else in danger, I'd send her home and put a prospect on her doorstep for the night to make sure she was safe. But she isn't anyone else. She's the blood of my club's traitor, and as good as Ghost is at his job, it's my responsibility to my club to be certain he's right about her.

I glance at the closed door that leads to my room. I hate that she's in there, pacing back and forth, filling it with the scent of cherry blossoms. A scent that invaded my senses the moment I was near her. A scent so sweet when this girl is anything but.

Tempe is feisty as fuck. She kicked me in the shins and tried to knock me out in my own damn clubhouse—my own fucking bedroom.

The girl is a fighter.

I'd be impressed if I wasn't so pissed off about it.

My phone rings, and I dig it out of my pocket to see Havoc's name flashing on the screen. He and Soul took a couple of prospects to check out the situation at Tempe's house and confirm her story.

After she mentioned her brother, everything hard about her demeanor crumbled, so it was difficult to get much else through her tears. But she said her brother was supposed to be hiding and that the men didn't know he was there. With any luck, they still haven't found him.

"Talk to me."

"Well, she wasn't lying." Havoc sounds out of breath. "Four guys were ready and waiting when we got here."

"Who are they?"

"They scattered before we could get a good look at them. Their lookout must have tipped them off because they bolted the second we pulled up."

I look over at Ghost. "Pull the traffic cam footage in that area, see if you can trace any plates or figure out what direction they went. And let me know once you figure out what's on the flash drive."

Havoc's search of Helix's old room confirmed what Tempe was sent here for. He found a flash drive hidden in the wall, and I don't like that Helix has been dead for almost a year, and I still haven't uncovered all his lies.

Ghost nods, walking away with the drive in hand.

"We've got another problem," Havoc says. "Her mom's gone."

"What do you mean, gone?"

"No body."

I shake my head. "You think they took her hostage."

"Not likely. If the puddle in the kitchen is any indication, Tempe's right; there's no way someone can survive that amount of blood loss."

"So they took a body?"

"Looks like it."

I drag my hair off my forehead; not sure what to make of that. One less body is a good thing. But it also means they had a reason to hide it.

"And her brother?" I ask.

"Found him in the laundry hamper like she said. Soul's trying to talk to him, but he's just a little kid, so he's not saying much."

Because he's probably traumatized.

At least he's alive.

As much as everything about this pisses me off, nothing gets under my skin like the fact that these assholes used some little kid to manipulate the situation.

"What do you want us to do with him?"

I know my answer before I say it, and I hate that it's my only option, but I don't have any other choice when it's two in the morning and the kid's not old enough to fend for himself.

"You have the truck?"

"Yeah."

"Bring him here."

"You got it. Anything else?"

I tip my head back and take a deep breath.

Not my house.

Not my mess.

Not my problem.

Except it is. Tempe has ties to the Twisted Kings, whether she's involved or not. We can't leave traces of what happened tonight in her house.

"Have the prospects hang back and bleach the floor. I want it fucking sterile. The last thing we need is the cops coming around and blaming the club for the mess. They've been itching for a reason to get to us. We don't need to hand them an excuse."

"You got it, Prez."

I end the call as a bad feeling settles in my gut. The same one I got right before I was almost blown up last year. Something nasty is on the horizon.

It figures.

The moment things settle, shit gets rattled around again.

Pushing off the wall, I stare at the door to my room, knowing nothing but problems are on the other side of it. But that's the job. Being president means I walk headfirst into everything.

I open the door, and Tempe looks up at me from where she's sitting on the edge of my bed. She jumps up when I step inside, and at least she's stopped crying.

She's a tiny little thing, even if she's filled with fire. Her eyes burn as she watches me from across the room. Her wavy, brown hair falls just below her shoulders, and it's messier now that she's been running her fingers through it. She chews her lower lip, and I hate how she's so naturally pretty. It's disarming.

Unassuming.

Dangerous.

"Your brother's fine." I don't know why I feel the need to reassure her when she broke into my club, but I do. "Soul's checking on him."

"Soul." She repeats his name on a sweet little exhale that pisses me off.

"My VP."

She wets her lips, her eyes glossy. "And the men…?"

"Gone. Same as your mom."

Her eyes widen. "She's alive?"

"Doubtful."

Any momentary light in her eyes fades. At least she doesn't ask me why they'd carry out her mom's dead body because I don't have any answers for her right now.

Tempe nods, tucking her hands in her pockets. "Are you going to let me go then? I told you everything I know. You just confirmed it."

I shake my head. "Not yet."

"But Austin—"

"Is coming back here." I cut her off.

"And how long are you keeping us? I have to work tomorrow." Her fiery temper flares, arguing with me like it's going to do her any good.

"You're calling in sick."

Her eyes narrow.

"Is there a problem, wildfire?"

"Why do you keep calling me that?" She rolls her shoulders back.

Stepping further into the room, I give in to the gravity that pulls me to her, watching every hint of her reaction at my approach. Her fingers clench. Her chest rises and falls with her shallow breaths. A faint red blush paints the apples of her cheeks.

"Because you've got that spark about you." I stop in front of her. "Doesn't seem like much at first. Just a little ember flicking around in the wind. But that's all it takes sometimes."

She tips her chin up. "To what?"

"To burn everything down."

I step back before I'm caught in her orbit. Her pull is too strong. Her big hazel eyes shine with the tears she's holding back, and if I'm not careful, she'll find a way to use that against me.

Walking over to my dresser, I pull out a cigarette.

"You smoke?" Her face scrunches.

"On occasion."

I've quit so many times over the past five years, I stopped counting. And even if it's been a few weeks, tonight has me reaching for all my bad habits again.

"Want one?" I hold the pack out, and she scowls in disgust. "Guess that's a no. Walk with me."

She wraps her arms around her stomach and follows me out of the room. If I were smart, I'd keep her locked in there so she doesn't get any ideas about running, but the space is too small with her in it. I can't fucking breathe.

She follows me back to the main part of the clubhouse. The party is still raging in the background, and only my men know what's really going on. I could have shut it down, but it's better to pretend things are normal. The last thing I need is rumors spreading.

"Drink, Prez?" One of the prospects yells from the bar when he sees me pass.

I shake my head. "Maybe later."

Another prospect looks Tempe up and down, but when my eyes meet his, he backs the fuck off.

She follows me outside, and it's quieter out here.

Mayhem is fucking a patch bunny on the porch, so I lead Tempe away. Her wide eyes and rosy cheeks tell me she didn't miss it, but she doesn't say anything.

"What are we doing?" she asks when I finally stop at the end of the long driveway.

I light my cigarette and hold in a deep inhale. It burns my lungs and gives me everything I need right now. A nicotine buzz. Clarity.

"My guys will be back with your brother any minute." I take another drag. "We're waiting for 'em."

"Then what?" She clutches her arms around her stomach as she shivers.

It's not that cold, but she's probably coming down from the adrenaline.

"You have a lot of questions for a girl who broke into my club trying to steal something." I flick my cigarette, watching the embers scurry off into the dark desert.

"And you have very few answers for a man wearing a patch that says you should have a lot more."

She glares at me, and I can't help smirking at her irritation.

At least the conversation is cut short by headlights in the distance.

Soul must have stayed back at Tempe's house with the prospects because it's just Havoc in the truck, rolling to a stop and hopping out. He circles the front, and when he pops open the passenger-side door, little feet jump to the ground.

I'm not good with kids—especially little ones. And I don't know what to make of the fact that Tempe's brother is wearing a superhero cape in the middle of the night as he walks at Havoc's side. But he keeps his gaze on the ground and refuses to make eye contact.

"Austin." Tempe's voice cracks.

She runs over to him, dropping to her knees and comforting him in her arms. He buries his face in the crook of her neck as she whispers something. All I can make out are the sobs. Quiet, painful. They cut deeper than Chaos's best knife.

I've seen death.

I've taken more lives than the number of years I've lived.

But something itches under my skin at the sight of Tempe with her brother.

Havoc walks past them, stopping beside me. "What's the plan, Prez? Want me to set them up in Tommy's old room?"

It's not a bad idea. The room's empty and at the end of the hall. I could have a prospect guard the door and lock them inside until I figure out what the fuck I'm going to do. But it doesn't seem like enough. Nothing does.

"It's fine," I tell him. "They can stay in mine."

Havoc's eyebrows pinch at my decision, but he keeps his thoughts to himself.

"Put Sonny at the door. I'll crash in Chaos's room for the night. We'll figure the rest out in the morning. I can't fucking think anymore."

"How long are they staying?"

"Until I figure out who sent her here."

"You think that's a good idea?"

"No." I brush my hair back. "But if you want 'em gone sooner, then get me some fucking answers."

Havoc nods, looking from me to Tempe.

She has her forehead pressed to Austin's, and she's talking to him about something. For the strong show she put on earlier, her defenses are down for him. A maternal soft side that's completely foreign to me, when my mom wasn't a great example of how a parent should love their kid.

A breeze kicks up, and it rattles my nerves.

Change is in the air. And if I'm not careful, it's going to wreck what's left of the club I'm barely holding on to.

5

Tempe

A LOUD KNOCK ON *the front door makes me jump, causing me to squeeze toothpaste all over the sink.*

It's ten o'clock at night, and I just got home from my shift at the bar. The last thing I'm in the mood for right now is a late-night visit from Mom's boyfriend.

She's been in town for three days and has already disrupted my entire life. But at least if she's here, I can keep an eye on my four-year-old brother. He needs some stability after she spent the last year dragging him around the country, moving to a new state every other month.

Another loud knock rattles the door.

"Coming," I mumble to myself, making my way into the hallway.

"Sorry." Mom darts out of her room, pulling her chestnut hair into a ponytail.

"I thought we agreed; no guys at the house."

Mom rolls her eyes, annoyed, but I don't care. She's twice my age and still acts like a teenager. Chasing every crush on a whim. Falling for every man who shows her an ounce of attention.

Grandma used to call Mom a love addict. She said Mom was born without a single defense around her heart, and it made her easily susceptible to sweet talk and a nice smile. But I think that's just an excuse. A substitute for the love she never got from her own father.

Not that I was willing to argue with Grandma about it.

"I'm serious." I frown. "No men."

"I know, Tempe." Mom pulls her robe closed over her chest before pinching her cheeks to draw some color to them. "I thought he was in bed. But don't worry, Austin and I will only be here a few more days. Josh said the apartment is almost ready."

Josh—Mom's boyfriend of the month.

Her excuse for moving to California next.

I'm not a fan.

I don't like how he stared at me when he stopped by yesterday, I don't like how he disregards Austin, and I don't like how he's showing up in the middle of the night.

"I'll make it quick," Mom says, hurrying down the hall when another knock comes at the door.

I make my way to the guest room where Austin is sleeping and peek inside. His eyes blink open as he sits up.

"Go back to sleep." I blow him a kiss. "Everything's okay."

It's not, and we both know it. Nothing's been right his entire life, and if my childhood is any indication, Mom's never going to change.

Austin curls into the blankets as I close his door and make my way toward the living room.

Mom is talking to someone, but I can't make out what they're saying. All I know is her tone is off.

Hushed.

Panicked.

I turn the corner and see she's standing in the middle of the kitchen with a man towering over her. He shifts, and I realize it's not Josh.

Four other men fill the living room, and I back myself into the hallway before they see me when I spot the guns in their hands.

"Please don't." They're the last words that leave my mom's mouth as the man standing in front of her pulls the trigger.

My ears ring with the sound, and time stops.

It takes a moment for Mom's body to process what just happened—the same way my mind is playing catch-up. She stands frozen in the kitchen, and I can't tear my eyes away from her.

Blood pools on her nightgown, spreading like paint. Reminding me of a street fair in San Francisco.

Red brushstrokes and splatter.

But then Mom blinks, and time speeds up again. Sound fills the room, and air floods my lungs. Mom falls to the floor, and I turn and run down the hallway, hurrying to my brother's room before they find us.

"Tempe—"

"Shh." I cover Austin's mouth with my hand and pull him from his bed. "My room, now. Get in the laundry hamper

and cover yourself with clothes. Don't come out until I say so."

I already hear footsteps making their way down the hall, and even if there's no way I'm escaping these men, maybe he can.

Austin follows me to the bathroom that connects my bedroom to his.

"Hurry." I rush him inside. "Remember, don't get out until I come get you."

"What's happening?" Tears stream his cheeks.

His voice quivers, and his little fingers grip my hands.

"It's going to be okay," I lie, leaning in to kiss him on the forehead before closing the bathroom door behind him.

Footsteps stop outside the bedroom door, and I back up. My breath catches in my chest, and I want to run, but there's nowhere to go before the door swings open, and I'm met with the barrel of a gun.

"Tempe." A little hand grabs onto my shoulder, and my eyes fly open.

Sweat drenches the back of my neck from my nightmare as I blink my eyes and jolt to sitting. It takes me a moment to realize that I'm not in my home—in my bed.

It takes a moment to process where I am.

The club.

Steel.

Looking around, I take in Steel's room in the daylight. The walls are a deep shade of blue, not gray like I first thought. It's even less impressive with the sunlight drawing attention to the cracks in the paint and dust-covered baseboards.

Austin blinks up at me, pulling the blanket up under his chin. "Did you have a bad dream?"

"No," I lie, forcing a smile. "Just sat up too fast. I'm fine. How about you? Did you get any sleep?"

He nods, chewing the inside of his cheek. His eyes are red and puffy from crying himself to sleep last night, and it makes my heart ache. Mom wasn't stable, but she was the only parent who stuck around for me and my brother when both our fathers cared more about themselves than their families.

Now she's gone, and I'm all my brother has left. I don't know how to be a parent or how I'm going finish my degree with a job and kid, but for Austin, I'll figure it out.

Austin drops the blanket to his lap, twisting the corner of it around his fingers.

"What's on your mind?" I roll onto my side, facing him, brushing his brown hair off his forehead. "Are you thinking about Mom?"

His big blue eyes gloss over with his nod. "I miss her."

"Me too." Tears sting my eyes as they start to fall from his.

"Are they going to hurt us too?" His voice quivers.

"No one's going to hurt you, Austin. I promise. I won't let them." I squeeze his hand. "That's why we're here, remember? They're going to keep us safe."

At least, I hope. The Twisted Kings can't be trusted any more than the threats outside this compound. But right now, I have no other option.

Austin wipes his cheeks dry with the back of his hand. "I can't find my Super Bear."

My gaze moves to his things on the floor.

"It's not in the bag?"

"I forgot it at your house."

Steel's men were nice enough to let Austin pack a bag before bringing him to the clubhouse last night, but from the collection of things he threw in it, it's clear none of them have kids. They didn't monitor what my four-year-old brother was packing. No clothes. No toothbrush. Nothing practical. Just a collection of random animals and his favorite blanket.

"I want to go home."

"We will." I rest my hand over Austin's. "Soon."

"When the bad men leave?"

A knot hardens in my throat as I nod.

Sitting up, I brush my hair back and spin my legs off the bed before he catches the tears trying to break through. I close my eyes and take a deep breath, finding any bit of strength to hold on to.

"Hey, you hungry?" I force a smile, glancing back at him.

He nods.

"Good." I hop off the bed. "How about I go find some food, and you can hang out here and watch cartoons while you wait for me?"

"I wanna come with you."

I want that too, but I don't know what I'm walking into when I step out of this room. Or if they'll even let me.

"This will be more fun. Breakfast in bed. Just like we did on Sunday."

Mom was out late Saturday night with Josh, so I watched Austin for her. He fell asleep in my bed watching cartoons, and when he woke up, we stayed there to eat breakfast. It helped take his mind off the fact that he didn't want to move to California with Mom's new boyfriend.

Now, he doesn't have to, but my entire chest burns with the reason for it.

"Okay." Austin rubs his eyes again. "Breakfast in bed."

I walk over to the television and turn it on, flipping through the channels until I find cartoons. Anything to distract him from where we are.

"This one?"

Austin nods, and I set the remote down.

"Don't leave this room, okay? Wait for me."

Austin pulls the blanket to his chin and rolls onto his side. "Okay."

I dig a hair tie out of my pocket and pull my hair up into a loose ponytail before walking over to the bedroom door. Closing my eyes, I take a deep breath and let it settle my nerves. Just because I can't leave doesn't mean they'd starve my little brother.

I don't think.

Reaching for the handle, I open it to find a guy I don't recognize standing on the opposite side. His patch tells me he's a prospect, so he's likely been standing guard all night.

I slip out into the hallway before he can stop me and close the door so Austin can't hear us.

"You're supposed to stay put." The prospect lifts off the wall.

He's a scrawny guy, but he towers over me as he steps close. His jet-black hair is slicked back, and his dark-brown eyes narrow.

"I know." I force a smile, hoping honey catches more flies with bikers. "But it's already past nine, and my brother is hungry, so I wanted to see if Steel could—"

"Steel wants you to stay put," he cuts me off, loyal as ever to his merciless leader.

"I've got this, Sonny." A voice comes from the other end of the hall, and I turn to see Havoc walking in my direction.

From what I gathered last night, when they got back from picking up Austin, Steel trusts Havoc, and my shoulders relax at a familiar face.

"My brother needs breakfast," I tell him.

"Food's in the kitchen." Havoc waves me forward before looking back at Sonny. "Stay there."

I don't like leaving Austin alone in this place, but I don't have a choice when I know he needs to eat.

Glancing from Sonny to the bedroom door, I pause, biting my lip, trying to decide if Havoc will just get the food for me.

"Don't worry," Havoc says. "The door locks from the inside, and only Steel has a key, so your brother will be fine."

Havoc's long dark hair is pulled back, and tattoos cover the full length of his arms. He's burly and big—solid muscle. But when I look into his eyes, there's a soft edge that has me trusting him, whether I should or not.

"Thank you."

He nods, leading me down the hallway.

In the morning light, the clubhouse is even less appealing than it was when I first came here. A few men and women are passed out on random pieces of furniture, but at least they're wearing more clothes than they were when I was searching for the bathroom.

The air reeks of stale cigarettes and leather, and my shoes stick to the floor with every step.

Havoc guides me through the bar to a door in the far corner of the room. "Food's in there. Help yourself. I'll let Steel know you're awake."

I nod, watching Havoc make his way back down the hallway.

I'm not sure where Steel slept last night since we were in his bedroom. The last time I saw him, he was ordering a prospect to fetch us fresh sheets and blankets. Then he left us to ourselves.

Pushing the kitchen door open, I find a few girls standing around drinking coffee. I recognize one as the blonde who was working behind the bar last night, and she doesn't appear any friendlier this morning. The moment she spots me walking into the kitchen, her smile drops.

Her bleached hair is brighter in the daylight, and without makeup, her face is washed out. But she's naturally pretty and has an hourglass figure, so I can see what Steel must see in her.

"Can we help you?" she asks.

"Reina, be nice." A girl with purple and blonde hair rolls her eyes.

"I'm just grabbing some food."

Reina lifts off the counter and walks over to me. She's wearing heels first thing in the morning, and each click of them against the tile is like a threat on her approach.

I stand up taller when she reaches me, refusing to back down just because she's feeling territorial.

Reina stops in front of me, scanning me slowly, before spearing me with her gaze. "You're cute, I'll give you that. But don't think that just because he fucked you once, you'll turn his head. Steel's spoken for."

"He didn't—"

"Don't bother."

She spins on her heels, walking out of the kitchen with her brunette friend right behind her. And I'm not sure what's more disturbing—the fact that she thinks I slept with Steel last night or that she thinks he's her man, and she still accepts that kind of behavior from him.

"Don't listen to her." The girl with purple hair walks over to me, offering me a friendly smile as she brings her coffee mug to her mouth. "Reina still thinks Steel's going to put a property patch on her back someday."

"Is he?"

And why am I asking?

Why do I care?

"Steel with an old lady?" She laughs. "No way."

That's not any more reassuring, but at least it's enough of a warning to stay far away from him.

"I'm Luna," she says.

"Tempe."

Luna smiles, and it lights up her cheeks. Her roots are blonde, but darker than Reina's, so I guess that's her natural color. The rest of her hair is streaked in lavender and pulled back, with pieces falling around her face. Her slippers are bright pink and fluffy. And she's paired them with an oversized Call of Duty T-shirt.

"Well, it's nice to meet you, Tempe." Luna takes a sip of her coffee before setting it down so she can dig through the cabinets. "Let's find you some food. They don't have much of a selection unless you're in the mood to cook something. Stevie won't be awake for another hour to get breakfast going for the guys since they're rarely up before ten. Granola bars?"

She spins with a couple in hand, and I take them. "That's perfect. Thanks."

Luna grabs her coffee and takes another sip. "No problem."

"I didn't sleep with Steel, just so you know." I don't think Luna cares, and I shouldn't need to explain myself, but I can't help it. "That's not why I'm here. It's just... things are complicated."

"Things usually are when you wind up at this place."

"I guess so." I bite my lip. "What about you? Are you seeing one of the guys? Or..."

"Or all of them?" Luna quirks an eyebrow when I don't finish my sentence.

"Sorry, I didn't mean—"

"You're fine." She waves a hand to stop me. "I get it. Guys like the Twisted Kings have a reputation for a reason. And I'd be lying if I tried to tell you it's overexaggerated because it's not. But it's not like that between me and them. Not that I've never had a weak moment of fun."

Luna winks, and I admire her unapologetic confidence.

"So you're a friend of the club then?"

"I help Ghost with surveillance, and in return, they give me a place to crash. They took me in when things got…" She pauses, her gaze drifting off with whatever she was just about to say.

"Complicated?" I finish her sentence.

"Yeah, complicated." Luna smiles. "But it's better now. And I've got a roof over my head while I finish up my degree, so that's all that matters."

"What are you stu—"

I'm cut off by the kitchen door swinging open.

Steel walks in, overtaking the room with one step inside. His gaze fixes on me for a long moment before he glances at Luna.

"Luna, give us a minute."

Short.

Demanding.

If I had to guess, everyone here is used to him bossing them around, but he doesn't have to be such a dick about it.

"Sure thing, Steel." Luna tips her coffee up at him, squeezing my shoulder as she walks by. "See you around, Tempe."

"See ya."

She walks around Steel, pausing with her hand on the door. "Open or closed?"

"Closed."

And when the door shuts behind Luna, trapping me in here with him, I'm ready to tell him exactly how I feel about him holding us hostage in this hellhole he calls a clubhouse. I'm all my brother has left, and even a Twisted Kings president isn't going to stop me from doing what I need to protect him.

6

Steel

Tempe stands in the middle of the kitchen like a bundle of dynamite. Her shoulders are rolled back, and her arms are gripping her middle like she's holding in an explosion. And when she narrows her pretty hazel eyes, I sense it.

A match being lit.

The fuse burning.

"You done in here?" I ask when she doesn't so much as blink while she stares at me.

"I guess." She shrugs.

"What's wrong?" *And why does she keep making it my problem?*

"Nothing."

I drag my fingers through my hair.

Games.

Attitude.

Everything about this girl is so fucking irritating.

It's not my fault she tried to steal from my club. It's not my fault she got herself into trouble. But here I am, dealing with her shit. And *she's* the one who is pissed at me about it.

"Fine. You want to know what's wrong?" She throws her arms to her sides and takes a step toward me when I'm quiet for a minute. "If you're going to hold us hostage, you could at least feed us."

I glance down at the granola bars in her hand. "Is that so?"

"Yes." Her spine straightens, and she gives me a sharp nod. "You're a rude host."

"This isn't a hotel, princess." I pop my knuckles. "And I'm not hosting shit."

I'm getting really tired of her pushing my buttons just to see what I'll do about it.

Taking a step toward her, I don't miss that her breath catches. That her cheeks turn a pretty shade of pink, complementing her perfectly puffy lips.

"You forget you're a little thief, Tempe." I tip her chin up, but she immediately pulls her face away from my grip. "You're worried about starving when you should be thankful that I was nice enough to give you a bed to sleep in last night."

My bed, on top of it.

It's going to take a whole new set of linens to erase her cherry-blossom scent from my room.

Tempe rolls her eyes. "I already told you I had nothing to do with what happened last night. I didn't want to steal anything. I didn't even know what they sent me to get. I told you everything I know—which is basically nothing. So if you don't like me being here, let us leave."

"Wish I could, wildfire."

Her eyes light up at the nickname I gave her, and I take another step closer. She backs up for every step I advance, but she can't hide.

There's no running.

Until I figure her out, I won't allow it.

"Why can't you?" There's the slightest quiver to her tone. "You know where to find us if absolutely necessary."

"Because you've already proved yourself to be trouble." I pause once she's backed against the counter. "Besides, if I send you back now, who's to say the guys who sent you here won't immediately show back up? You already folded for them once. I'm sure they could convince you to do it again."

"I—" Her eyebrows pinch as she cuts herself off, and something new washes over her expression. "They wouldn't."

She was probably going to argue and run that smart little mouth of hers, but her momentary confidence is replaced with something else.

Fear.

Tempe's tough. I'll give her that. But at my mention of the men who sent her here, her voice shakes and goes up in pitch. She chews the inside of her cheek, and her eyes dart around the room.

I'd like to think she's not this innocent, and she's just good at playing men. But her reaction is more proof that she's nothing like Helix.

"You think they'll come back?"

I could lie to her—soften the blow. But I'm not that nice, and after last night, this girl needs a dose of reality.

"Probably. They still don't have what they wanted."

"Which is what exactly?"

"That's none of your business." Just because they sent her here looking for the thumb drive doesn't mean she has a right to know we found it. Especially when I don't know what's on it yet.

"You're right. This isn't my *business*. This is my *life*." She narrows her eyes, but they're glossy from the tears she's holding back. "And you're holding me hostage until what—you decide if I'm lying to you? My mom is *dead*, and I'm all my brother has. Trust me, what happens to your club is the least of my concerns. I don't know what I'm stuck in the middle of, but I didn't ask for this, and neither did my brother."

Her shoulders are squared, and her face is a shade redder with her frustration.

"I have a right to answers if you're going to keep us here." She glares at me. "If I don't show up at work tonight, I'll get fired. And rent's already ten days past due. I don't know what those men want from you, but why couldn't you all just leave me out of it?"

Tempe dips her chin and rakes her fingers along her scalp, messing up her ponytail so she has to redo it. When it's slicked back again, she curls her arms around her body and deflates against the counter.

I don't know what to make of her. Her guard flies up as quickly as it crumbles. One second, she's fighting me, and the next, her eyes are begging me to help her. She hates me as much as I hate her, but we're both stuck in this fucked-up predicament.

Tempe is a walking contradiction.

A beautiful distraction.

The enemy.

She's going to make me lose my mind.

"I need some fucking coffee." I cross the kitchen and grab a mug, filling it up.

The first sip burns my tongue, but I take another right after. I'm running on zero sleep, and this girl won't stop talking.

Last night, I crashed in Chaos's room but couldn't sleep. There was too much going through my mind between the Trojan horse standing in my kitchen and the brawl with the Iron Sinners at Sapphire Rise.

Between exhaustion and upheaval, I can't think clearly.

Tempe could be putting on this act to save her ass, but with her brother involved, would she really risk it?

He's just a kid caught in the middle. A kid who's seen too much for his age. A kid who wouldn't talk to anyone but his sister last night because he probably doesn't trust us any more than the men who stormed his house.

Still, when she carried him to my room, he stared at me over her shoulder.

Watching me.

Seeing me.

They're both going to be the death of me if I'm not careful.

Taking another sip of coffee, my tastebuds numb as I swallow it down and turn to face Tempe. I sort through everything she just said and do what I do best: make a list in my head and take action.

"Ghost is looking into the guys who sent you here. We'll take care of that so you don't have to worry about it when you get home."

"And my job?" Her voice quivers, and it slices something inside me.

"I'll have a couple of guys get you to work tonight so you don't lose your job. They'll hang out and keep an eye on you, then bring you back here when your shift's over. That part's nonnegotiable."

I'm starting to believe her, but I've been wrong before, and I can't risk it.

"Here?" She glances around, taking in the kitchen.

"Something wrong with your accommodations, princess?"

"It's fine," she says, even as her pursed lips contradict it.

She opens her mouth like she's going to say more when the kitchen door flies open, and a superhero runs in.

Whatever smart comment she was about to say falls from her tongue the moment she sees her brother. She squats down, catching him and wrapping him in a hug. The girl is pure fire, but the second Austin is around, he puts it out.

"Hey, Prez," Ghost says, propping his forearm on the doorframe while Austin runs over to Tempe. "Sonny caught this guy sneaking out of your room."

"Austin." Tempe grips his shoulders, frowning. "I told you to stay put."

"He wasn't supposed to catch me. I'm wearing my invisibility cloak." Austin waves his cape around his legs. "I was careful."

"I'm sure you were." Tempe frowns. "Still, just because you're wearing an invisibility cloak doesn't mean you don't have to listen."

"Sorry, Tempe." He frowns, dropping his chin.

Invisibility cloak?

I can't figure out why this kid is always dressed like a superhero or what to make of it. And when I look up at Ghost, and he shrugs, I'm guessing he thinks the same.

"Can we eat yet?" Austin asks Tempe. "I'm hungry."

"Yes, I was just bringing these back to you."

She stands and grabs the granola bars off the counter to show him.

"Nola bars?"

"*Gr*anola bars. You like these ones."

He groans, and I don't know what makes me feel worse: holding a kid hostage when I don't even know if his sister is to blame or the fact that I'm apparently starving him.

Behind Ghost, a few patch bunnies walk by in bikinis. If I had to guess, they'll lay out in the yard and pretend it's closer to summer. They'll have their tops off the moment the guys start waking up, and it's a reminder of why Legacy keeps his kid out of the clubhouse.

Tempe and Austin can't stay here. Not that I can let them go either.

Fuck.

There's only one option, and I'm regretting it before the thought fully forms. She's more trouble than I have time for, and I'm planting dynamite in the center of my life by suggesting this to her.

"Grab your shit."

Austin's eyes widen. "That's a bad word."

Wonderful, the kid who won't talk to the guys says something to me, and he's judging me like his fucking sister.

I sigh. "*Stuff*... Get your stuff."

He smiles—*actually fucking smiles*.

Kids usually fear me or avoid me. Even Legacy's daughter keeps her distance because she senses I'm not a kid person. I'd rather wait to talk to them when they're old enough to not have to filter myself.

But this kid in his superhero cape, with his arms wrapped around his sister's leg, looks up at me with the brightest fucking eyes, and I hate that it does something inside my chest.

I squat down to bring myself to his height. "Austin, right?"

Austin nods, burying the side of his face against Tempe's leg as she holds her hand on his cheek.

"I'm Steel."

"Mr. Steel." He laughs. "That's a funny name."

"Yeah, I guess so." I shake my head, not prepared to explain road names to a four-year-old. "It's my last name. But you can call me Jameson if you like."

No one calls me by my first name but my grandma, and Ghost must not miss me caving for this kid because he chuckles.

"Okay, Mr. Jameson."

Mr. Jameson. Like I'm not president of the most feared MC on the West Coast.

"No mister. Just Jameson. So how about it, you hungry, Austin?"

"Yes."

"You like pancakes?"

His eyes widen, and a smile curls in the corners of his mouth. "They're my favorite."

"Mine too." I stand up, looking down at him and Tempe, but I don't know how to read the way she's looking at me. "Grab your things. I need to touch base with the guys, but we'll head out in thirty."

"Okay," she says, sounding a little nervous. "Where are we going?"

Someplace that is going to make this a hell of a lot more complicated than it already is. "My house."

7

Steel

"Take your fucking time, why don't you." I lean back in my chair, lighting a cigarette.

I swear I'm going to quit smoking.

Just one final nicotine hit to burn this morning from my lungs, and then I'll throw away the pack.

Being in the same room as Tempe is borderline torture. She talks back, doesn't shut up, and makes me question every decision. She's a wildfire ripping through all my good intentions, and I fucking hate it.

I'm the president of this club.

My word is law, and people don't question me.

Until her.

She has the nerve to show up on my doorstep and be pissed about the fact that I'm making her play by my rules on my turf. I'll let her leave when I say she can fucking leave. And if she doesn't like it—good. Maybe then she'll learn not to fuck with the Twisted Kings.

Soul is the last of the guys to walk through the door and sit in his seat on my right at the long, oval-shaped wooden table. It's a thick maple with the Twisted Kings' crowned skull and wings carved into the center of it.

Beside Soul is Ghost, with an empty chair on his right where Chaos, my road captain, would be if he wasn't behind bars.

To my left is Havoc, with Legacy, my treasurer, beside him. At the end is Mayhem, the tail gunner, sitting in for Chaos until he returns.

Sometimes, church involves all voting members, but today, it's only those with rank because I'm trying to keep what happened last night under wraps until I figure out what to do about it. With everything that's gone down in the past forty-eight hours, I don't know who I can trust.

Soul leans back, rubbing his temples. "If I'd have known we were having church at nine-thirty in the fucking morning, I wouldn't have gone to bed an hour ago."

"You can sleep when our enemies aren't stealing shit from our club." I take another drag of my cigarette, and Legacy hitches an eyebrow at me because I just told him yesterday that I was done smoking.

"Enemies?" Soul grins, leaning back in his chair and lacing his hands around the back of his head. "Is that what you're calling the girl who kept your bed warm last night, Prez?"

Soul being Soul was bound to give me shit. If Chaos wasn't behind bars, he'd be fucking with me too. I glance at his empty seat at the table and remind myself I need to call the lawyer today and figure out the next steps.

"Better than having her wandering the grounds getting into more trouble." I take another drag of my cigarette, slowly exhaling the smoke before turning to Ghost. "Did you figure out what's on the drive yet?"

Ghost shakes his head. "Not yet. The encryption is a spiderweb of tripwires. If I'm not careful, I'll trigger the code that wipes the data."

"Helix wasn't that smart."

"Nope." Ghost shakes his head. "Which means that even if he is the one who hid the drive in his room, he's not the one who encrypted it."

"Then who did?"

"Still trying to figure that out." Ghost leans forward, crossing one tattooed arm over the other on the table. "Doesn't look like any of the signatures I'm used to."

"The Iron Sinners?"

"Not unless they have someone other than Richter doing their tech work."

Richter's been with them as long as I've been alive, so that's not likely.

"All right. Well, keep me updated."

"Will do, Prez." Ghost nods, sinking back in his seat.

His fingers tap away on the arms of his chair while I move on. Ghost would rather be behind a laptop, phone, or any kind of screen, but I don't allow distractions in church.

"Any other updates on what went down with the Sinners last night?" I look around the room.

Legacy leans forward, raking his dark-blond hair off his forehead. "The contractor called first thing this morning.

We're looking at thirty thousand to fix the hole they blew in the wall between the VIP room and the bathrooms."

"Fucking hell." I tip my head back and scratch my jaw, itching to grab another cigarette. "See if you can get him down to twenty and then get started. And figure out a way to do it without closing the doors. Sapphire Rise is one of the few businesses on the Strip that's still floating after Zane had the city enforce their new building regulations."

Rick Zane owns half the casinos in Las Vegas, and he's made it his mission to push the Twisted Kings off the Strip to advance his interests. It's been going on for a while now, but lately, his attempts are getting more aggressive.

"Kansas said one of the strippers broke a finger in the scuffle. She wants us to pay for it."

"If it'll keep her quiet, make it happen." I might not like it, but it's easier than her making a fuss about her lack of health insurance. "Mayhem, when's the next shipment coming in?"

"Next week. But Victor's now saying we're going to have to meet 'em halfway."

"Why?"

"The Road Rebels have been running into issues on the New Mexico and Arizona border. The furthest they'll take it is Santa Fe. They said they don't have the backup if shit goes sideways. If we want it, we're going to have to go get it."

I don't like my guys transporting shipments across state lines, which is why we usually meet the Road Rebels out in Pahrump and pay them transport fees.

"We need the shipment," Legacy cuts in. "Cash has been running low since we lost the guns we had coming from up north."

"Understood. Mayhem, take backup and meet 'em in Santa Fe." I glance at Havoc. "Get him whatever he needs to be ready for whatever Victor is worried about. We can't risk losing this shipment too."

Havoc nods, and I turn back to Mayhem.

"Tell The Road Rebels we're only paying a third of the transport fee for the trouble, and get it done."

"Want me to join them?" Soul asks.

I shake my head. "I need you here while we figure out who sent Tempe to the clubhouse last night. If you can search her house for anything they might have left behind, we might find something that leads us to them."

"Doubt we will if they're good."

"Then let's hope they aren't." Because that would mean Tempe isn't leaving anytime soon.

"So what's the deal then? You're keeping her here until we figure this out?" Soul smirks, baiting me.

"Not much of a choice." I nod. "Except tonight, I need a couple of prospects to take her to work. She's got a shift at the bar."

"You're holding her hostage but letting her go to work?"

"It's the only way to see if the guys from last night will show their faces."

"So she's bait." Havoc shakes his head, and it's clear he doesn't like the idea. "Don't you think you're taking this a little too far, Prez?"

"Is there such a thing?" I pull out another cigarette and light it, mentally restarting the clock once more for quitting. "Helix was working against us for eight years under our fucking noses. I'm not taking that chance again."

"And what if she's just like dear old dad?" Soul asks.

We're usually in agreement, and I don't like that my second-in-command is questioning this.

"Then I'll deal with it. But she's not walking out of here until I know she won't be dragging more shit back to our doorstep."

"Who says her being here won't do just that?"

Taking a long drag, I look around the table, reading my men. They're split, and I don't blame them. I don't do *gray areas*, and that's what Tempe is. An unknown.

But this is my call, and I'm making it. She's the daughter of the man who nearly ripped my club apart, and I'm keeping her close until I know for sure she's not just like him.

"You saying we can't protect what's ours?" I challenge.

"I'm not saying—"

"Then what the fuck are you saying, Soul?" I put my cigarette out and rest my elbows on the table. "If they come for her, I expect you to do your fucking job and protect our club. But I'm not sending her back home where they can use her against us again. Especially with how close they got the first time."

"Understood." Soul leans back in his seat. "But where you gonna keep her? Your room couldn't hold down the four-year-old this morning."

"You haven't heard?" Havoc grins, tipping his chin up at me. "Prez is putting the girl up in his house."

Soul's face is blank for a minute, and then it cracks with the biggest smile as he tips his head back and laughs.

"Steel's putting up a girl? We're all fucked."

A few of the guys start laughing with him, and I know I'm screwed, but I can't come up with any better options.

"You want her gone?" I say. "Then everyone do your fucking jobs and figure out who sent her here in the first place."

"You got it, Prez." Soul grins, shaking his head.

"Get to it." The guys disperse, but I hang back, watching them disappear into the different parts of the clubhouse through the windows that look out from the room where we hold church.

Ghost is the last to leave, and he pauses in the doorway like he's going to say something. But he doesn't.

And when I see Tempe and Austin come out from around the corner with his bag in her hand, I'm frozen for a moment. Her hair is down again and messy. Her eyes are even puffier this morning. Her gaze meets mine through the glass, and as she wets her lips, I have to remind myself what I'm doing this for.

Who I am.

What I represent to my brothers and my family.

I was young when I was given this throne, and I've failed my club a few times since. My VP betrayed me right under my nose, and I didn't see it until there was already too much damage. I won't let that happen again. No matter how much this girl makes me question what I'm doing as she holds her brother at her side.

Standing up, I make my way out of the room and walk over to Tempe. Her cheeks are pink at my approach, and there's something so innocent about how she blushes in my presence.

I want to convince myself she's working against me so I don't have to admit she's chipping away at something I didn't know was there before I met her.

Women don't affect me, and yet, this girl and her brother have me making stupid decisions.

"Come on." I walk straight past her, not waiting for her to follow.

They stick close as I guide the way out of the clubhouse to my truck.

Propping the door open, I wait for them to climb in. Austin is first, settling in the middle, but Tempe pauses, turning to face me.

"Don't think I can't see through this just because he can't." She crosses her arms over her chest. "You're not doing us any favors by keeping us here, Jameson, so don't try to pretend you are."

Jameson.

No one calls me by my first name, and it takes me a second to remember I told her brother to call me that.

"You're right." I grip the car door. "I'm not doing you a favor. I'm just keeping my club safe and you alive."

"For how long?" She quirks an eyebrow in a challenge.

I rest my forearm against the door, and it brings me closer. I'm towering over her, and as a breeze kicks up, tossing her hair around, I'm hit with her cherry-blossom scent.

"Depends."

"On what?"

"If you're a good girl or not."

Her cheeks burn with her blush now, and I really shouldn't enjoy finding out how much Tempe likes being called that, but it has my blood pumping hot through me.

Tempe rolls her shoulders back. "Guess you'll have to wait and find out."

A devious smile ticks up in the corner of her mouth, and I'm so fucking tempted to put this girl on her knees and tame her smart little mouth. But she climbs in the truck and avoids my gaze as I shut the door behind her.

She's fearless when she should be scared.

Outspoken when she should be quiet.

Tempe is a spark blowing in the wind, hovering over the sagebrush, ready to light my whole life up in flames.

8

Tempe

JAMESON GRABS AUSTIN'S BAG out of the back of the truck, and I try not to notice how his arms flex with his grip. The same way I tried not to breathe him in when he stood so close I could feel the heat radiating off him. It was like the earth in the middle of summer, all while he held my door open.

This man throws my senses off balance.

Studying Jameson from the other side of the truck, I can't figure him out.

He doesn't trust me, but he's helping me.

He hates how I talk back, but it cracks through his cold demeanor.

He doesn't seem to care what people think of him, but he still tries to hide the fact that he smokes with cinnamon gum and cologne.

Nothing about him makes sense, and I wish my mind would stop nagging me to figure him out.

Jameson circles the truck with Austin's bag slung over his shoulder, and his gaze pauses on where a sliver of my stomach is showing. It's clear this curiosity goes both ways, but we won't act on it.

I know better than to let myself go there with a man like him, and his immediate scowl is proof he hates himself for showing interest.

Still, something about Jameson intrigues me. He adjusts his cut and his T-shirt stretches with his strong shoulders. A man bred from danger, and yet, he makes me feel safe.

He shouldn't.

If he decides I'm the enemy, I have no doubt he'll make me suffer.

"Let's go." Steel tips his chin at the house.

It's nicer than I expected for being located on the Twisted Kings compound. The gray siding is highlighted with white shutters and brightened by the flowerpots on the porch.

There are a few houses on this stretch of dirt road, but they're spaced apart, and it's quiet out here. Off at a distance, I can make out the clubhouse in the desert, but it's far enough away that I can't hear anything. There's room to breathe. It's desolate, but I don't mind it.

"This is your house?"

"Yep." He unlocks the door and waits for me and Austin to walk in before following. "But I don't crash here often."

"Of course you don't," I mumble.

"Meaning?"

I didn't think I was loud enough for him to hear me, but I'm starting to learn there isn't much that Jameson misses.

"I'm just not surprised." I shrug. "No time to stay in your actual house when the clubhouse is so... convenient? You forget half my DNA came from a man like you. God forbid you care about something more than the Twisted Kings for five seconds."

"I'm nothing like Helix." Steel's voice drops, and I realize I've hit a sore spot.

"I'm not saying you don't have your differences," I clarify. "But a biker is a biker. Nothing matters more than the patch on your cut. Regardless of who has to live with that sacrifice. At least you're smart enough not to have kids who you'll just disappoint... You don't, do you?"

Jameson shakes his head, looking more confused now than anything, even as I'm insulting him.

"Good." I smooth my fingers over my shirt, realizing I'm rambling. "Maybe consider keeping it that way for their sake."

He stares at me for a moment, probably trying to decide what to make of my word vomit.

"You're awfully judgmental for someone who met me yesterday."

I shrug because he's not wrong. "Be less of an asshole, and maybe I'll get a different opinion."

"Says the girl who broke into my clubhouse."

"Can't break in if all the doors were open."

Jameson's eyes narrow, but there's amusement in his gaze. A showdown we both keep walking into, and I wish I didn't like fighting with him as much as I do.

I press my lips together, and his leather scent floods my nose with my inhale, making me realize we're somehow now face-to-face. My neck is craned back to look up at him. I don't know when we got so close, but our gravitational rage pulled us together.

"Do you have a pool?" Austin pops up beside us, breaking the tension.

I take a step back and get some air while Jameson closes the front door before looking down at Austin. "Nope."

"It's March. You don't need a pool." I pat Austin on the head.

"But summer's hot."

"We won't still be here this summer."

Austin frowns, probably disappointed because this is exactly how Mom operated, shuffling him from one place to the next.

It's just one more reason that I need to find a way to create stability for my brother once we leave here.

"Jameson, is that you?" A woman's voice comes from the top of the stairs, and when I look up, I see her peeking over the railing. "Oh my, we have guests."

She hurries down the staircase, tucking her gray hair behind her ears as she does. She twists her strands around one of her hands and then uses a clip to pin it back. The woman has the same gray eyes as Jameson, but unlike his stone-cold gaze, hers is warm.

"You didn't tell me people were coming over." She squeezes his arm when she reaches the bottom of the stairs.

"Tempe, this is my grandma." Jameson nods at her. "Grandma, this is Tempe and her brother, Austin."

"Tempe, what a beautiful name." She reaches for a hug and pulls me in, being the exact opposite of her standoffish grandson. "You don't hear that often. The last Tempe I met was—"

"Helix's kid." Jameson finishes her sentence.

She pulls back and looks at me, her eyes widening. "Oh my, I haven't seen you since you were two. You're all grown up."

Her eyes dart between me and Jameson.

"Long story," he says.

"I'm sure it is." But she doesn't seem worried about it. Stepping back, she looks down at my brother. "You must be Austin."

He curls against my leg and nods.

It takes him time to warm up to people. Which is why I'm surprised he's been so comfortable around Jameson today. It's rare he'll talk to a stranger until he has time to assess them, but he's already his bossy little self with the president of the most feared MC on the West Coast.

"It's nice to meet you, Austin. I'm Pearl, Jameson's grandma."

"I'm hungry," he says back.

"Austin, that's not polite." I brush his cheek with my hand. "Sorry about that, he hasn't had breakfast."

"It's no problem, dear." She waves me off, reaching her hand out toward Austin. "How about I get you some breakfast? You can help me cook if you like."

"Pancakes?" he asks her.

"Of course." She leans down to whisper, even if we can all hear her, "They're my grandson's favorite."

She juts a thumb in Jameson's direction and smiles at Austin, who is still holding my leg. He looks from Pearl to Jameson, and it isn't until Jameson nods at him that he lets go and takes Pearl's hand.

I can't figure out why Austin trusts him, but he does. And as much as Jameson pisses me off, I'm starting to wish I could trust him as well. He might be dangerous, but in the past twenty-four hours, the men outside these gates have done worse to me than the Twisted Kings.

"We're going to make some breakfast," Pearl announces, looking down at Austin as she leads him toward the kitchen. "I like your cape."

He swishes it out with his free hand. "It's my invisibility. But don't worry, it's off now. You can see me."

"Well, good because you're a handsome young fellow to look at."

They disappear around the corner, and I'm still frozen in place, recovering from the whiplash of going from the clubhouse to this. A home that feels nearly suburban on the inside. The warm greeting of a woman, unlike the glares from the patch bunnies in the kitchen.

The two environments are night and day. Jameson Steel might be the most confusing man I've ever met.

My eyebrows pinch as I look up at him. "You live with your grandma?"

He sighs, scratching his jaw. "She lives with me."

I can't help but smile because the entire scene is so out of left field for a leather-wearing biker, it's hilarious. "That's... sweet. Guess there's a human beneath that president patch after all."

"Don't get any fucking ideas, wildfire." He shakes his head, tossing Austin's bag over his shoulder. "I'll show you to your rooms."

Jameson leads me up the staircase, which is lined with photos I assume are of his family members. The men have Jameson's strong, square jawline. And the women have a familiar fierce intensity in their gazes.

I suppose being a strong woman is necessary to spend time here.

On the upper level of the house is a long hallway with four bedrooms and a bathroom.

"This one's my grandma's room, and that's her crafting room." He points from the first door to the second, stopping at the two at the end of the hall. "You and Austin can have these two."

Jameson drops the bag inside one, standing in the doorway watching me as I make my way into the other.

It's small but surprisingly decorated. The curtains let in light but keep the harsh sunbeams out. The bed in the center has a large quilt stretched across it with vines and a sunflower stitched into it.

Spinning around, I find Jameson propped against the doorframe, watching me. "Where's your room?"

"Downstairs." He juts his chin toward the staircase. "But like I said, I don't usually stay here."

I hum, scanning the room once more. "Understood."

"Tempe." Jameson steps into the room, dropping his voice slightly, and my chest tightens when he gets close.

He dips his chin and drags his fingers through his hair, thinking over something.

"Yeah?"

His gray stare darts to mine. "Tell me you aren't like your father."

Doubt flashes in his gaze. Vulnerability I'm guessing he doesn't often show when, in his business, it could cost him his life.

"I'm not like my father." I stare into his eyes and try to convince him it's the truth, even though I'm sure it's hard for him to accept, given how I came here. "I'm just trying to survive for me and my brother, Jameson. I didn't want anything to do with this. I promise I'm not working against you or your club. I just want my life back. And I just want to give Austin his."

He nods. "All right then."

"Do you believe me?"

"I'd like to, which is why I'm letting you stay here with my only living family." He wipes his palm down his face. "Don't make me regret trusting you."

Trust.

It's a fragile concept between the two of us.

He doesn't want to trust me because of my bloodline, and I don't want to trust him because of his club. But right now, we have no choice.

"I won't."

"I've gotta take care of some business, but I'll have a prospect pick you up in time for work."

"You aren't staying for breakfast?"

He shakes his head. "No time. I'll grab something later."

I get the feeling that's not unusual for him, but I don't say anything. I've already got enough responsibility with a little brother to raise. I'm not taking more on. Especially a biker who makes my body question why I've spent my life avoiding them in the first place.

9

Tempe

"What's your favorite, good-looking?" The blond frat boy across the bar grins at me, thinking he's original.

They always do.

The pickup lines, the pretending to care about my favorite drink, the *what time do you get off tonight* questions. None of them seem to take the hint.

I'm not looking for a one-night stand, much less a boyfriend.

Forcing a smile, I ignore the fact that this guy's pearly whites make me want to punch him in the face. "I don't know. Guinness, I suppose."

It's not, even if I don't mind it.

But if I had to guess, Frat Boy is a Bud Light or Corona drinker. Something light enough for him to handle while still feeling tough because he's holding a beer.

"I'll take a Guinness." He grins.

Of course he will.

As expected, he'll order my "favorite" to try and impress me. Which is as satisfying as his sour face when he takes the first bitter sip. Just as I thought, he wouldn't know real alcohol if it was sitting right in front of him.

"Something wrong?" I wipe down the bar with a wet rag.

He shakes his head. "Nah. All good."

I bite back a smile and walk away.

Dirty Drakes pulls in the worst of the locals, but at least messing with them makes for good entertainment.

"Hey, Tempe, you headed to the back?" Marley asks.

"Yeah, what can I get you?"

She holds up a wad of soaked napkins. "Towels? The tap's leaking again."

I look at the puddle of stout on the floor and sigh. "Sure thing."

Walking into the back, I grab my hair tie out of my pocket and pull back the waves falling in my face. I'm only an hour into my shift, and I have the feeling it's going to be a long night.

I glance up at the clock, and it's Austin's bedtime, so I hope he isn't giving Pearl any trouble. He always fought Mom on going to bed, and since he doesn't know Pearl well, I'm not sure how that's going to go.

At least he seemed happy to stay with her for the night so I could make it to work. Like Jameson, he instantly trusted her. He helped her cook pancakes and then asked her a hundred questions about her knitting room.

I don't know what I'm going to do with him once we leave here, but I need to find someone I can trust to watch him while I'm at work. At least my classes are online, so I can do those at night when he's sleeping.

This newfound responsibility is heavy inside me. I'm twenty-two, and my entire life just turned upside down.

So long as I can pull my brother through this, I'll keep it together for both of us.

He hasn't cried since this morning, and part of me is waiting for the floodgates to open. For the shock to wear off and for him to realize I'm all he has left.

Am I enough?

Can I be?

I'm better for him than my mother was for either of us, but that doesn't mean I'm prepared for this.

I catch sight of myself in a mirror that hangs in the back room, and there are dark circles around my eyes. I'm wearing zero makeup, and I had to borrow one of Marley's uniforms since I don't have any clothes at Jameson's house. My outfit is skintight because she doesn't like her Dirty Drakes T-shirt baggy like I do.

Next time I see Jameson, I need to convince him to let me get some of my things from my house. Austin hates sleeping without his Super Bear, and I'm in desperate need of clothes.

Grabbing a stack of towels and napkins, I head back out front and catch sight of the two prospects sitting in the corner of the bar.

Sonny is the opposite of his name, hanging like a dark storm cloud over the room, just like when he was standing outside Jameson's door at the clubhouse guarding it. I've yet to see him smile, and he watches everything around him, looking prepared to strike the moment something happens.

Reyes is the opposite, grinning and laughing at something one of the waitresses just said to him. He's friendly, but a little too much so. I don't like how his eyes skimmed my bare legs in my uniform or how he's watching the waitress's ass as she walks away.

I remind myself that Jameson trusts him—both of them. I have no choice but to do the same, whether I want them here or not.

Circling behind the bar, I meet Marley with the stack of towels and cover the spill on the floor, helping her clean it up.

A few new customers make their way inside, and I catch Sonny discreetly taking a picture of them. He's been doing that all night. Keeping a lookout and reporting to Jameson.

"That guy's giving me the creeps," Marley leans close and whispers, her gaze following mine to Sonny across the room. "Want me to have security kick 'em out? He's been watching you all night."

"It's fine. He's a..." I chew the inside of my cheek, deciding what sounds the least suspicious. "Friend."

Her eyebrows pinch. "Since when are you friends with bikers?"

Marley's worked at Dirty Drakes longer than I have, and she knows I avoid anyone in a cut.

"He's a family friend." I wipe the counter, trying to avoid her gaze so she can't see I'm lying.

"Whatever you say." Marley pulls her red hair back and starts stacking clean glasses.

"Hey, how was that date the other night?" I change the subject. "It was with that tall guy who was built like a football player, wasn't it?"

"Yes, and it was so good." She grins. "He scored all night long. If you know what I mean."

I shake my head and laugh.

Marley's dating life is so much more interesting than mine. I'm not a virgin, but I rarely date. There's no time. And now with Austin, there will be even less.

A phone ringing on the other side of the bar catches my attention, and I look up to see Sonny lifting his to his ear. It must suck being a prospect, sitting here all night drinking water, watching out for some girl just because their president told them to.

But I guess they signed up for it.

A group of out-of-towners walks in, and Marley and I get back to pouring drinks. It's always easy to separate the locals from those passing through because out-of-towners aren't here long enough to see past the bright lights and ringing slot machines.

"What can I get you?" I place two napkins in front of a couple wearing matching light-up cowboy hats.

"Your darkest stout and a vodka cranberry."

"You got it." I mix her drink first, then grab a beer glass, but when I pull the handle, foam comes out. "Shit, the keg's empty."

"Want me to take care of it?" Marley asks.

I shake my head when I see her serving a group that just walked in. "I've got it."

I wave at my customers for them to give me a second and head into the back room. The wall that backs to the bar is lined with kegs, and I head toward the one that needs to be swapped. But the moment I reach it, I hear the door open again.

"Marley, I told you I had it."

There's no response as a body presses close behind me, and I spin around. A man I don't recognize has me cornered. His dark hair is shaved down to his scalp, and his beady eyes make the hair on the back of my head stand on its ends.

"You've been a bad girl." He grabs me by the throat and slams my back against the nearest wall.

I scratch at his wrists, but it just makes him grip on tighter.

"Think you're brave with your bodyguards out front, do you?" the man asks, pressing close.

"Who are you?"

He tightens his grip on my throat, and his eyes narrow. "Who do you think?"

"You work for him?" I choke out. "The man from last night."

"No, he's like me. Just someone getting the job done for our boss." He ticks his head to the side. "Where's the package?"

"I don't know." My nails dig into his wrist, but he refuses to release me. "They have it."

"The Twisted Kings?"

I try to nod but can't with how he's choking me.

"I'm here to deliver a message. Bring us the package, and we'll let you live."

"I—" His fingers grip tighter. "I can't."

The man's teeth clench, and he's holding me so tight my vision is getting darker. Spots form in the corners of my periphery, and all I see is the man's eyes gleaming with fascination as he chokes me.

His nails dig into my neck, breaking skin, just as a loud bang rings out across the room.

One second, I'm pinned to the wall, and the next, the man's being pulled off me.

I reach for my throat as I choke for air, collapsing with a deep inhale. Light spots the corners of my vision as I find my breath, and for a moment, I think I'm imagining Jameson in front of me.

Not Jameson... Steel.

He pops his knuckles, and he's not the man who put my brother and me in his house to keep us safe. He's the embodiment of the president of the most feared motorcycle club on the West Coast.

Jameson's fist connects with the side of the man's face, and bone cracks. Light leaves his eyes as his body crumples to the ground like dead weight.

One hit and Jameson knocked him out cold.

He rubs the back of his knuckles with his other hand, turning back to me.

"You okay?" He tips my chin up so I'm forced to meet his gaze.

"I—" I'm still processing what just happened. "I'm fine."

He releases my face, and I look down to see his knuckles are bleeding. He hit that man so hard, it broke his skin open.

"Are you okay?" Before I think about it, I reach out and grab Jameson's hand to examine the cut. "You need antiseptic and a bandage."

Jameson chuckles, and when I look up into his eyes, there's amusement in them. I've seen a few sides to this man in the past day, but *friendly* isn't one of them, so it's disarming.

"I've been hurt worse." He pulls his hand from my grasp.

"Doesn't mean you should ignore it." I narrow my eyes, circling around him to the first aid kit hanging on the back wall. "Just because it isn't a bullet wound doesn't mean it can't get infected."

I pull out an antiseptic wipe and a Band-Aid.

"Hearts?" he asks, spotting the cartoon hearts on the Band-Aid.

I shrug. "Marley thought it was funny. Nothing lightens the mood from a bar fight like a Band-Aid with hearts on it."

Jameson watches me wipe the cut on the back of his hand with the antiseptic wipe. "You clean up lots of guys after bar fights?"

"No." I glance up at him. "You're an exception."

"Is that so?" He smirks.

I nod. "That's so. Can't trust you to do it yourself, tough guy. Besides, it's the least I can do to thank you."

My gaze moves to the body on the ground, and Jameson's fingers wrap around my hand. The other one rests over where I'm still wiping the back of his knuckles.

"Are you okay, Tempe? Really?"

"I'm fine. Just a little out of breath." I force a smile, and he luckily accepts it.

Stepping back, I'm still a little hazy, but I distract myself with the Band-Aid, picking at the corner to unwrap it.

Jameson chuckles. "No thanks on the Band-Aid, wildfire."

"But hearts..." I tease, and he shakes his head.

I don't argue because there's no point. I tried, and at least he let me clean his cut.

Jameson reaches into his pocket, pulling out his phone, while I make my way over to the trash to throw away the antiseptic wipe.

"Havoc, I need you to bring the van to Dirty Drakes and pick up a package... No, the other kind of package... Yeah... Sonny's gonna keep an eye on it. I'm heading back now."

He hangs up as the back door swings open, and Sonny and Reyes walk in.

"Where were you?" Jameson snaps at them.

"Sorry, Pres—"

"Stay here until Havoc arrives." He cuts them off, and his tone is pure ice.

Jameson turns his back on the prospects, focusing his attention on me.

"What are you going to do with him?" I ask, glancing down at the unconscious man.

"Nothing for you to worry about." Jameson puts his phone away. "Let's go; your shift is over."

"No, it's not."

He steps toward me, tipping my chin up. "Yes, it is. Tell your boss you're feeling sick. Or whatever excuse they'll believe. We tried this your way, but we're doing it my way now."

He nods toward the body on the floor, and I swallow hard when I realize this isn't him being overbearing; he's trying to keep me safe. For whatever reason, Jameson is looking out for me. And somehow, I trust him to do it.

10

Steel

BY THE TIME TEMPE meets me outside the bar, she's back wearing the same jeans and shirt she was wearing last night. And when I glance down at her outfit, she frowns.

"It's all I have." She crosses her arms over her chest. "It's not like I had a chance to pack a bag. I need more clothes."

Glancing up at her, I realize that even though the guys had Austin pack a few things before bringing him to the clubhouse, Tempe has nothing.

"Come on." I hand her a helmet. "We'll grab some of your things."

She hitches her eyebrow, drawing my attention back to the scar that cuts through it. "And put it where?"

"How much you planning on packing, princess?"

She rolls her eyes, and something about her annoyance is my favorite form of entertainment.

"It's not just me, Jameson. My brother needs his favorite bear, *a toothbrush.* A booster seat for riding in your truck. I swear it's like you've never been around a kid." She's not wrong about that. "They require *all the things*. I don't know how much, except that it's probably more than your bike can handle, *Steel*."

She calls me by my road name just to pick at me, and I can't help but chuckle at the attempt.

"Fine. I'll have the guys take you to your place tomorrow. Just get on the fucking bike, Tempe." I don't like that she's out here in the open. "You ever been on the back of a motorcycle?"

She shakes her head.

"First time for everything." I swing my leg over my bike and start the engine while Tempe fights with the helmet. Her honey-brown hair waves out around her shoulders, and her ass wiggles as she adjusts the strap.

She's too fucking tempting for a girl who annoys the living hell out of me half the time.

A complete contradiction. Sour and sweet. Gentle with her brother but feisty with me. Hating me one moment and cleaning out the cut on my knuckle the next.

It's fucking confusing.

"Need help?" I ask when she's still fighting with the buckle.

"Nope, got it." It clicks.

Tempe is a lot like me, refusing assistance and being a stubborn asshole about it. Except on her it's cute.

I don't like cute.

But damn, *this girl*.

Tempe walks over, pausing when I reach out my hand to help her onto the bike.

"Climb on, wildfire. I don't bite unless you want me to."

Her eyes narrow. "Does that kind of talk actually work on women?"

"You tell me." I wink, and even if she groans, I don't miss she's biting back a smile. "Watch out for the exhaust pipe. It gets hot."

Tempe swings her leg over my bike and slides behind me. There's a gap of space, and I sense her nerves, so I grab her thighs and tug her flush to my back. The heat of her core makes me question what the fuck I'm thinking by doing this.

I don't let women on my bike. It gives them the wrong impression. But Tempe breaks all my rules, and when her body melts to mine, I swear it's like she's always belonged right there.

"Gotta hold on tight unless you want to fall off." I move her hands to my stomach, and I swear she ignites an electrical current through me. "Lean when I lean, and we'll be good, all right?"

Her arms circle my waist, and her chest presses to my back. "I trust you."

Three words have never sounded more dangerous.

By the time I'm walking into the Shack, I can still feel Tempe's arms wrapped around my body. I can still feel the quick breaths with every sharp turn. The heat of her body pressing to my back was hotter than the middle of summer in Vegas. And it has my fists clenching when the door swings open, and I'm faced with the piece of shit who had her pinned to a wall by her throat a couple of hours ago.

The Shack sits on the opposite side of the compound from the neighborhood, and it's bigger than its name gives it credit for. The building is a large, wide-open space with a concrete floor and a few strategically placed drains. It serves one purpose, and one purpose only.

Something it's going to live up to tonight.

My men brought Banks back here from the bar, but they haven't been able to learn anything more than the name stitched into his Iron Sinners cut.

Not for a lack of trying, if his bloody face and the knife handle sticking out of his thigh are any indication.

Havoc stands in front of him with his arms crossed over his chest, and if I had to guess, he's the reason Banks is missing three of his toes. Havoc is a peaceful guy so long as you don't threaten the club. But once you do, a military war machine unleashes.

Havoc is patient, and it's not something his enemies appreciate about him when he cuts them apart piece by piece.

One limb at a time.

"Prez," Havoc says, not taking his eyes off Banks.

Legacy and Soul stand behind Banks, and Ghost is to the side of the room spinning a knife, watching.

Being in church or in the Shack is the only time Ghost's full attention isn't on one of his devices. And even if people think his road name comes from how quiet he is, the truth is closer to the things he's done between these walls.

"Is he talking yet?"

Soul grabs Banks's hair and tips his face to the ceiling. "Not yet. But what do you say Banks, ready to behave?"

Banks grinds his teeth, not answering, and Soul shoves his head forward again. His shoulders sink with his exhaustion as blood drips down from a gash in his forehead.

Peeling off my leather jacket, I drape it over a chair at the side of the room, circling Banks and popping my knuckles.

He's scrawny but tall. And he was strong enough to overpower Tempe, even if the claw marks on his wrists and forearms are proof she fought back. The red gashes fuel my rage as I take him in.

Stopping in front of him, his eyes flare when he looks up at me.

Fear.

Before I got here, I'm sure he figured he had some time. Maybe he assumed his perseverance would wear my men out, and they'd let him go. But one look into my eyes, and he must be able to read my mind because there's no coming out the other side of this after he put his hands on her. He'll be taking a dirt nap by the end of tonight for fucking with something that's mine.

Mine?

That's a dangerous thought.

"Knife?" Havoc offers one to me.

But I shake my head when I'd rather use my weapon of choice—my fists.

This club is my blood, so for that reason, I give my sweat, bones, and soul for my men. A weapon is a cop-out when my father and grandfather sacrificed their lives for their brothers.

At the end of the day, I'm not Jameson.

I'm not even Steel.

I'm the flowers on the grave. The memory of what once was. Here to honor those who came before me and to pass that tradition on.

I *am* a Twisted King.

Not by choice, or patch, or oath. But by *blood*.

There's nothing more important than my brothers.

My club.

But when I look into Banks's eyes, and I'm reminded of the fear that flooded Tempe's gaze when he choked her—when her eyes started to fade out—I snap.

I don't know if it's for my men or for the little thief and her brother, but I grab Banks by the throat and tighten my grip with all I have.

"Who sent the girl to my club?" I slam my knuckles into the side of his face so hard his eyes roll back. "Who?"

I loosen my grip just enough for Banks to choke on a breath. "Fuck off."

"Wrong answer." My grip tenses and his eyes bulge.

Spit trickles from the corner of his mouth as his cheeks turn bright red.

Rearing back, I slam my fist into the side of his face again, ripping open an already angry gash on his cheekbone.

The punch is hard enough that I almost lose him, so I have to slap his face and wake him the fuck up. There's no sleeping through this.

Not until I'm done with him.

Banks blinks, coming to, and I grab him by the throat again.

"You feel that, Banks? That burning in your lungs? It's spreading through your chest, isn't it? Your eyes are pushing against their sockets like they're going to explode."

I allow him one gulp of breath before doing it all over again.

"I could do this all night. Want to know why?" I lean in, not releasing him for an answer. "Because you fucked up. And it wasn't even for patching into the wrong club. Or being loyal to a shit leader. It's because you tried to take what's mine."

From all around, I feel the guys watching me, weighing what I said. But I don't take it back because it doesn't matter if Helix betrayed us, Tempe is the blood of the club.

My club.

"How does it feel struggling for air like she did?" I press my thumb to his windpipe, and his mouth widens as he searches for breath. "How does it feel to be powerless? Because only a cunt uses an innocent woman as a shield and is willing to threaten a kid."

My fingers ache, but I don't let up. I watch the tears spilling from Banks's eyes and appreciate every drip of spit dribbling from his lip as he chokes for air. He deserves to reap what he's sown, and when he's laid to rest in this unholy ground, he'll pay for his earthly sins.

"Steel, you're losing him." Soul takes a step forward, but I don't let go.

I didn't walk in here to torture him. If he was going to give up information, he'd have done it for my men.

I'm here to end this piece of shit. To remind the world what happens when they fuck with the Twisted Kings.

Banks's cheeks turn a shade of red that reminds me of the Painted Desert. A shade I appreciate as he stares me down through the last seconds of his life.

To the earth, we are born, and that's where our bodies all eventually return. But our souls are another story, and as the last twitches of this asshole's miserable life start to fade, I watch with hope that he's descending to hell.

Banks stops wiggling, and even if his eyes are wide open, he's no longer there.

Releasing him, I flex my fingers and let them stretch. They're cramped from my grip, but it's still not enough to release the tension. I wish it would have taken longer for this piece of shit to die so I could have enjoyed it.

"We could have gotten more." Soul feels for a pulse, but he isn't going to find one. "Seven more toes and ten fingers at least."

"He wouldn't have talked." And I was done letting him fucking breathe after what he did to Tempe. "There's a reason Titan sent him. He was low enough on the totem pole to be disposable but reliable enough that if he got caught, he wouldn't be a liability."

"You're probably right." Soul steps back.

Havoc shakes his head. "Let's hope so."

My men are questioning my motives. And it's all because of the brushfire ripping through my life in the form of Tempe Evans.

"I'm right." I crack my knuckles. "Besides, at least now we know the Iron Sinners are behind all this."

"We could have at least kept him around long enough to see if he could tie them to the flash drive." Legacy tucks his thumbs in his pockets.

I glance over at Ghost. "Let him worry about that."

Ghost nods. He's been working on it all day and getting nowhere, but I know he will. He's never let me down.

"What do you want us to do with him?" Havoc glances at Banks's body.

"Send a message. I want the Iron Sinners to know we're done taking hits. No more defense. It's our turn."

11

Steel

It's three in the morning when I finally make it through the front door. Any other night, I would have crashed in my room at the clubhouse, but something felt empty about it when I got there. So I turned around and made the short drive to the neighborhood.

It's the strangers in my house.

The unease of the night still wearing thin on my bones.

That's all that makes sense when there's no other reason I'd be compelled to show up at a house I barely ever sleep in.

Peeling off my cut, I hang it right inside the front door. As I do, movement in the kitchen draws my attention.

The house is dark, so I reach behind my back and pull out my gun, holding it firmly at my side as I quietly make my way through the house. The compound is fenced and monitored from every corner, but it doesn't mean no one has ever found a way to sneak past.

Peeking around the corner into the kitchen, I spot bare legs sticking out the bottom of the refrigerator, so I holster my gun.

"You're up early." I step into the room.

Tempe lets out a little yelp as she jolts upright. Her frame is lit by the glow from inside the refrigerator.

"Jameson." Her eyes are wide when she spots me leaning against the doorframe.

I never should have told Austin my first name because every time Tempe uses it, something warm churns in my chest. A biker's life shouldn't be comforting, yet somehow, that's what her presence is.

"Don't look so surprised, wildfire. I live here, remember?" Walking into the kitchen, I slide onto one of the barstools at the kitchen island.

"I know. But you're the one who said you 'never stay here.'" She throws up air quotes, tossing my words back at me.

"Maybe I'm just keeping you on your toes."

After all, it's what she gets for keeping me on mine.

Tempe rolls her eyes, tugging at the hem of her T-shirt. It hits her mid-thigh, brushing against the smooth skin of her legs. And the cool air from inside the refrigerator makes her nipples peak against the fabric.

"Your grandma gave it to me to sleep in. Hope you don't mind." She brushes her hands over the front of the T-shirt, and I realize it's one of mine. "I didn't have anything comfortable to sleep in."

"It's fine." Albeit tempting as fuck. "You looking for something to eat?"

I tip my chin at the still-open fridge.

"Not really, I just couldn't sleep." She looks from me to the food and shakes her head. "Thought a snack might help take my mind off things."

Tempe shuts the refrigerator and tugs her hair out of the messy bun, only to wrangle the waves right back on top of her head in a fresh knot.

"How are you doing?" I ask.

It's bad enough I'm here—bad enough I'm letting Tempe and her brother live in my house. I shouldn't give a shit how she's doing, but I can't seem to help myself after what happened at the bar tonight.

Tempe grazes her fingers across her neck, skating them back and forth over the faint bruising already starting to show. I wish I could bring Banks back from the dead just so I could suffocate the life out of him all over again for putting his hands on her.

"I'm doing okay." But her eyes don't match her tone in the dark kitchen as they trail off.

"And Austin?"

Her gaze snaps to mine, and her eyes gloss over. "He's in shock, and I don't blame him."

I nod, not sure what else to say.

I've been that kid—frozen in time. Born into circumstances that only twisted and became more fucked up the older I got. He's going to become tough quickly, and that's not always a good thing.

"Thanks for everything you did at the bar."

"Don't mention it." I stand up, circling the island to get a glass of water.

I'm too fucking sober, and the room's too hot with Tempe standing in the middle of it.

Grabbing two glasses out of the cabinet, I fill them up and hand one to her.

"Why were you there, anyway?" Tempe's eyes pinch as she watches me take a sip. "I'm sure you have better things to do than check in on your prospects."

I drain the glass and set it down, wishing she'd stop seeing through everything. "I was around the corner and figured I'd drop in on my way back to the clubhouse. It was on my way."

Kind of.

It would have been quicker to head straight out of the city, but I couldn't seem to help myself. After checking in with Kansas, I had every intention of heading back to the club. But something pulled my bike in the direction of Dirty Drakes instead.

Tempe is a magnet, and I'm the metal that can't escape her pull.

"Well, you had good timing, so I guess it worked out." She lifts off the counter, setting her water glass down. "Sorry, I'm keeping you up. You must be tired. You don't need to entertain me. I'm heading back to bed soon."

"I'm usually up this late." If anything, this is early.

Her gaze drifts around the kitchen. "Are you hungry then? I was going to make a grilled cheese, if you want one."

Between Stevie cooking for the guys at the clubhouse, and my grandma always having food packaged in the refrigerator, I'm used to people cooking for me. But her offer feels different. Like genuine kindness when all I've done is add to her problems.

"You don't have to do that."

"It's fine." She waves her hand, walking back over to the fridge. "You're letting us stay here. It's the least I can do."

"Thought I was holding you hostage?" I smirk.

She narrows her eyes, playfully glaring at me over her shoulder. "Technically, yes. But I guess after everything that's happened, I get it. And I appreciate what you're doing for me and Austin."

For now.

Tempe's got a life. A brother to raise. Wounds to heal.

And my world is no place for a girl who is eight years younger than me, with her whole future ahead of her.

"Go, sit. You've had a long day, Jameson. Let me make you something to eat."

I chuckle, sliding onto the stool closest to the stove. "I'm still getting used to you being nice to me."

She rolls her eyes. "I could say the same for you."

Tempe moves around the kitchen like she already knows where everything is. She grabs two plates from a cabinet and then bends over to grab a frying pan. Her ass peeks out as the T-shirt rides up, and it's borderline torture when I know I can't do anything about it.

I've been so tired and busy lately that I haven't even had the energy to get laid. And with Tempe roaming my kitchen like it's hers, making me a sandwich, every nerve in my body is on edge.

"Pearl said we've met before." Tempe pops back up with a pan and sets it on the stove. "I didn't realize my mom brought me around here, but I guess I was only two, so I don't remember it. And back then, we never stayed in one place long. You lived here then, right?"

"Born and raised." I knock my knuckles on the counter. "Did you move around a lot as a kid?"

"Too much." Tempe huffs. "I can't imagine living in one place. I would have given anything to spend a full school year in one city growing up. My mom's boyfriends never lasted that long."

"So you and Austin...?"

"We're technically half-siblings. I was eighteen when she had him."

"You seem close though."

"We are. Mom was never that reliable—for me or him. So I tried to make up for it whenever they came through town." She shakes her head as she butters the bread. "I guess now I'm all he has. Maybe I'll actually give him a full school year in one place."

"What about his dad?"

"He's not much better than Helix. Or so my mom told me. I never met him, and I don't know who he is, except that she met him in Austin."

"Texas?"

"Yep." She plops one sandwich in the pan, and then the other, and they start sizzling.

"So your name... Tempe."

"Helix was riding through Arizona when they met, and she followed him back here. She said it was fun times until it wasn't, which is how she operated with men."

I try to picture Tempe's childhood, moving around nonstop. Parents who couldn't commit to the responsibilities they bred. It's the opposite of how I grew up, and also somehow, the same.

"Mom always said she was going to settle down." Tempe shakes her head. "*She was going to change.* When she showed up last week, she swore this move was different. I didn't believe her, and now…"

"Now, what?" I ask when she doesn't finish her sentence.

"Now I guess she'll never prove me wrong." Tempe flips over the sandwiches. "Austin deserves so much more than this. More than she gave him, and more than I can."

"You offer him plenty. Don't doubt yourself, wildfire."

She rolls her eyes. "You don't know me, Jameson. I don't even know that side of me. I've never raised a kid. What if things get hard and it turns out I'm just like her?"

"You standing here is already proof you're not." I shrug. "You're strong, Tempe, even if some days you feel like you're faking it. Even if it's just a front you're putting on for those around you. Strength isn't always apparent. Sometimes, you just have to manifest it into existence when life throws a curveball. And I've already seen enough to know you're more than capable of doing that."

"You have a lot of faith in me."

"I know a fighter when I see one." I smirk. "Got the bruises on my shins to prove it."

She laughs, and the sound lifts a weight off my shoulders. "Thanks, Jameson."

"Anytime, wildfire."

Tempe's still grinning when she turns back to the sandwiches. She checks the bottoms of them and turns off the stove when they're brown. The moon shines through the window, offering her enough light to see as she moves around.

She walks over with my plate, setting it in front of me, and the breeze of her movement kicks the napkin across the counter. She tries to catch it, not realizing until it's too late that she's pressed her chest against me with her efforts.

Her lashes flutter as she looks me in the eyes. We're face-to-face. So close I can feel her sweet little exhales escaping her lips, and I'm teased with every brush of her pebbled nipples poking through her T-shirt as her chest expands.

So close I can hardly resist when her gaze drops to my mouth, and she wets her lips.

She's the daughter of the man who betrayed my club.

Baggage I can't take when my shoulders are already burdened with enough weight.

A girl who comes with expectations a man like me can't live up to.

But when her hazel eyes flit back to mine, I'm tempted to grab her hips and lift her onto the counter. To claim this girl like I wanted to do the second I met her.

I didn't ask her to rush my life, but she did.

Tempe is a breath of fresh air in a room without oxygen. A spark when I've been walking in darkness. She's fire when not even the Vegas sun has been able to heat the coldest parts of my chest up to this point.

I want to make her leave as strongly as I want to keep her safe.

I want to push her away, and I want to hold her close.

She makes me want everything.

"Sorry." Tempe backs up, and I miss her body heat the moment she does.

But she doesn't circle the island like I expect. She takes the stool next to mine. And when she sinks her teeth into her grilled cheese, avoiding my stare, I know why Soul's been giving me such a hard time about the fact that I haven't let this girl out of my sight since she first broke into the clubhouse.

I have no doubt Tempe was put on earth as the weakness of man. And if I'm not careful, she's going to become mine.

12

Tempe

Havoc grips the steering wheel as he makes a turn. The dog tags around his neck shift, and I'm tempted to ask him about his time in the service, but I keep my questions to myself. He's shown kindness to me and my brother, offering to escort us to my house to gather some of our things. But I still don't know whether he's actually friendly or just doing his president a favor.

At least I feel safe around him. He's Jameson's sergeant at arms, the club's protector, and for the time being, mine.

"How's Prez treating you?" Havoc asks, glancing over at me when I've been staring at him for too long.

"Good." I shrug. "He's busy, so we don't see him much."

"He went home last night." A hint of a grin curls up in the corner of Havoc's mouth.

"He did." And I still don't know why.

When Jameson first brought us to his house, he made a point of telling me he never sleeps there. So I'm not sure what to make of the fact that he came home last night.

It could be that he doesn't trust us, but that's not the impression I got.

"Jameson's going to show me his motorcycle." Austin smiles, changing the subject. "He said it's superfast."

"When did he say that?" My eyebrows pinch.

"This morning."

After sharing grilled cheese sandwiches in silence last night, I went to bed. And by the time I woke up and showered, Jameson had already left.

"Do you think it's faster than the fastest superhero?" Austin's eyes widen. "Do you think he'd break the speeding limit?"

Havoc looks down at Austin. "Bet if you asked him, he'd be willing to test it out."

"I wanna go with him."

"There will be no motorcycle racing for you, mister." I pat Austin on the head. "Especially if you're trying to break a speeding record."

"Why not?" Austin frowns. "Jameson can do it."

"Jameson isn't four years old."

Austin crosses his arms over his chest and dips his chin. "I'm almost five."

"Don't worry, bud." Havoc nudges Austin with his elbow. "Plenty of time to ride in life. Better to start with something that doesn't have an engine. Besides, gotta get to know the bike first."

Austin's face brightens as he looks up at Havoc. "Do you think he'll show me the parts?"

"I'm sure he would."

Austin smiles, facing forward, and I wonder if Jameson realizes what he opened himself up to by offering to show Austin his bike. If not, he's going to quickly learn what happens when you make promises to a four-year-old.

Havoc takes the final turn down my street, rolling to a stop at the curb. The two bikes that were following us circle to park in the driveway.

The entourage is a little embarrassing. But when I look at the house sitting in broad daylight, and I remember what happened last time I was here, I'm thankful I'm not alone with Austin.

Havoc cuts the engine. "The guys are gonna do a quick sweep, and then you can pack your things."

Ghost and Sonny climb off their bikes and enter the house while I help Austin out of the truck. He jumps into my arms. They're almost instantly tired with Austin getting bigger by the day, but I don't set him down.

When the guys step back out of the house, they're frowning.

"Someone cut the feeds," Ghost says, looking at his phone. "Explains why they stopped recording in the middle of the night. I'm gonna replace them and add a few cameras to the perimeter."

"You're surveilling my house?"

Ghost's cool blue stare lands on me. "Just in case they come back."

My spine prickles, and I hold Austin tighter.

"And the house?" Havoc asks.

"It's clear," Sonny answers, coming to a stop in front of us.

I take that as my go-ahead, but he holds a hand up when I start to make my way toward the front door.

"What?"

"You should prepare yourself before going in there." He looks from me to Austin. "They left a bit of a mess."

I close my eyes and take a deep breath. I shouldn't be surprised, but still, it stings. Just last week all I could think about was work and school. And in one night, everything changed.

I blink my eyes open to find Austin staring at me, and it takes all my strength to bury the tears stinging as they fight to get out.

Setting him on the ground, I crouch down to bring myself to his eye level. "How about you stay out here with Ghost while I get your things?"

"But I want Super Bear." He frowns.

"I'll get him for you."

After everything he's already witnessed, I can't have him seeing this too.

"Hey, Ghost." Havoc tips his chin at Ghost's motorcycle. "Austin said he wants to learn to ride. How about you show him that Evolution engine you just rebuilt?"

"The flying one?" Austin's face lights up when he looks at Ghost's bike.

"Flying one?" Ghost looks from Austin to me.

"Your bike is black and purple," I explain. "One of his favorite superheroes flies around on a purple bike."

And everything with Austin boils down to superheroes.

"I like that." Ghost looks back at him with an amused smile. "Come on. Let's check it out."

Ghost leads Austin over to his motorcycle, and Austin dives into a story about the Avengers as they squat down to look at the details.

"Thanks," I say to Havoc.

"No problem."

He guides me toward the house, and the moment I walk through the front door, I'm thankful Sonny warned me before I brought Austin in here. They didn't just toss the place, they destroyed it.

Frames are broken; glass is shattered. The television is in pieces, and every dish in the kitchen is smashed on the floor. Someone must have cleaned up the blood because it's no longer there, but I swear I can still see it.

Mom crumpled on the floor.

A metallic scent in the air.

I clutch my stomach as I take it all in; my head swims with the destruction.

"This isn't about you," Havoc says, coming up beside me. "They're just trying to make a point to the club."

"Looks like they were loud and clear."

Havoc nods, frowning as he looks around.

My dad was a biker, so I know the danger that comes from associating with the Twisted Kings. But to see it permeating my life when I've worked so hard to steer clear feels like a wrecking ball knocking me in the chest.

It doesn't matter how much space I've maintained between me and my bloodline; there's no avoiding it now.

And all I can do is trust the very club I've spent my life avoiding with the hope that they'll keep us safe from whatever my father's sins are raining down on me and Austin.

"I'm going to grab what I can from the bedrooms," I tell Havoc before making my way down the hallway.

There's no use digging through the kitchen or living room with the state they're in. I already know that once Steel lets us leave the compound, I'll be starting over. New furniture, new dishes. I can barely afford rent, so I don't know how I'm going to swing it. But I'll figure it out as I always do.

Like I did when I was eighteen and had nothing because Mom never stayed in one place for more than a few months. I fought for the life I built once, and I'll do it again if I have to.

I'll create a stable life for me and my brother.

Walking into the guest room first, I'm thankful it's the least destroyed room in the house. It's turned upside down, but Austin's belongings are in one piece.

I grab Super Bear first and start packing. Since Mom was always moving around, he already doesn't have much, so it makes it easy to fit all his belongings in the two bags he arrived at my house with.

When I move to my room, it's in worse shape than Austin's. The mirror above the dresser is shattered, and *whore* is spraypainted on the wall above my bed. I'm sure they thought they were being cruel with their threat, but it's been a year since I've had sex. So if anything, it's a reminder of my pathetic dating life.

Moving to my closet, I find a pile of shredded clothes on the floor. Luckily, they didn't destroy everything, so I pack what can be salvaged.

The bathroom is next, and toothpaste is still smeared on the sink from when I accidentally squeezed it out of the tube. I brush off the nerves that prickle my skin with the reminder of that night, grabbing my makeup and our toothbrushes quickly.

Swinging the bags over my shoulders, I make my way down the hallway to find Havoc pacing in the center of the living room, talking on his phone.

When he spots me, he pauses. "Let me get those."

Havoc walks over and grabs the bags, carrying them like they weigh nothing.

"Yeah, she's right here." Havoc listens to the person on the phone before handing it out to me. "Prez wants to talk to you."

I take the phone from Havoc, and he walks out the front door.

Through the window, I see Austin sitting with Sonny on the front step while Ghost is installing a camera at the front of the house.

I bring the phone to my ear and sink against the wall. "Hey."

"You got everything you need?" Jameson's voice is nearly drowned out by what sounds like a party in the background.

His life is wild.

Untamed.

Everything I don't want.

"I got enough."

"Good." A door closes on his end, and he must have stepped away because now it's quiet. "Don't leave anything you might want later."

"I didn't." And I know why he's saying that as Ghost moves inside to install another camera.

There's a good chance I'll never come back here.

Jameson hums, quiet for a moment on the other end of the line. And even though he doesn't say anything; the silence is comforting. I still don't know if I can trust him, but in this moment, he's the person who is here for me.

"Curveballs, Tempe, remember? You've got this," he says after a long pause. "The men who did that to your house are going to pay."

I don't ask how because I already know. And even if it's wrong, I'm thankful.

I want them to.

I cast my gaze over the room—at the mess left behind just to prove a point. A life they destroyed without caring. Either because of who my father is or because they want revenge on his club.

It's a mess I'm left to clean up.

"Curveballs," I repeat, taking a deep breath.

If only they'd stop coming.

13

Tempe

WHEN WE GET BACK to the Twisted Kings compound, Havoc doesn't take us to the neighborhood like I expect him to. Instead, he pulls the truck to a stop outside the clubhouse.

The lot is empty compared to when I first arrived here in the middle of a party. The few bikes and trucks are parked under a canopy at the side of the building.

"I thought we were going back to the house."

Havoc swings his door open to climb out. "We will, but Steel thought you might be hungry."

He walks around the truck and opens my door. The aroma of a grill filters through the truck as I undo Austin's seat belt, and he hops out of his booster seat.

"Burgers?" Austin jumps out of his seat.

"And hot dogs," Havoc answers.

"Yes!" Austin jumps up, landing in his superhero pose.

"Are our bags okay out here?" I glance at the back of the truck.

"It'll be fine. The compound's on lockdown to outsiders right now."

The mention of a lockdown should probably make me feel trapped or nervous, but instead, I grab Austin's hand and feel safe for the first time in a few days.

Havoc leads us through the clubhouse, and it's eerily empty. Apart from a few guys playing pool, everyone is out back. The large glass doors that look out at the empty desert at the back of the clubhouse are wide open, and it's a warm day. It's the perfect time of year in Vegas, when you don't have to hide from the sun because it's not yet scalding.

People are everywhere, laughing, barbecuing, and enjoying themselves.

I recognize a few of the men, but many others are new faces. The same goes for the girls walking around in bikini tops like it's the middle of summer.

There are multiple grills going, and music blasts through the speakers. Everyone is relaxed like it's a big family get-together. I almost feel like I'm an outsider intruding, but deep down, there's this strange familiarity, and maybe I'm recognizing my roots for the first time. Seeing a side of what the club offers that extends beyond whatever illegal activities they take part in.

Out here there's comradery.

Security.

Family.

Maybe I'm starting to understand the appeal.

"A pool." Austin bounces up and down, tugging my hand.

I follow his gaze to a patch of grass in the distance, where a little blonde girl is splashing around in a kiddie pool.

"Please, Tempe. Can I go play?" He squeezes my hand. "Please. Please."

I glance down at his T-shirt and shorts, wishing we had a bathing suit. But when I look up to find the other kids aren't in swimsuits either, I'm thankful.

"Go, have fun." I lean down and give him a kiss on the forehead.

He darts away, running across the yard to meet the other kids at the pool, and I see Pearl sitting in a lawn chair beside it. She waves at me before going back to the book she's reading.

"I didn't realize anyone had kids," I say to Havoc.

"Most of the guys don't." Havoc points to the blonde girl making room for Austin in the pool. "But that's Legacy's kid, Bea. She's a sweetheart."

Austin sits down in the water facing Bea, showing her his cape. He still refuses to take it off. And it's a reminder that no matter how comfortable he seems to be around the Twisted Kings, he still has his guard up after everything that happened.

"Tempe." Luna pops up from where she's sitting in a lawn chair. "You're here."

She jumps to her feet, pulling her purple hair into a ponytail. As she walks over to me, she ties a knot in her T-shirt, hugging it to her stomach. It's roomy, so her arms swim in it. And it has the words "Good Game" in graffiti font across the front.

Havoc slips away as Luna walks up, making his way over to where Jameson is sitting, drinking a beer. He and a couple of other guys are laughing at something Soul said while Reina is propped on the arm of Jameson's chair, smiling at him like he's the center of her universe.

It's strange seeing him in this environment, where he's not Jameson.

He's Steel. Their leader.

His men surround him, and women watch him from every corner of the yard. He demands the attention of the entire party while sitting back and not having to ask for it. No matter where he is, they all seem to take notice.

Jameson takes a sip of his beer, and his gaze moves to Havoc on his approach before catching mine from across the yard.

His stare lands like dynamite inside my chest.

Grey, stormy eyes.

An ocean in the middle of a hurricane.

It makes sense why women would lose themselves at sea for this man.

Turning my back on Jameson, I smile at Luna, trying to ignore the inevitable pull of his presence.

"You're still here." She pulls me in for a hug. "I thought you left."

"We did, kind of. Steel moved us to his house for my brother's sake."

Her eyes widen as she looks from me to him. "His house?"

"Yeah."

"Where Pearl lives?"

My eyebrows pinch. "That's the place."

If it's possible, her eyes get even bigger. "Good lord, girl, we need to get you a drink so you can tell me all about it."

She snatches my hand and drags me toward the outdoor bar. The moment we walk up, we're each handed a beer.

Across the lawn, Austin is still playing in the pool, and he's now soaking wet. But at least he's laughing.

"Spill," Luna says, clinking her beer bottle against mine. "You're living with him?"

"It's not how it sounds." I laugh, realizing she's making way more of it than there is. "We can't go back to my house right now, so he's doing us a favor."

Luna hums, smirking at me.

"I'm serious."

"Oh, I'm sure you are." She bites her lip, playfully mocking me. "It's *club business*. Of course. You be sure to keep me updated on how that pans out."

I roll my eyes, trying to ignore what she's insinuating. It's clear Jameson doesn't let many people stay at his house, but she's making it something it's not. Something it can't be.

Glancing over my shoulder, I see Jameson is standing now, talking to Havoc. Reina has taken his seat and is pretending not to be watching his every movement. I'd judge her, but I'm no better, staring at him from across the yard.

I take a sip of my beer and try to cool my thoughts. A man is the last thing I need in my life right now. Especially a biker.

If I'm going to build a more stable life for Austin, I can't be chasing love like my mom did. Things are complicated enough without adding lust to my problems.

"It's different around here today." I look around, pausing at where Austin and Bea are still playing.

The two of them have squirt guns now, and they're in a battle with a couple of Jameson's men. One must be Legacy because Bea is using him as a shield. He has the same dark-blond hair and bright-blue eyes she does.

"Yeah, it's calmer around the compound when the guys are in lockdown."

"It's nice."

She nods.

"All done." I jump as someone stops at my side, and when I turn, I see Ghost looking down at me.

He's so quiet, I never hear him coming. And even when he's in the room, it's almost like he isn't.

"What's done?"

"The cameras at your house. We'll know if anyone else shows up from here on out."

"Thanks." I'm not sure why he's reporting to me when I didn't ask him to do it.

"Hey, Ghost." Luna smiles, the faintest blush climbing her cheeks when she breaks the silence. For all of her usual confidence, she looks nervous for the first time since I met her. "I gathered all the footage you were looking for from Sapphire Rise. It's in a drive for you."

"Thanks, Luna." He nods.

They stare at each other for a moment, and I feel like I'm standing in the middle of something. But then Ghost's phone pings, and it splits his attention. He pulls it out, glancing at the screen. Then he disappears in Jameson's direction without another word.

Luna watches him leave, gnawing at the inside of her cheek.

"What was that all about?" My eyebrows pinch.

Her focus snaps back like she's coming out of a trance. "What? That? Nothing."

"Nothing?" I repeat, smiling and taking another sip of my beer.

Luna sighs. "Really, nothing. Ghost is Ghost."

"Meaning?"

"He wouldn't notice me if I danced around naked in front of him."

"I highly doubt that."

She frowns. "I'm serious. Any girl who's tried with him has been shot down."

"Have *you* tried?"

She takes a sip of her beer, not answering.

"I take your silence as a no."

"I don't want to make it awkward. Ghost is the one who brought me in here. He helped me during a tough time, and now he's mentoring me through my tech classes." She sets her beer down on the bar, dragging her thumb through the condensation. "These guys get a bad rap for the things they do, but they do a lot of good as well. Like taking me in when I needed it and giving me a place to crash so long as I helped around the clubhouse. It's not just bikers and prostitutes like the world seems to think. We're a community. I can't risk losing it over a little crush. If Ghost wants something, he knows where to find me."

"I respect that." I lift my beer, and she clinks hers against it. "Now give me some of that confidence, please. I could use it."

"Like you need confidence." Luna slides closer, nudging me on the arm. "I heard you nearly knocked Steel on his ass when you met him. You're a badass, Tempe."

My face pinches. "Let me guess, Ghost told you that?"

"Don't worry, he's not a gossip." She takes a drink. "He just tells me things."

"Because he *doesn't* like you."

Luna smirks, glancing over at Ghost for a split second before turning back to me. "That's beside the point. Ghost said you're tough as nails, which is a lot coming from him. How did you learn to fight anyway?"

"Self-defense classes in high school." I wave my hand up to the gash that cuts through my eyebrow. "My mom didn't always have the best taste in guys. After one did this, I figured I should learn how to stick up for myself if she wasn't going to."

Luna stares at my scar, almost looking like she sees herself in it. "Maybe sometime, you can teach me a few things. If you don't mind, that is. These guys look out for us, but they won't always be there."

"Of course." I squeeze her hand.

Unlike the majority of the clubhouse girls, who look at me like I'm an outsider—an enemy trying to steal their men—Luna treats me like a friend.

"Starting a fight club, wildfire?" Jameson's voice comes from behind me, and it makes me jump.

I spin to find him leaning against the bar watching me.

"Find me later, Tempe." Luna winks, walking away at Jameson's interruption.

"So?" His gaze moves to my scar, and I wonder how much he heard. "Self-defense classes?"

"Any girl hanging out with bikers should know how to throw a punch. Just in case."

Jameson hums, amusement playing in his gaze, and I appreciate that my fiery side doesn't scare him.

"Maybe I'll have to stop by and check it out then." He smirks.

Stepping closer, I scan him over, wetting my lips as we lock gazes again. "I could use a target to show 'em how to take someone down. You volunteering?"

"You want to fight me, Tempe?" Jameson leans closer, brushing my hair off my cheek and leaving a path of pure fire in its wake. "Think you could take me?"

"Maybe." I shrug, playfully. "Guess we'll have to find out."

14

Steel

THIS LITTLE FIRECRACKER THINKS she's tough, and something about it is really fucking hot. But at the same time, I'm not thrilled to find out *why* she's such a fighter.

When I first walked up behind Tempe and heard her telling Luna about how she got the scar that cuts through her eyebrow, it took everything in me not to immediately hunt down her mom's ex-boyfriend to teach him a lesson. I probably would have if Tempe wasn't standing in front of me looking so damn distracting.

She must have changed her clothes at her house because she's wearing a flowery sundress that blows around her thighs with the slight breeze. Her chin is tipped up in a challenge, and the sunset draws out the blonde streaks in her honey-brown hair.

Tempe's cheeks are the prettiest shade of pink as her hazel eyes blink up at me. Her hair is down and wavy and wild like her spirit when she's being feisty. I'd love to feel her silky strands, her soft skin. The contradiction of her prickly attitude.

My gaze drops to her mouth when she wets her lips, and her eyelashes flutter.

I'm standing close—too close.

I can't help it.

I walked over here to get a beer... at least, that's what I told myself. But really, I'm here because of *her*.

I've been on edge since Havoc called me from Tempe's house and told me someone flipped it. I don't know if they were looking for something specific or trying to prove a point. But if that was the case, they made it.

She and Austin aren't going back there unguarded. The neighborhood she was living in is bad enough, but the lack of a security door or any type of alarm system grinds my nerves, thinking she was living in that place as long as she was like that.

I'll help her find a better place.

A nicer neighborhood.

Somewhere to go when she inevitably leaves.

My gut sinks, and I take a step back. This girl is a sinkhole, and I'm riding straight for her.

"So that's how you learned to fight?" I ask, curious now. "Self-defense classes?"

"How much did you hear exactly?" She narrows her eyes.

"Enough to know Helix wasn't the only piece of shit your mom dated."

Tempe lifts her beer to take a sip, but it's empty, so I nod at Reyes working behind the bar, and he gets her another one.

"Unfortunately." She takes a sip, and a bead of condensation drips onto her chest. "They weren't all violent, but she had a thing for bikers."

"Being a biker doesn't give a man an excuse to hit a woman."

Tempe nods, and I'm starting to understand why it's so hard to break through her defenses. She thinks all men are like her father and that all bikers are like the man who hurt her, when that couldn't be farther from the truth.

"I'm not saying all bikers are bad." Tempe frowns. "But try telling my mom's long list of exes that."

"Give me a list of names, and I will." *Happily.*

She shakes her head but keeps her lips sealed because she's smart enough to know what I'd do with that information.

"Well now you know why you shouldn't mess with me," she teases.

"Learned that lesson the first night we met." I rub my jaw in the spot she almost got me with a right hook. "You've got solid technique."

"I thought I did." She sighs. "But it didn't do me any good at the bar last night."

Her fingers find her throat, and my fists clench at the reminder of the man who choked her.

"Don't beat yourself up about that." I tip her chin up when she drops her gaze to the ground. "Knowing what to do and actually doing it when shit goes sideways are two different things. All you can do is give 'em hell if they come for you. But you won't always win."

"You probably do."

"Not always." I shake my head. "Your father was proof of that. Lost a lot of good men because of him."

Tempe's eyebrows pinch. "What did he do exactly? If you don't mind me asking."

I brush my hair back, taking a long pull of my beer. I've asked myself that same question many times over the past nine months, and every time I think I've got it figured out, something else comes to light.

Like his daughter ending up at my clubhouse.

She might not be involved with the men who sent her here, but I'm pretty sure they targeted her for a reason. Either to complete a task or to get under my skin. And it's working.

I set my beer on the bar and swish it around. "Helix thought he was owed something because of an agreement he had with my father. He wasn't."

"We aren't owed anything," Tempe mumbles, surprising me.

"Not everyone feels that way."

"Do you?" She tips her chin up. "What do you think you're owed, Jameson?"

"Not a damn thing, wildfire." I can't help but chuckle. "Some people—like your father—look at this patch as an excuse to let out the worst version of themselves. But I got this patch from my father, and him from his. I was born to wear this cut. So do you want to know what I see when I look at it?"

She nods.

"Honor." I plant my hand over my president patch. "I'll die for my brothers without hesitation because loyalty is the most important thing to have in this life. The men who understand that know we aren't owed a damn thing. We're all here because there are worse places we'd be if we weren't—if we didn't have each other. We're a family. No one comes before anyone else. We survive *together*. It's an honor to wear this patch, but your father didn't understand that."

There's no use sugarcoating the truth. I have nothing good to say about a man who would betray his own club. A man who willingly took the lives of his brothers in an attempt to overthrow me.

Besides, Tempe strikes me as a girl who can handle a little honesty.

She blinks up at me. "Do you blame me for having his blood in my veins?"

I take a deep breath, tipping my face up to the cloudless sky.

I'd like to hate her for being a product of Helix. I probably should when he's the reason I'm incapable of trusting anyone but myself lately. But the more I'm around her, the clearer it is—Tempe is nothing like her dad.

"No." I drop my gaze to hers. "I don't blame you for it."

"Good." A faint smile brightens her hazel eyes.

"We've come a long way, haven't we, wildfire?" I chuckle, taking a sip of my beer.

"We have."

Her eyes brighten like gems that house the souls of men who have fallen into their depths. The desert sky could be void of the sun, and she'd still brighten it.

A breeze kicks up, and Tempe sets her beer on the bar. She reaches for the hair tie around her wrist, wrangling her hair into a bun on the top of her head. A few pieces fall around her face, and my fingers itch to brush them back. To feel her skin. To get a hit of that electrical current that vibrates between us.

The club has always been my entire life.

My purpose.

Women were there to fill a void, like booze was there to loosen my nerves.

But when I look at Tempe, I'm faced with something I didn't realize I've been hiding from. A man beneath the president patch. One who might want more than I've been giving him.

A man I lost at twenty-one when my father took a bullet to the forehead. A man I was still figuring out, so this is what I became instead.

A mask of myself.

Tempe looks around the yard, and I follow her gaze. She watches Austin and Bea in the kiddie pool, smiling at the sight of them having fun.

Legacy is acting as a barrier between them and a couple of the guys with water guns, and he's soaked, taking the brunt of the battle.

I never got it before.

Family.

Kids.

I had my brothers, and that was enough.

Maybe it always will be. Because I have no other choice when the club has to come first to a man in my position.

But when Austin looks up and spots Tempe standing next to me, he smiles with the full force of the sun. He waves at us, and my chest expands.

Like his sister, Austin sees straight past my cut. He sees the parts of me I've been avoiding, and he hands me his full trust. He's still too young to understand the terrible things I've done. Some of it for good reason, but others not so much.

Austin smiles at me, and I don't want to fail him. I don't want either of them to suffer any more than they have—especially for the sins of my club.

"Cute kid." Reina slides up beside me, cutting through my thoughts.

Her smile is as fake as her bleach-blonde hair as she looks from Austin to Tempe.

"Thanks." Tempe forces a smile.

"You coming back, Steel?" Reina rests her hand on my arm. "It's getting lonely over there without you."

She doesn't really care where I am, but she's being territorial because she sees Tempe as a threat. Rumors have been spreading over the fact that Tempe and Austin have been staying at my house, which explains Reina's desperate attempt to claim me.

If she knew me at all, she'd realize jealousy just gets under my skin. No one owns me but my patch.

I shake her off in irritation. "Seems like you and Havoc were getting along just fine without me."

"Oh, come on, Steel. You know how it is. You never cared before."

"And I still don't." I take a sip of my beer.

Reina fucks all the guys at the club, even if she tries to pretend that she doesn't when she's working an angle with me. It didn't bother me when I was still letting her climb into my bed, and it sure as fuck doesn't bother me now. But she's too blind to what this really is to see that.

I'm not looking for an old lady. Especially one who doesn't fucking understand me.

Reina narrows her eyes, her glare landing on Tempe. "Don't tell me you're being like this because of this homely whore. She's just using you, Steel. Everyone can see it."

"And you aren't?" I snap, and Reina tenses when she realizes she's struck a nerve. "Get out of here before you're looking for a new place to live."

It's cold.

Harsh.

I should feel bad because I'm not usually mean to her, even when she's pulling this jealousy act. But she crossed a line, and she fucking knows it.

My brothers might give me shit about Tempe, but they know better than to tell me what to do or question my choices. Reina doesn't.

At least she scurries off, glaring at Tempe as she goes. But it's clear I haven't heard the end of this from her. She's going to be a problem I don't want to deal with, and I should have seen it coming. The moment Reina started spreading rumors that she was going to wear my name on her back someday, I should have cut her off.

Tempe spins to face the bar, draining more of her beer.

She's clearly annoyed, and it's a reaction I'm used to when I've seen Reina pull this shit before.

"Sorry about that."

I don't apologize to anyone, but for some reason, I just did.

"It's fine." Tempe shrugs, turning to walk away, proving it's not fine at all.

I follow her when I should probably just let this go, snagging her arm right as she dips inside the empty clubhouse. "Wait."

"For the record"—she spins the moment I grab her—"I'm not using you. You're the one who won't let me leave."

Her voice cracks at the end, and she avoids looking directly at me.

"I'm aware."

"Good." She rolls her shoulders back. "Because I don't need anyone thinking I'm a charity case. I got myself this far without anyone's help. I sure as hell don't need yours."

"Tempe." I lean in, reaching for her hand, surprised when she doesn't pull away, even if she still refuses to look at me. "No one's questioning that."

"She just did."

"Reina's just being jealous."

Tempe pulls her hand from my grip. "Because she thinks she's your girl, Jameson."

"She's not."

"You're wrong. She is. *They all are.*" She chuckles, shaking her head. "I don't hold it against you though. This is your world. You belong to your people either because you're their president or because you *saved them* from something, and it makes them want to protect you."

"I don't belong to anything but my club, Tempe."

She shakes her head, and even if she's smiling, there's only sadness in her gaze when it meets mine. "You say that like you aren't confirming everything I just said. You don't just belong to your club, Jameson, you *are it*. It's why girls like Reina will never be able to see the difference whether they have your name on their back or not. You, Jameson Steel, *are* the Twisted Kings. You're what they belong to. And I'm an outsider—a threat."

Tempe steps toward me and places her hand on my arm. The lightest grip has my insides rattling.

"I don't need you to apologize for her or try to explain it away as something it's not. I'm not blind, and I'm not stupid. Whatever lines you think you draw are blurry at best. And honestly, there's nothing wrong with that. It's your club, and I respect what you do for them, just like I respect what you're doing for me and Austin. But I need it to be clear that I don't need you to save us. I was doing fine on my own before you, and I'll continue to do so for me and my brother. I'm not one of your people. I can't be."

She looks toward the kiddie pool, stepping through the door onto the porch to yell, "Austin, time to go."

"You don't have to—"

"We do, Steel." She uses my road name like she's trying to prove a point, and I hate it. "This is your life. My father's life... but it's not mine. And that was a good reminder of it."

Austin runs over to Tempe, grabbing her leg and soaking it with his wet clothes. She drops her irritation for him and pats him on the head, even as he starts to complain about having to leave so soon.

And as I watch them walk away, every step eats away at a piece of me.

This is your life.

It is, and that's always been more than enough. Except right now, it isn't.

15

Tempe

At twenty-two, I shouldn't be so jaded. But putting up defenses is what feels safe, and it's the only way I survived my childhood, so I can't seem to help it.

I learned at a young age that trust is delicate. People enjoy breaking it more than building upon it.

Mom's half-hearted promises.

Men constantly coming and going.

After a while, I learned not to count on anyone but myself. I survived, earning every inch of my thick skin in the process.

So I can't figure out how Jameson gets under it so easily.

He asked for my trust, and I wanted to think I was handing it to *him*, not his club. I wanted to think there was still a man beneath the skull and wings on his cut. I forgot for a second that these men plant their roots here, watering them with the blood of their traitors, sacrificing everything until that's all they are: a Twisted King.

Jameson probably thinks I left the barbeque because of Reina, but she was just one more reminder of how little I fit into this place. How this is all temporary for me, but for them, this is everything they believe in.

I understand his loyalty.

I even understand Reina's jealousy.

What I can't do is make myself a part of it. No amount of explanation erases the fact that this is his home, not mine. I need to stop getting so comfortable when I'll be gone soon.

Once Jameson takes out the threat, Austin and I are leaving. It's just the two of us, and I can't let myself think anything more than that.

Luna bounces up and down, circling the punching bag. It's unnecessary in a fight, but I'm getting the impression she'd rather be moving around than sitting still. Finally pausing at the other side, she plants a right hook on the bag with all her strength, hitting the bag so hard her purple hair almost falls out of her bun with the sheer force of it.

"Nice." I watch her continue to circle before she jabs at it again.

Nothing clears the mind like movement, so I'm thankful Luna is apparently as active as I am. She showed up at the house this morning to see if I wanted to work out and asked if I was still willing to teach her how to throw a punch.

It was the perfect excuse to get out of the house, even if we are still on the Twisted Kings compound.

There are several buildings scattered across the property, and the gym is one of them. It looks like an old barn that's been converted. The doors are wide open since it's a nice day outside, but the large air conditioning unit proves it must get blistering hot in here in the middle of summer.

Austin is building tents and car ramps with the mats in the corner while Luna and I work out.

"That was good." I smile when she hits the bag again. "Remember, the key is to punch *through it*. Pretend you're trying to hit whatever's on the other side."

Luna nods, readjusting her stance. She winds her arm back and strikes the bag again, harder this time. It swings, making the rafter creak.

"That's it."

She shakes her hand, rubbing her knuckles. "That hurts."

"A little bit. But the goal is that it hurts them more."

Luna laughs, stepping back so I can get a few jabs in. One punch after another, my thoughts drift with the rhythm.

I still remember when I first learned how to throw a punch. Helix was passing through Houston, and we were living there at the time. He showed up for my ninth birthday party and took me on an errand when it was over.

We stopped by a gym so he could meet up with the owner, and when he was done, he held one of the punching bags and walked me through how to punch someone without breaking my hand.

It's one of the few good things he showed me, even if Mom wasn't happy about it.

She said men want a lady, not a warrior, and that's one more thing I didn't agree with her on. If she was the picture of a lady, then it was nothing to look up to. Men walked all over her, and she accepted it.

I refused to be like her—to be anything less than my unapologetic self for a man—even if it meant I couldn't be loved.

I strike the bag again, and my knuckles burn. My entire body aches as I hit it over and over. My lungs sting as I work through it, but it feels good to get out of the house and move.

Landing a final punch, I grab the bag to steady it.

"Damn, girl, you can hit." Luna wipes her hair off her sweaty forehead, smiling as she takes a sip from her water bottle.

"Clearly." Jameson's voice comes from across the barn, and I look to see him standing with Havoc in the doorway.

I'm drenched in sweat from working out, and my hair is sticking out in all directions, but I don't try to fix it as he walks up to me.

"Jameson!" Austin runs through the barn, always so happy to see him.

He holds up his hand, and Austin gives him a high five.

I should be comforted by the trust my brother shows him, but when this is over, Jameson will be another man he'll lose from his life.

Jameson squats down so Austin can show him his red toy car, and he points out a couple of parts when Austin asks what they are.

"Do you think the car can jump as tall as me?" Austin asks, holding his arm up.

"Only one way to find out." Jameson stands back up, planting his hand on Austin's head and shaking his hair around. "Go build a ramp, and we'll test it."

Austin runs off, and Jameson makes his way over to me.

"You're good with kids." My gaze moves from Jameson to Austin.

Jameson glances at Havoc when he laughs at my comment.

"What?"

"Nothing." Jameson shoots Havoc a glare, watching him walk to Luna before glancing back at me. "I was wondering where you went."

"Luna asked if I'd work out with her for a bit, and I needed to move around. Nice gym." I wave my arms out. "Hope you don't mind."

"Of course not."

"So what brings you here?" I ask. "Pearl knew where we were going, so I assumed she'd tell you where we went."

"She did. And I remembered Luna asking you to teach her a few things, so I figured I'd see if you still need my services."

"You were serious about that?"

Jameson might have volunteered himself during the barbeque, but I assumed that was just flirtation. Especially since I haven't seen much of him since.

"I'm always serious." Jameson shrugs. "Use me all you need, wildfire."

Those words should not be as hot as they are. But coming from his mouth in the middle of this warm barn has my body burning up.

Jameson's black T-shirt hugs his muscular arms, and his square jaw ticks with his smirk. His ocean-gray eyes brew in a challenge.

"You sure?" I hitch an eyebrow. "I won't take it easy on you, and I wouldn't want to embarrass you in front of your friend."

Jameson steps closer. "Please do."

My eyebrow quirks, and I look up at him.

Touching him might be the most dangerous thing for me, but I can't resist his challenge.

"All right." I take a step back, and his gaze skims me. "Try to get me then."

Jameson drags his teeth over his bottom lip, and I'm tempted to let him win. My body feels like it's been in hibernation, and this man drags it out of hiding. He looks me up and down, and my skin prickles.

"You gonna knock some sense into him, Tempe?" Havoc asks, chuckling from the edge of the mat.

I look over my shoulder and see him sitting next to Luna.

"That's assuming there's any sense to be knocked into him." I glance at Jameson. "Guess we'll find out."

Jameson grins as he starts to circle. We don't take our eyes off each other as we play this game of cat and mouse.

"You scared, Jameson?" I ask when he's yet to move in.

"Should I be?"

I shrug. "Don't worry, I won't be mean."

"What do you consider mean?"

"Kneeing you in the nuts."

Jameson laughs. "How kind of you."

"Not really." I smirk. "I just don't want to face the wrath of your fan club if I accidentally take you out of commission."

"Good to know you show mercy, wildfire." Jameson starts to close in. "Let's see what you got."

I turn my back on Jameson so I'm facing Luna, and he pauses behind me.

"Most men attack women from behind," I say a moment before I feel the heat of Jameson's body on me.

He circles an arm around my neck, and the full force of his chest presses flush to my back.

"You need to protect your airway first." I grab his arm with both my hands and turn my chin to the crook of his elbow. "Tuck your chin."

He's holding me tight but still cooperating so I can show Luna the steps, which I appreciate.

"Got it." She watches me, gripping the edge of her seat.

"Then you need to get leverage." I step to the side to bring my leg behind his. "You need to take away his balance."

With my leg behind Jameson's, I jut my knee forward to force his to bend.

"Then you get big." I straighten my leg at the same time as I stretch my arms out, knocking Jameson off me, and he barely manages to find his balance to stop himself from falling to the mat. "From there you would use some of the moves we were doing earlier. But I don't think the patch bunnies would appreciate it if I broke his pretty face."

Luna and Havoc burst out laughing.

"Pretty?" Jameson winks.

"Don't get any ideas." I roll my eyes.

I really shouldn't be flirty with a man who is all wrong for me, but I can't seem to help it.

"Nice." Luna smiles, looking up at Havoc. "You gonna let me practice on you now?"

Havoc tips his head back and laughs. "Sure thing."

They make their way to the middle of the mat while Jameson and I step off to the side.

"Thanks for taking it easy on me so I could show her."

"I only went a little easy." Jameson shrugs. "You still got me good."

"I'm surprised you don't mind."

Most men I've met are intimidated when I show any hint of strength or confidence, but Jameson isn't.

"What can I say…" Jameson follows me to the bench so I can grab my water bottle. "I like when a girl can hold her own."

"Unfortunate necessity sometimes."

Jameson's jaw clenches, but he doesn't respond. He waits for me to take a drink and then walks with me to the barn door so I can get some fresh air.

Luna and Havoc are still fighting each other in the center of the gym, and when his body slams to the ground, the thud echoes through the barn.

Jameson leans against the barn door, watching me take another drink of water. "What are you thinking?"

"That I can't believe you grew up here." I look around at the wide stretch of empty desert. "I guess I'm not the only one with an unconventional childhood."

"I guess." He shrugs. "It's good and bad, depending on how you look at it."

I nod. "When I was a kid, I'd have given anything to live in suburbia and have a normal, boring life. But I guess looking back, I can't imagine not growing up how I did. How else would I have learned all the useless, odd skill sets I picked up from childhood?"

"Such as?" He crosses his arms over his broad chest.

"Taxidermy, for one." I shiver at the thought.

Jameson's face pinches. "Taxidermy?"

"Yeah. That's something I wish I knew nothing about. I was vegan for a year after my mom dated that guy." I hold up a finger, counting the odd things I've learned through the years. "Knife throwing, glassblowing, card counting... And then there was the Houdini wannabe she had a one-month fling with who taught me how to pick every kind of lock you can think of. I could win an award for all the random things I know."

Jameson chuckles, looking out at the desert.

"What about you, Mr. President?" I tease him. "Any fun tricks up your sleeve?"

He watches me, dragging his teeth over his lower lip, and my core flutters, considering whatever just crossed his mind. Luckily, he doesn't share it.

"When I was thirteen, my dad taught me how to make stained glass." Jameson tucks his hands in his pockets.

My eyebrows pinch. "Because that's a necessary life skill for a biker?"

"His response would be *you never know*." Jameson shakes his head. "Really it was because he was working with a guy who owned a window shop, and Dad was transporting product with the glass shipments. We spent so much time there that I picked up a few things."

Something about his confession makes him feel less like a figurehead and more human. It makes me want to learn more.

"Jameson. Tempe." Austin runs up, cutting off our conversation. "The ramp is ready."

"All right, show us." I squeeze Austin's shoulder.

But as soon as I start to move, a bang at a distance freezes me in place.

Instinct tells me to run. To duck. To grab my brother. But I can't seem to make my body do any of those things.

I'm still processing the first bang when there's a succession of others at a distance, and Jameson's body slams into me so quickly, it takes me a moment to process what he's doing.

He has one arm around Austin and the other around me as he puts himself between us and the gunshots without hesitating for a second. He shoves us back into the barn, shielding us as gunshots continue to ring out from all around.

His body is flush with mine as he presses me to a beam, and only when the gunshots stop does he take a step back.

"Austin." Jameson looks down at my brother first. "Are you okay?"

Austin's hands are shaking, gripping my arm.

"I—" Austin's voice stutters, and he doesn't take his eyes off Jameson as I drop to my knees and start patting Austin's shirt, checking for injuries.

"Nothing, he's good." I pat his arms and stomach and then rest my hands on mine. "We're both okay."

Except we're not. None of this is.

Looking up at Jameson, I process what just happened. His hand is on my shoulder; his body's between us and the doorway.

"You protected us," I whisper.

He kept us safe.

16

Steel

My patch gives me strength.

It gives my men hope.

The Twisted Kings are my family as much as my own blood.

The responsibility of leading them is what I was born to do, and I'm damn good at it.

At least, I thought I was.

The attack on the perimeter of the compound was another reminder we've been on the defense for too long. War is on the horizon, and our enemies have proven they'll show no mercy.

My fingers clench, and I can still feel Tempe and Austin shaking in my arms. I didn't think fear was something I could feel, but when that first gunshot rang out, all I could do was throw myself at them.

Tempe doesn't want anything to do with me or my club, but she was all I saw in that moment. Her and her brother—with those eyes that see straight through me. I had to protect them.

What is it about her?

The girl makes me borderline happy.

Content.

At peace.

What the fuck am I going to do with that?

The attack is proof I can't offer her the same. It's in everyone's best interest that I get her out of here as soon as it's safe, and that thought burns in my chest.

A buzzer sounds and another gate opens, letting Havoc and me deeper into the prison.

The guards pat me down, even after they sent me through the metal detector because they like fucking with us. Especially when they know we have no choice but to cooperate if I want to talk to Chaos.

Havoc grits his teeth as the guard knocks him hard in the nuts on a final pass before they let us through.

Another guard leads us into a large cement room with tables, chairs, and bars on the windows. Chaos is sitting at one in the corner, talking to Tanner Monroe, the club's attorney, as we make our way over to them and sit in the chairs on the other side.

Chaos's hair is a touch longer than it's been in a while, marking the amount of time he's already spent in here, and reminding me I'm failing him every day he does. He rubs the back of his tattooed hands and looks up at me.

"How are you doing?" I tip my chin up.

"Just fine, Prez." Chaos leans back in his chair, crossing his arms over his chest, grinning. "Although I'd be better if Monroe could get me a conjugal visit."

Chaos doesn't let anyone see him stressed—or serious for that matter. He'll make light of any situation to prove it's not getting to him. But deep in his eyes, I see it—I owe him. He took the fall for the club so we wouldn't lose our entire shipment, and now he's paying for all our sins.

It was supposed to be a simple trade: guns for coke. But someone tipped off the cops, and the Soulless Riders blamed us and started shooting. We clipped a couple of them but had to split before we could clean up the mess.

Chaos led the cops in one direction while Mayhem got the rest of our men out of there. He went down so no one else would.

"I already told you; you aren't married," Monroe says.

"We'll get you plenty of pussy when you're out of here," I promise, looking at Monroe. "Where are we on that?"

"The judge will hear the next appeal in two weeks." Monroe straightens his tie. "But we have a problem."

"What now?"

"They say they've got a witness. Someone can place Chaos at the gas station."

That is a problem.

The only reason we've gotten this far is that the cops arrested Chaos a few miles away. They locked him up for the drugs in his saddlebag but couldn't tie him to the bodies we'd left behind.

If they do that, there's a chance they'll use him to make an example, and that's not something I'm willing to accept.

"Who's the witness?"

"Don't know. They're protecting them."

I shake my head. "Then figure it the fuck out. Chaos gets out in two weeks, Monroe. Or it's on you."

Monroe has worked for the club for a long time, so I don't feel bad threatening him. He covers for us, and we cover for him. No one's hands are clean.

"You got it, Steel." He stands up, nodding at me once before leaving.

"You think he'll take care of it?" Chaos watches him go.

"He has no choice."

I have enough to make Monroe suffer if he tries to turn on us. And as much as I'd hate to do it, given how many years we've worked together, I will for my brothers.

"How are things on the outside?" Chaos asks, lacing his hands behind his head. "Any more noise at Sapphire Rise?"

I shake my head. "No, it's been quiet. Kansas is keeping it under control."

Chaos tips his head back and laughs. "Only you would actively avoid a strip club, Prez. The girls could help you relieve a little tension."

"All those girls do is give me a fucking headache."

"That's because you don't use 'em like they want you to."

"Like they want *you* to," I remind him.

The girls at Sapphire Rise treat Chaos like he's a god, and given how he looks after them, it makes sense. But I've got enough to worry about without adding the club's strippers to the list of my problems.

Chaos narrows his eyes, scanning me over. "What's got you so fucking uptight? You'd think you're the one in the jumpsuit."

"Ghost still can't crack the drive." I dip my chin, shaking my head. "And the Iron Sinners showed up at the compound to send another message."

"What the fuck?" Chaos's eyes burn with rage when I look back up at him.

"It was just a couple of guys on the perimeter, shooting the dirt to get our attention. Still. Too fucking close."

"No one got hit?"

I shake my head.

Havoc leans back in his chair, crossing his arms over his chest and smirking at me.

"Don't fucking start," I say, already knowing what Havoc's thinking.

"Start what?" Havoc smirks. "I've never seen you so protective, Prez. Knight in shining armor if I've ever seen one."

"Oh shit, is this about the girl?" Chaos rests his elbows on the table, leaning forward.

I haven't mentioned Tempe to Chaos, but I'm not surprised he's heard about her when Soul likes to gossip.

"I was doing my job and making sure they didn't get shot."

"A little too well I hear. Playing house with her and the kid." Chaos shakes his head. "How hard did you get hit in the head when you took down the Sinners at the strip club? I've heard your bed at the clubhouse has been empty."

"I'm staying at my house. Didn't know it was such big fucking news."

"I'm not complaining." Havoc grins. "I'm happy to keep Reina's mouth busy while you're gone."

"Fuck, that girl can give head." Chaos rubs his hand down his face.

"Are you two done reminiscing about blow jobs or are we here to talk business?"

"Can't we do both?" Chaos looks at Havoc, who shrugs. "Besides, this isn't about blow jobs, Prez. This is about you. We've protected plenty of people, but you've never put them up in your house."

"She has a kid."

"Exactly. Fuck that shit. Kids are—"

I slam my fist on the table, cutting him off. "Don't."

Chaos leans back, grinning before pretending to zip his lips. "My bad. Didn't realize I hit a sore spot."

I hate that he's calling me out.

Even more, I hate that he's right.

There's no shortage of people who the Vegas cops don't give a shit about. We're always protecting our community. We do the work the law won't. But I've never let anyone stay in my house before. I've never cared enough to.

I'd like to think I still don't.

But then Tempe will pour me coffee in the morning. And even if she doesn't talk to me, we silently sit across from each other and drink it.

Or Austin will wake up screaming in the middle of the night—and I'll wait at the bottom of the stairs until I hear Tempe soothe him long enough that he's stopped crying.

And I care just enough to have a second cup. Or to sit on the staircase for an extra hour to make sure everyone gets back to sleep.

I care just enough to find my way back to the house every single night to make sure they're okay.

"No one's judging," Havoc says, looking over at me, playing peacekeeper as always.

Chaos shakes his head. "Not judging. But I swear, if Jameson Steel claims an old lady while I'm behind bars, I might just stay in here. You get too much good pussy to be locking down one chick. It'd be a fucking tragedy."

"Just focus on getting out." I stand up. "I mean it, Dean; the club needs you. Jokes aside, this isn't where you belong."

It's rare I call the guys by their legal names, but Chaos has a way of steamrolling through serious situations, and right now, that could get him into trouble. I need him focused on getting back to his brothers.

Chaos stands up, nodding. "You got it, Prez."

A buzzer rings, letting the visitors know it's time to go. The guards drag Chaos away a little rougher than need be to prove a point to us. But while I'm sure it's intended to piss me off, all it does is remind me why I'll fight like hell to get him out.

Forces from all sides are trying to tear my family apart, but I'll keep us together.

No matter what it costs me.

17

Tempe

Sonny is quiet driving me home, and Reyes leads the way on his bike as we enter the Twisted Kings compound. He makes the turn into the neighborhood, and the lights of the house come into view at a distance.

The two of them have become my personal escort service now that I'm back to working the occasional shift at the bar.

Jameson fought me on it at first, but when my manager threatened to fire me if I didn't turn in a doctor's note, I didn't have a choice, and he was finally understanding.

Still, he refuses to let me go to work alone. And secretly, I don't mind. Working at a bar has never been an ideal job. It's just something to cover the expenses of my physical therapy degree. But after everything that happened, I dread work even more.

Thankfully, it's been quiet, and no one has shown up again to threaten me. But I need to start looking for something safer with more regular hours. If only receptionist jobs paid as well as serving alcohol to handsy out-of-towners.

When we pull up to the house, I'm surprised to see Jameson's motorcycle already parked in his spot in the garage. He sleeps here every night, but it's rare he shows up before three in the morning, so it's odd that he's home when it's not even past dinnertime.

"Thanks for the ride." I smile at Sonny before climbing out.

He nods, giving me his usual silent goodbye before pulling away.

We spend every car ride between the compound and work together, but I still don't know much about him. The most I've learned is that he did a stint for robbery a few months ago, and while he was in prison, he met Chaos, who offered him an opportunity with the club when he got out.

I'm pretty sure he told me that story to scare me away from asking for more details, but half my DNA comes from a man with a much worse record than his, so it didn't.

Shutting the car door behind me, I make my way up the front steps of the house. Things have been tense between me and Jameson since the attack on the compound, and he's been so busy I've barely seen him these past few days.

It's a good thing. Or so I keep telling myself.

I make my way into the house and find Pearl in the kitchen, humming while she cooks. She's the exact opposite of her grandson—warm and inviting. She's welcomed us into her space like we've always belonged here, and the company is nice.

Sometimes I wonder if Jameson sees how much Pearl worries about him. She mentioned in passing that he isn't hiding his stress and that he's been more distant since my father betrayed him. From what she said, he took that hard, and I'm starting to understand the depth of it.

Jameson gives all of himself to the club. So for his own vice president to turn against him, it must have hurt.

"Where's Austin?" I glance at his favorite barstool.

Pearl looks over her shoulder, jutting her chin to the hallway. "He's in the den with Jameson watching a movie. I hope you like tacos; they'll be ready in ten minutes."

"Love them."

Pearl hasn't made a bad meal yet. And she cooks much better than I can.

"Need any help?"

She shakes her head. "No, but if you can wrangle those two, that would be great."

I head toward the den in the back of the house, pausing to notice the fresh-cut flowers in the middle of the dining room table.

I've never lived anywhere that felt like *home*. My houses and apartments were temporary landing places while I figured things out—something I'm still doing apparently. But being here with Jameson and Pearl feels like family. Even if Austin and I are technically outsiders intruding.

Turning the corner into the den, I find Jameson and Austin sitting on the couch. Austin is up on his knees watching the battle scene, and Jameson is leaning back with his arm stretched across the back of the couch.

"I'd freeze him." Austin holds his hand out like he's reenacting the action on the screen, pretending to freeze the villain.

I pause in the doorway when Jameson chuckles. It's a sound I've never heard, even if he's laughed before. This time there's no sarcasm, no irritation, no holding back. Just genuine amusement.

"And what about when he unfreezes?" Jameson asks.

Austin sinks back on the couch thinking about the question. "I'd kick him."

Jameson shakes his head. "Gotta learn to fight first if you're gonna do that."

"Will you teach me?"

"Why don't you ask your sister?" Jameson looks over at him. "She's a fighter."

"You're bigger."

"It's not always about being bigger. It's about being smarter than your opponent."

"Tempe's smart."

"That she is." Jameson smiles. "And fearless."

Fearless.

The word swells in my chest. A man who demands the respect of his club, and he's sitting here singing my praises.

Austin sinks back on the couch, curling his legs to his chest. "Tempe stood up to the bad man."

"The one who came to your house?"

Austin nods.

"That's because your sister will always fight for you. Don't you forget it."

"Would you?" Austin blinks up at him. "If the bad man comes back, will you help her fight him?"

Jameson's jaw clenches, and he swallows hard. "With all I am."

Tears sting my eyes when I watch them. It's easy to judge Jameson for his club because then I don't have to face this side of him. The man he is when he lets his guard down. When he lets us see he's human.

A man with honor.

A man who has done nothing but help us when I'm the one who threw his life into upheaval.

Lifting off the doorframe, the floorboard creaks beneath me, and Jameson catches me wiping a tear from the underside of my lashes when he looks my way.

Luckily, Austin doesn't seem to notice as he flies off the couch and runs for me.

"Tempe."

"Hey, kiddo." I crouch down and give him a hug. "Pearl said it's dinnertime."

"Yes!" He bounces up and down. "I'm hungry."

Austin lets me go and darts from the room as Jameson lifts off the couch.

He always takes his cut off when he walks into the house, and it's obscene how this man wears jeans and a simple gray T-shirt. It's no wonder the club girls fight over him.

Glancing away, I swallow that thought.

"Tempe—"

"Dinner's ready," I cut him off, forcing a smile. "I hope you're hungry."

I leave the room before he can stop me. Every second alone with him lately has my mind spiraling, and the more I give in, the harder it's going to be to leave.

Jameson's helping us out to save his club. That's it. That's all this can be.

Pearl's tired when we finish dinner, so I offer to clear the table and do the dishes. It's the least I can do to help when we're staying here.

Pausing halfway through cleanup, I finish Austin's bedtime routine with him. Except tonight, since Jameson is here, he wants him to read him his story, and Jameson surprises me by agreeing to it.

I'm finishing drying the final dish when Jameson's footsteps sound from above, and he makes his way back downstairs.

Glancing up from the dishes, I spot Jameson walking down the steps.

"Austin likes you." I turn to face him.

"Against better judgment." Jameson sets Austin's cape over one of the chairs in the kitchen.

"I need to start working with him on taking the cape off."

"If he likes it, who cares?" Jameson shrugs.

"He starts kindergarten this fall, and kids are mean."

"I guess you're right." Jameson holds the counter, leaning against it. "Why's he always wearing it anyway?"

"Superheroes make him feel safe. He didn't have much of that growing up."

"He has that now." Jameson tips his chin up. "He has you."

"I guess." I make my way over to the couch and sink onto it.

Jameson grabs a bottle of whiskey and a glass out of the cabinet and meets me on the couch, pouring two fingers and taking a sip.

"Want some?" He holds his glass out, and even if I'm not usually a whiskey drinker, I take it.

The energy is different when I'm alone with Jameson. The air is thicker, and I can't deny the tension. Taking a small sip, I let the whiskey settle my nerves before handing it back to him.

"Thanks."

Jameson nods, taking the glass. "How's Austin doing with everything?"

"Some days are better than others." I brush my hair back. "He still wakes up every morning asking for her."

"Your mom?"

I nod.

"It's strange how the brain resets like that. How you can fall asleep and forget. And then it's like you're losing them all over again."

I turn to face him. "You sound like you know something about that."

"I do." He sets his glass down but doesn't elaborate.

My gaze drifts while the constant hole inside me widens. "The other day Austin asked me if this is what it takes to become a superhero. He asked me if that's why all this happened. Because he thinks you don't get your powers until you've lost something big. He's still too young to know the difference between a hero's origin story and real life. How am I supposed to explain all this to him? I don't have the answers he's looking for."

"He's not looking for answers, Tempe. He's looking for comfort. He's trusting you to keep him safe."

I curl my legs up under me. "I'm not a superhero, Jameson."

"You are to Austin. He sees you stepping up for him—being there for him. You're grieving your mom's loss just as much as he is, but you put him first no matter what you're feeling. Your actions say more than words ever could."

My heart hurts when I think about my mom. How I'm all he has left, and I'm still nothing close to what he deserves.

"You're his superhero, Tempe, and it gives him hope. Let him have it."

I shake my head. "If anyone is his superhero, *you are*."

"I'm no hero." Jameson scratches the scruff on his jaw.

"Your men think you are."

"My men *know* I'm not."

I mull over that confession, wondering what side of Jameson they see, and wondering if maybe he's right. Maybe he never shows them the parts of himself we get to see. The man who strips his cut off when he walks through the front door and leaves the club outside it.

I can't imagine how hard that must be on him. While Austin relies on me, Jameson has an entire club resting on his shoulders.

"How heavy is it?" I glance at Jameson.

"How heavy is what?"

"Your men rely on you. The women rely on you. Your whole club does. Hero or not, you're responsible for them. And when things go wrong, you're the one who carries the burden. How heavy is that weight?"

Jameson stares at me, and it's impossible to read his expression. His gray eyes soften, and I sense his defenses slowly coming down, no matter how much he fights it.

"Heavy enough that it's easier not to focus on it."

I absorb that.

The weight he carries. The responsibility. The burden.

I resented the Twisted Kings because of my father, but Jameson offers a different perspective on his club. The more time I spend with him, I understand that he does so much more than enjoy the perks that come with being a biker.

Jameson is there for the people who depend on him. He helps them when they have nowhere to go. And for the first time, I'm seeing the full burden of that responsibility sitting in front of me.

Turning, I sit on the edge of the couch and widen my knees, pointing to the ground at my feet. "Come here."

Jameson's face pinches. "Why?"

"Just come sit on the floor." I roll my eyes.

He's so used to issuing orders that he finds it impossible to let anyone tell him what to do.

Jameson reluctantly climbs up, standing in front of me. I sense an internal battle waging in his eyes before he turns and sits with his back against the couch between my legs.

I place my hands on his solid shoulders, and he stiffens for a moment before relaxing as I knead my fingers into his thick muscles.

Steel—living up to his name.

"What are you doing?"

"Thanking you for everything you've done for me and my brother." I rub my fingers over his shoulders, digging my thumbs into his shoulder blades as he relaxes into it. "I think a lot of people want things from you, but very few people actually thank you for it."

"Here we are again..." Jameson chuckles. "You're keeping me on my toes by being nice to me."

I bite back a smile. "Against all odds."

Jameson groans when my thumbs dig deeper, and my chest tightens at the sound.

"You keep doing that, and you can be nice all you want."

I knead deeper just to get him to make that sound again.

His chin drops, and he sinks into the feel of my touch. I run my thumbs up the back of his neck, slowly feeling his muscles relax beneath my hands.

"You do so much for your men, and they probably don't even notice. They expect a lot out of you because they know you'll live up to those expectations."

"And what are your expectations of me, Tempe?"

I rake my fingers up into his thick hair, dragging them slowly back down again, and appreciating how I have the power to make this man melt beneath my touch when he is an unmovable wall in any other situation.

"I don't have expectations, Jameson. Life taught me better than that. I just want to make it through the day. And then the next day. And the next. And hopefully, through all of it, I'll slowly build a better life for me and Austin."

"All by yourself?"

"If that ends up being the case, then yes." I rub his shoulders. "My life comes with baggage, and after what happened, there's even more of it. I don't expect anyone else to want to take that on with me."

"What if someone wants to?"

I shrug. "I guess that's on them."

Jameson lifts his head, staring straight ahead. "And what if they've got even more than you?"

I pause, resting my hands on his back, feeling his body expand with every deep inhale.

"I honestly don't know." I sigh. "A few months ago, I might have said it didn't matter. But that was before Austin became my responsibility. He deserves better than I had, and I'll do everything to make that happen—sacrifice anything. Even having a relationship if it comes down to it."

Jameson hums, and I glide my fingers over his shoulders.

"Feel any better?"

"Much." He brushes his palm along my shin.

It's a gentle graze at first. A friendly thank you for helping him release a little tension.

But when his hand doesn't leave my bare skin, and he tightens his hold, I dig my thumbs into his shoulders, and static crackles between us.

"I'm not the only one taking care of everyone around me, Tempe. You do plenty of that too."

"Yeah?" My voice shoots up slightly as his hand moves up my leg.

"Mm-hmm." He brushes his thumb over my calf, kneading it, teasing me with slow strokes. "Who makes you feel good when you've taken everything on? Who takes care of you?"

I swallow hard as he moves down my leg, gripping my foot and kneading the arch.

"Myself, I guess."

Jameson rubs up my foot—my leg. His other hand does the same, and my head is light. It's been so long since I've been touched that I've forgotten how it felt. And Jameson's firm grip and purposeful strokes are unlike anyone else.

"That's a shame," Jameson says, pulling my legs further apart as he rubs them, and I'm suddenly very aware of how his body is warm against my core with how I'm spread open.

He leans back when I've stopped massaging him, laying his head back on my thigh and looking up at me. But I don't lean away; I don't back up. I stare into his eyes and lose myself in the ocean of his gaze.

His hands roam my legs, and I lose all sense at his touch.

"Thank you, wildfire."

"For what?"

A smirk climbs up in the corner of his mouth. "Lifting the weight."

"Even if I'm one of the people who makes it heavier?" The tension between us is so thick, the heat of him has me in flames.

"Especially then."

Before I can shoot off another sassy comment, he reaches up and grabs the back of my hair, pulling me to him.

18

Tempe

JAMESON'S LIPS MEET MINE, and my heart leaps to my throat.

We're stripped of who we are and fall into this moment. Two people with responsibilities we still don't fully understand and didn't have a choice in accepting them. Weight we've been carrying around, unwilling to share the burden when it's hard to trust anyone but ourselves.

Tonight, we shoulder it together. We bend to the pressure. We submit.

Jameson's fingers thread through my hair, and he holds me to him. The scruff of his jaw is rough like he is. Burning me from my cheek to my soul.

I part my lips, and he drinks me in. His tongue reaches for mine, and I cup his face in my palms. The most delicate kiss from a man with blood on his hands.

Hands that keep me safe.

Hands that make my skin prickle.

Our teeth clash, and our tongues tangle. And even if the kiss is awkward and upside down, it wakes my every nerve ending.

He smells like leather even out of his cut. He tastes like whiskey mixed with the cinnamon gum he was chewing after dinner. And he feels like my body's favorite drug as he kisses me slowly.

With purpose.

Jameson's warm back presses to my core, and when he lightens his grip on my hair, I pull back to look down at him sitting on the floor between my legs. I stare into the gray eyes that stole my soul the moment I first looked into them.

I promised I'd never give myself to a man like the ones my mom always fell for.

Promised I was smarter than to hand my heart to a biker.

Looking into Jameson's eyes, I don't know where I went wrong—or if this even is. All I know is that I need more of him.

"You're supposed to hate me, Tempe." He blinks up at me. "Why are you kissing me back?"

"Maybe because you're good at it." I smile, brushing my fingers over the stubble on his jaw, pulling his mouth to mine again.

Except this time, he's anything but sweet. His fingers twist tight in my hair. And even if I'm the one hovering over him, he's the one who claims me.

Jameson pulls away just long enough to turn around, and he picks me up so fast that my head rushes as he lifts me off the couch. I wrap my legs around him, and my core grinds against his body. Beneath his hands, I feel the full year it's been since I've been touched.

All the anger I've harbored toward this man slips away, and I lose myself in him for the night. I lose the responsibilities I'll wake up to in the morning. I let myself be his.

"Jameson." I moan against his mouth when his hand strokes my thigh, and he pulls back. "Please don't stop."

His eyes are closed when I tip my forehead to his. I sense him holding back with all he has. But his body tells me what he doesn't want to as his hard cock puts pressure on my core.

"I'm a bad idea, Tempe." He teases my lower lip, slowly peppering kisses along my jaw. "I'm not good for anyone."

"I'm no picnic myself." I tip my head back when he kisses the center of my throat. "Besides, it's just one night. I'm sure you do this all the time."

Jameson pauses, looking me in the eyes. "You're wrong. I never do *this*."

I don't know what to make of his comment, but it feels a little like a challenge I can't resist.

"Are you scared, Steel?" I smirk, dipping my mouth by his ear and run my tongue along the shell of it. "Is the president of the Twisted Kings afraid of what could happen?"

"Are you testing me, wildfire?"

"Maybe."

Jameson spins me around, pinning my back to the wall so hard it knocks the air from my chest. He uses the wall as leverage to pin me with his body, and one hand finds my jaw, gripping it hard.

He drags his thumb roughly over my lower lip. "Most people know better than to test an MC president."

"And what if they don't?" I tease.

"Then I'm happy to teach them a lesson."

He grazes his thumb up and over my mouth, and when he pauses at my lips, I part them. He presses his thumb over my tongue, and I close my mouth around him. He pulls it out slowly, and I suck on it as he does, eliciting the most intoxicating growl from him.

"Are you worried I can't handle you, Jameson?" I wet my lips.

"I wish you could." He rubs his wet thumb over my mouth, fixating on where he's smearing my ChapStick. "You have no idea how much I wish you could."

"I promise I'm not as innocent as you might think."

"You're a good girl. Or, at least, too good for a man like me."

I tip my chin up, sinking against him, and my whole body hums with everything I've wanted since the first moment we caught gazes across the bar. Even if back then I didn't see it.

"I'm not scared of you." I run my fingers through his thick hair, scratching his scalp. "Besides... I'll let you in on a little secret. Even a good girl wants to be fucked like she's bad sometimes."

I'm never this confident. But with Jameson pinning me against a wall, I want to tease him. To tempt him. To challenge him until he makes me pay for all of it.

"Are you trying to tease me, wildfire?" He cups my jaw and presses me to the wall. "You should be careful with this smart little mouth."

"Make me."

He smirks. "You really don't want me to do that."

"Or do I?"

"Let's find out." Jameson grins, setting me down slowly. "Get in my room, wildfire."

I wait for him to take it back, but he doesn't, so I slowly make my way toward his bedroom. Jameson snatches the bottle of whiskey as he follows me.

With every step, my mind begs me to turn back. But my body hasn't felt this alive in a long time.

Jameson demands control, and I need that.

To be mindless.

To be free.

I don't know what's to come when I leave the compound. But for tonight, I don't want to think about it.

When I reach his moonlit bedroom, I'm reminded of his room at the clubhouse. The decorations are simple and impersonal. It's neat, but not because that's how he is. More so because he never spends any time in it.

Still, it feels like him. A room needs nothing more than Jameson Steel in the flesh to make a statement.

Stopping in the center, I spin around to face Jameson, who's leaning against the doorframe, holding the bottle of whiskey in his hand. He pops off the top and brings it to his lips, taking a sip as he watches me.

"You look good in here, wildfire."

"And yet, you're still standing over there. Do you always play hard to get, Jameson?"

"I'm anything but hard to get when it comes to you."

"Then why aren't you teaching me my lesson yet?" I drag my teeth over my lower lip, holding my hands behind my back and testing him.

Jameson smirks, wiping his mouth with the back of his hand as he lifts off the doorframe. He eats up the space between us in four steps, towering over me.

"You want to play this little game?" He tips my chin up, forcing me to look at him. "Then strip for me."

I bite my lip, reaching for the bottom of my T-shirt and stripping it off, tossing it to the side. My nipples peak under my lace bra in the cool bedroom.

He shakes his head when I pause. "You're not done yet."

I reach for the button on my pants, slowly unzipping them. Taking my time to dip my thumbs into the band and slowly dragging them down my legs. The moon shines through the windows, painting me in the glow of the desert at night when I stand in front of him in nothing but my bra and underwear.

"You think it's cute to tease me?" He reaches into his back pocket and pulls out a knife, flicking it open. "I said strip. That means everything."

One hand holds the bottle of whiskey while he uses the other to trace the knife along my ribs. He sweeps the blade up between my breasts, hooking the lace bow between them. With a swift tug, he slices through it, popping my bra open.

My nipples pebble with his attention as he slowly drags the knife down one breast, teasing my nipple with the tip and then trailing it over my stomach. He pauses at the thin strap that holds my underwear to my hips, cutting through that too.

"That's better." He smirks, tossing his knife to the dresser. "Now, get on your knees."

Slowly, I drop to my knees in front of Jameson.

He's still fully clothed as he stands over me. His jaw clenches, and he's everything that embodies the title on his patch.

Ego.

Confidence.

Power.

"How can I serve you, President?"

Jameson swallows hard, watching me, slipping his belt from the loops with his free hand.

"You're too sweet to be a bad girl." He tugs his belt off, tossing it to the side. "But you like playing with fire. You like seeing how hot you can stand the heat before it burns you. I warned you not to push this."

"Maybe you aren't the only one who enjoys a challenge." I tip my chin up.

"We're about to find out." Jameson grips my jaw. "Open."

He taps his thumb on my lips, and I part them. The moment I do, he hooks his thumb over my teeth, holding my jaw wide as he lifts the whiskey and dribbles it over my lip, spilling a shot into my mouth. It coats my tongue and drips down my chin.

"Swallow." But he doesn't move his thumb, so I have to close my lips around it, sucking as I swallow the alcohol down.

My head swims as I take a breath.

"Good girl."

He brings the bottle to his lips next, taking a drink. But instead of swallowing, he holds my mouth open and leans down, feeding me the shot straight from his lips. He presses his mouth to mine, forcing his tongue into my mouth as I swallow the whiskey down.

Claiming me.

Consuming me.

Jameson's chest rumbles with a low growl, and his fingers lace into the back of my hair, deepening the kiss. Whiskey coats my throat—our lips. It drips down my chin and over my breasts, and when he pulls back, I'm lightheaded.

"Your mouth is so pretty when it's pleasing me." Jameson sets the whiskey down on the dresser and reaches for his zipper. "Let's see what else it can do."

He pulls his cock out, stroking from base to tip. "Put your pretty lips around my cock, and thank me for forgiving you for your family's sins."

I muster all my confidence, wanting to be everything he sees in me and more. Wanting to play into this fantasy so I can spend a night outside of my head. At his mercy. Used and pleased at his discretion.

Tomorrow, we can go back into battle. But right now, this is just us lifting the weight.

He grips his cock, and I know there's no way I'll be able to take him down my throat. The sheer size of him makes me wonder how much I'll be able to take in general. But as he pumps slowly up and down his length, I want to take him in every way.

Jameson angles my chin up and taps my mouth. "Open."

I do as I'm told, and the second my lips part, he shoves his thumb into my mouth, rubbing it over my tongue. With every stroke, I stick it out farther, seeking his touch.

Jameson strokes himself, stepping closer, squeezing his cock to pull a bead of cum from the tip. He watches it drip onto my tongue, but he refuses to release my jaw so I can swallow it down.

"What is this needy tongue of yours begging for, Tempe? A shot of whiskey or my cum?" He smears another drip of cum over my lips. "Or maybe both?"

I can't answer him with how he's holding my jaw, but I want *everything*.

"You think you know me, wildfire. But you have no idea who you're dealing with. No idea the things I've wanted to do to you. You really should have thought twice before giving me permission."

He pulls my mouth open wider.

"You should have known better than to make yourself my plaything."

Pulling his thumb out, he replaces it with the head of his cock, and I wrap my lips around him. But when I try to take him deeper, he grabs the back of my hair and holds me in place.

"Don't be so greedy. Play with it."

I do as I'm told, closing my lips over the head of his cock and swirling my tongue around the tip. Teasing him. And I can't figure out why he won't let me take him deeper.

Jameson stands over me, and I stare up into his eyes. His body tenses with every swirl of my tongue. Every flick gives me a reaction, and I crave them all.

Flattening my tongue, I rub it over the leaking slit, tasting him mixed with the whiskey. And when my lips suction as I swallow, a growl vibrates his chest, so I do it again.

But before I can do more, he pulls my hair, tugging me off him.

"I wasn't done."

"Neither am I." He grabs my jaw, leaning down to brush his mouth over mine. "Get on the bed."

19

Tempe

STANDING UP, I STEP backward until my calves hit the bed, and I sink onto it. My palms find the comforter, and I scoot back until I'm in the center while Jameson stays where he is, watching me with his cock in his hand.

The full intensity of his focus is on me, and I've never felt as desired as I do when he strokes his hard cock.

A man everyone wants, but tonight, he's mine.

I press my thighs together, and he immediately shakes his head.

"Spread your legs, Tempe. Let me see your pretty pussy drip."

I slowly spread my knees open, dragging my hand over my stomach and walking my fingers down. My pussy aches with the need for him, and when I dip my fingers inside myself, Jameson's jaw clenches.

"You have a lot of patience," I say, pushing my fingers in deeper, watching him tighten his grip on his cock.

"Patience is a virtue." His gaze meets mine. "And very effective."

"How?"

"Because anticipation makes everything better."

Jameson steps forward, reaching behind his back to strip off his T-shirt. Moonlight cascades over his chest, reflecting off the solid ripples of his muscles that draw a beautiful path to his perfectly chiseled abs. His arms are covered in ink, with the Twisted Kings patch prominent on his right shoulder.

Jameson strips off his pants next, and he's an unholy sight.

A god to his men.

A blessing to women.

Mine for the night.

"Be a good girl and give me a taste." He pauses at the foot of the bed, dropping a knee onto it.

I pull my fingers out, and he grabs my wrist, sucking them into his mouth and rolling his tongue over them.

"Such a sweet cunt." He drags his tongue over my fingers once more before moving lower, tugging my hips and pulling my pussy to his face.

He dives between my legs, licking the full length of me before slowly circling my clit. My hands fly into his hair as he draws figure eights.

"Whiskey tastes better on you." He grins, and I look down, realizing it spilled all the way down the front of me when he poured it into my mouth.

Jameson sucks on my clit, and my back arches.

"Yes." My eyes seal shut, moaning when he does it again.

But right as I start to build, he pulls back, refusing me my release.

"Please don't stop." I thrash my head in irritation.

"No?" He nips at the inside of my thigh. "Why not?"

"I need it." I dig my fingers into his scalp.

"How bad?" He brushes his tongue over my pussy, holding my hips to the bed when I try to lift them in search of friction. "I want to hear you beg."

"Please, Jameson." I tip my head back as he teases my clit with his tongue. "Please let me come."

"Better." He drives his tongue inside me, his fingers flicking my clit as he fucks me with his mouth.

But right as I'm about to come again, he pulls back, pinning my hips to the bed.

"Fuck." I slap my hands over my eyes, tipping my head back in frustration. "Why are you doing this?"

"I told you I'd teach you a lesson, wildfire. You need to learn it's not smart to test a patient man. I could do this all night. Until your cunt makes a mess of my bed, and you're begging me to put you out of your misery with my cock." He drags his tongue over my pussy. "You might be wild, but I'll enjoy the challenge of making you submit."

"Please, Jameson." I dig my fingers into his hair again.

He doesn't take his eyes off me as he nips at the inside of one thigh then the other. He watches me as he slowly skates his tongue in, sucking my clit into his mouth and humming.

This time, he doesn't let up. He makes artwork with his tongue. And when I finally reach the precipice, I come so hard my vision gets dark.

White noise fills my ears, and I'm floating.

Jameson lifts, bracing his hand on the bed for leverage. He pinches my nipple, and my body is so incredibly sensitive from my still-fading climax that it makes me scream. His nose moves down the side of my neck as he breathes me in. Moving his hand to my other breast, he pinches that nipple even harder.

"I warned you we shouldn't do this." He looks down at me writhing for him. "I'm no good for you."

"You're not all bad."

"You sure about that?" Jameson reaches for my jaw, grazing his thumb across it as he tips my head back.

His fingers tighten as his hard cock puts pressure between my legs. I rock my hips along him, chasing that fear mixed with excitement.

His hips shift forward, teasing me like he's going to push in before resisting and pulling back.

"Please." I tip my head back when he continues to torture me.

"That's a good girl, begging for my cock." Jameson circles my clit with his thumb. "Open your legs, and let me see how much you want it."

I widen my legs further, looking down as Jameson slides himself through my slickness. He coats his cock in my excitement, grazing up and down. But every time I lift my hips, he pulls away.

"Please, Jameson."

"What do you need, wildfire?"

"I need you to fuck me." I grab his shoulders, and my nails dig in so hard I nearly break skin.

It draws light to Jameson's eyes, and I watch him break beneath what he's been resisting.

One moment.

He's holding back, and then he's thrusting in. A strong, brutal shift that kicks the air from my lungs. It might even stop my heart.

He fills me to the fullest.

"Fuck." Jameson freezes when he bottoms out.

My legs curl, and I drag my nails down his chest. He's larger than he looked, and my entire body aches with how I'm forced to stretch around him.

I tip my head back, and a tear slips out as I try to adjust, but Jameson reaches up and wipes it away.

"Look at me, wildfire."

Blinking my eyes open, I'm met with his gaze. He's settled between my legs, not moving while I adjust. Even as my pussy squeezes him, desperate for the friction, he waits for me.

Jameson brushes his lips over mine.

Gentle when he rarely is.

Sweet when I didn't think it was possible.

A whiskey kiss that strikes a match to my heart.

"You okay?"

"Yes." I kiss him deeper, and he starts to move.

He tucks his arms under my knees to curl my legs up, driving himself to the center of my being as I chase what's building with every roll of his hips. He buries his face in the side of my neck, kissing the path up and down it.

Maybe Jameson's right—I'm a spark in the wind. Because my body is burning up with need as he forces me to take every hard inch.

Every *bare* inch.

"Jameson—" I pant, my eyes widening, "you're not wearing a condom."

"No, I'm not." He lifts, pulling out almost all the way, watching where we connect as he slowly pushes back in. "I don't have any at my house."

"Why?"

This time, when he pulls almost all the way out, he pauses with just the tip inside me.

"Because I don't fuck people here." He thrusts in again.

But that's exactly what he's doing—fucking me here—in his bed.

Fucking me so hard I can barely breathe. Not stopping even if he's aware of what he's doing.

It's reckless. Careless.

And I stupidly let him.

Jameson tilts his hips and finds a spot I didn't know existed as he strikes me deeper. His cock pulses against it over and over. But right as I'm about to fall over the other side, he pulls out.

"No." I grip the blanket in frustration. "I was about to come."

"I know." He smirks, grabbing my hips and spinning them in a windmill until I'm on all fours. He grabs my hips and thrusts in again, claiming me deeper from this angle.

"Are you going to try to stop me, wildfire?" He grabs my arms and pulls me up so I'm kneeling, forcing my back to arch. The stubble on his jaw scratches my neck when he kisses the path up it. "Or are you going to be a good girl and let me fill you with my cum?"

I already know my answer, and it's terrifying.

"I'm yours."

"Good girl." He reaches down and circles his finger over my clit. "You feel so good squeezing my cock. I think this pussy was made for me."

Jameson claims my body like he runs his club.

With all of him.

He widens his knees so he can fuck me deeper, stretching his palm over my stomach. We become one, from our breath to our heartbeats.

Tipping my head back against his chest, I reach up and pull him in for a kiss. I need the intimacy, to feel like this man can be contained, even for just a minute. That in my hands, I can hold him in place and make him feel less infinite.

We're expanding.

Becoming.

What? I don't know.

All I know is my core aches with his hard thrusts, and my skin burns with his rough kiss. My body splits like the start of a new moment in time.

I sink into the illusion that he isn't just doing this to prove a point. That he wants me here for more than to get revenge for his club. That he's fucking me for more than just a release.

Maybe he feels this too.

I drown in the illusion that his kiss is from the heart.

His tongue dips into my mouth, and I suck on it like I wanted to do with his cock, but he denied me.

A man with unmatched patience, yet relentless when he lets loose.

Jameson groans, spinning me back down onto the bed so he can claim me fully. He tilts my ass and strikes the nerves that have me seeing stars. His pelvis grinds against my clit with every thrust, and it's almost too much for my body to handle.

"Fuck, Tempe. Give me that tight little cunt. Let me feel you come."

My mouth opens as my climax hits, but sound doesn't come out. My ears ring, and my body shakes with the most intense release to ever shudder through me.

"Such a good girl."

His words.

His praise.

His touch.

Jameson shifts, and his body tenses as he curls his face into my neck. He fills me up just like he promised. Not considering the consequences.

I should care, but I don't. I want him on me—inside me.

I've never let a man fuck me without a condom, but I want to hand everything to this one.

Maybe it's his patch and the attention he demands.

Maybe I'm no better than anyone else in his life, taking what I know he'll give.

Or maybe I'm naïve enough to think this could be more.

Jameson lifts, looking down at me as he brushes my hair from my face. There's something in his eyes I can't quite read. Emotion from a man who so rarely shows it.

Pain from his past.

Pressure from his present.

Obligation from his patch.

Jameson needed the same thing I did tonight. To pretend nothing outside this room exists, and we gave into it.

He traces my cheek, tucking my hair behind my ear. "You break all my rules, Tempe. All my fucking rules."

"You break mine too."

20

Steel

THIS LIFE NEVER STOPS.

Never slows.

My club requires my attention every minute of the day, and up until now, they've had it.

Waking up with Tempe in my bed a couple of days ago was a mistake I shouldn't have made, and there's no taking it back.

She's splitting my focus, and now, every time I blink, I see her kneeling in front of me. Offering everything I can't have if I'm going to be the kind of man my club needs.

Not that I can scrub my thoughts clean either. There's something innocent behind the mile-high walls Tempe builds. Something soft underneath the ruthless fighter. And no matter how hard her life has been, her touch heals, and her kiss cracks me open.

I tried my best to resist her—to be patient.

I tried to stay in control, but she snaps it.

She showed affection to a man who's better at killing people than loving them.

Maybe she just caught me at the end of a hard day. A difficult month. An impossible year.

A weak moment.

My traitor's daughter dropped to her knees, and I stared into the eyes of the blood that tried to destroy me and my men. She blinked up at me, and I wanted to forget the war I've been fighting since I first slipped on my president patch at twenty-one.

I wanted the peace she was offering.

Comfort.

Something a man as strong as me was weak enough to give in to for a moment.

She parted her lips, and I felt the pause in the universe. I gave in to what I'm not allowed to want—things I never knew I did.

I don't fuck women bare, and I certainly don't fuck them in my actual bed.

I sure as hell don't let them stay at my house.

She breaks every rule I've ever set.

Tempe might think of herself as another check mark on my mind-numbing list of conquests, but she's so far from it that I'm not sure who I am anymore.

What we did was more than sex, and I learned at a young age the danger of wanting more than that from a relationship.

My dad gave his whole heart to my mom. He never strayed and never wanted more than she gave him. He wanted a family, and they had it—first me, then my brother.

But life's unpredictable whether you're in the club or not. And when we lost Wyatt when he was only a year old, Mom never recovered. It didn't matter that I was five and barely understood it. I felt the impact in every day that passed.

Mom rarely left her room after his funeral. She didn't even want to see me when I tried to bring her things I thought might help.

My favorite stuffed animal, my favorite blanket, a hug.

That's when I learned that people don't have to be dead to become ghosts. I watched her become one right in front of us. Haunting the house with her cries. Turning the air cold.

Dad tried to hold it together, but the pieces were everywhere. Our love wasn't enough to fix her. My love wasn't enough to fill the holes.

I still remember that day I learned that love doesn't last.

A breeze ran through the house when Dad and I got home because the back door had been left open. Dad walked in first, and I was right behind him. We had been at the shop, where I played with my toy cars while Dad fixed his motorcycle and talked to Helix.

I sorted the wrenches, making an obstacle course for my cars. It was like every other day.

When the nightmares take over, I can still see my mom's feet floating in the air. Her nightgown blowing in the breeze while her body swayed.

Her twisted face. Her discolored skin.

The final transition to the ghost she was already becoming.

Loving us wasn't enough to keep her here, and I learned not to trust feelings of comfort ever again.

Whoever says it's better to have loved and lost doesn't know how heartbreak can level someone.

It's why I don't entertain relationships. Especially ones that end with me putting my name on some girl's back. My dad did that and look where it got him.

Call me cold.

Call me heartless.

Call me incapable of emotional commitment.

It's better than the alternative.

But the fact that Tempe and Austin are living in my house is starting to get to me. And having her in my arms kicked up something in my chest I thought I was numb to. The two of them make me doubt myself, which is dangerous for an MC president.

So from now on, I need to be smart.

I need some distance.

The past couple of nights, I've slept at the clubhouse because it's better than the alternative.

For a split second, Tempe made me feel safe.

Safe is dangerous in my world.

So I slipped out of my bed before she woke up, rode to the club, and haven't returned since. It's better that she hates me than expects what we did to change something.

"Smoking again?" Legacy is the first one to church, and he doesn't miss that I'm already on my second cigarette.

"I'm quitting."

Maybe if I say it enough times, I'll believe it.

"You know..." Legacy leans back in his chair, watching me. "Sometimes life's little surprises are a good thing."

"I don't know what you're talking about."

"Tempe." Legacy taps his hand on his knee. "And Austin."

I take a drag of my cigarette, wishing the rest of the guys would show up so I could get church started.

"They're leaving soon. Ghost is making progress on the drive, and then I'm cutting 'em loose."

Legacy hums, not saying anything, even as his eyes pass judgment.

"This isn't like it was with Bea, all right." I take another drag. "She's your kid, and you had no other choice but to take her in when Sera bailed. But Tempe and Austin are Helix's family, not mine."

"That's where you're wrong, Jameson." Legacy shakes his head. "They're his blood, but they're not his family. We decide who we let into that circle, the same way we decide who belongs to this club."

"I'm not claiming her." I put out my cigarette, itching to reach for another if Legacy wouldn't give me so much crap about it. "I'm just helping her out."

"So you keep telling yourself." Legacy combs his fingers through his hair. "But everyone deserves a slice of life that's just for them. I didn't realize that until Bea came around. Before that, this club was everything to me, just like it is to you. I didn't think anything could come above it. But Honey Bea... I'd give my blood, life, and soul for that little girl's happiness. She's the sunshine I didn't think I needed, and you deserve that too. Something that gives you purpose outside of this club. Something that makes you happy."

"This club *is* what makes me happy."

"There's more to life than that."

I tip my head back and take a deep breath. "Not for me."

Not if I want to keep my men safe. They rely on me not to be distracted, which is exactly what Tempe and Austin do—distract me. Ever since they moved into my house, my attention has been in two places.

I need them gone so I can get my head on straight.

"Just think about it," Legacy says. "Once you accept what I'm telling you, you'll kick this foul mood you've been in lately."

"What he needs is to get laid." Soul walks into the room, wiping his blond hair off his forehead.

If he only knew that's where my problems started.

Fucking Tempe reminded me that I'll never be the kind of man who can give a girl like her the life she deserves.

"Helpful as always, Soul." Legacy shakes his head.

"Just doing my part." He shrugs. "You could use some pussy too. All this family bullshit at the club is killing the mood."

Thankfully, the rest of the guys start to filter into the room before Legacy and Soul can get into it. They have opposite views on family, and there's no use trying to sway either of them from their opinions.

Ghost is the final one to walk in, shutting the door behind him.

"You cracked the drive?" I ask as he takes a seat.

Ghost has been working on hacking the flash drive for weeks, but it's been one firewall after another.

"Yep, but you're not going to like it."

"Didn't think I would. What's on there?"

Ghost leans forward, planting his elbows on the table. "Everything there is to know about Sapphire Rise. The building plans, the books, the permits."

That's not what I was expecting Ghost to say.

"What the fuck would Helix or the Sinners want with inside info on a strip club?"

"That's the part you're not going to like." Ghost leans back. "They wouldn't."

"Then who—" I don't finish the question when the realization hits me. "Rick Zane."

"Fuck." Soul slams his fist against the table, no happier about it than I am.

"At least now we know who's funding the Iron Sinners' payroll," Ghost says.

Not that it makes this any better.

Rick Zane controls most of the Strip, and he's been trying to push the Twisted Kings businesses off it. Something he's been succeeding at, no matter what we do to fight back. While the Iron Sinners keep us distracted, he sends the city after our businesses one by one.

Code violations.

License lapses.

He seems to know every issue we have the second it happens, and now we know how he's been doing it—insider information.

"Zane's involvement makes sense." Legacy's eyebrows pinch. "The Sinners have had more resources lately, and now we know where they're coming from."

"If that's the case, then it's also going to make 'em that much harder to take down," Havoc adds.

He's right. War costs money, and if Rick Zane is funding our enemies with bottomless resources, it's going to be a fucking nightmare.

"The timing on this brings up another issue." Ghost looks around the room. "Their last target was the tattoo shop. They shut us down for a code violation."

"I'm aware."

"That was after Helix was already dead." Ghost looks at me. "Someone else had to have leaked that information."

"If there's someone else on the inside, why'd they send Tempe to retrieve it?" Havoc speaks up. "Anyone in here could have gotten the flash drive without raising any red flags. All they had to do was strip the info off Ghost's computer and get it out. It doesn't make sense. Why hide it and have her come here instead of just taking it to the Iron Sinners the second they had it?"

That's a good point, and I don't have any good answers. "Don't know."

"You're sure she's not in on it?"

"I'm fucking sure." It comes out louder than I mean for it to, but I don't take it back because he needs to get it through his head. "And I don't appreciate that this is still in question."

Havoc nods, sitting back. But his expression tells me he's on the fence.

"I don't know why they sent Tempe here, but she's not a part of this. Anyone who doubts that can get the fuck out of this room." I pause long enough for anyone to leave, but they don't. "If you want to protect the club, figure out who is leaking insider information to the Sinners. And I don't care who is bankrolling them; find me a way to take down Titan and his men."

"What about Zane?" Soul asks.

I push my hair back. "One problem at a time. Right now, he's using them to do his dirty work, and he's being smart about it. First, we take down the Iron Sinners, then we'll deal with Zane. Agreed?"

Everyone nods.

"Get to it."

Slowly, everyone leaves the room.

I can tell a few of them doubt me even if they don't say it. But I can only control so much right now, and in time, they'll understand, like I do, that Tempe had nothing to do with this. So long as they do their jobs, convincing them is a problem for another day.

As everyone disburses, I make my way to the bar in the front of the clubhouse. I need a shot to dull my headache.

Every time I think I've put the club back together, something else tears it apart. Dad made this look easy, but maybe he was just more fit to be a leader.

"Hey, Steel."

I glance over and see Wren, one of the newer patch bunnies, sliding onto the barstool beside me. Her red hair is in a tight ponytail that shows off her bright-blue eyes.

She leans forward to show off her big fake tits, and that used to be enough to do it for me.

A new face.

A nice rack.

A good time.

But right now, all that means absolutely nothing.

"Want some company?" Wren asks, smiling.

I'm still staring at her, processing her question, when the door to the clubhouse opens, and Tempe steps inside.

She's messing with her hair when she walks in, tying it in a knot on the top of her head as she scopes out the room. And when our eyes connect, her stare drifts to Wren sitting beside me, and I immediately sense a shift in her posture.

I should fuck Wren. Or, at the very least, make Tempe think I am. It would push her away so fast, she'd never fall for my bullshit again. But the thought of touching another woman when I know what it's like to be lost between Tempe's legs has me questioning my existence. And now that I've felt that, I can't let it go.

"Sorry, sweetheart. Busy." I stand up, making my way over to Tempe, who refuses to look at me when I stop in front of her.

Once more, she starts messing with her hair, pretending not to notice me leaning against the wall beside her.

"What are you doing here?" I ask.

She glares at me. "Looking for Havoc."

His name coming from her mouth nearly makes my jaw crack with how hard I'm clenching it. "Why are you looking for Havoc?"

Tempe narrows her eyes even more, crossing her arms over her chest. "Because the washer at the house broke two days ago, and Havoc brought the laundry to the clubhouse. I need to get my uniform for work."

"Why the fuck would you go to Havoc with that and not me?"

"Really, Steel?" She tips her chin up, and I get the full force of her irritation. "When was I supposed to ask for your help with this? Or better yet, *how*? You still have my phone, and you haven't been around for days."

"I've been busy."

She glances at Wren, who's still sitting at the bar. "Yeah, I can see that."

"It's not—"

"I don't care. We agreed to one night, remember?" Her eyes narrow. "I didn't walk into this expecting you to change your ways. So don't worry, I didn't catch feelings. That night was the same thing for me as it was for you, and we're not talking about it again. Just let me deal with my business, and you can go deal with yours."

She takes a second glance at Wren before turning to walk farther into the clubhouse in search of Havoc.

I could stop her—I *want to*. But I also know there's no point when I can't live up to what she's looking for.

I warned her, I'm not a good man.

If only I didn't hate that about myself right now.

21

Tempe

Work finally feels like a routine again.

Serving drinks.

Fending off handsy frat boys.

Spending the night cleaning up sticky floors and beer-drenched bar tops.

Sonny and Reyes chauffeur me back and forth from every shift, and thankfully, it's been quiet. I don't know how much longer Jameson will consider Austin and me at risk, but if it stays like this, he might send us away soon.

It's clear that's what he wants.

The second we slept together, he slipped back into his routine of living at the clubhouse. He ignores me, and even if I know Austin has seen him in passing while I'm at work, he avoids the house when I'm there.

It's only a matter of time before we're no longer worth the trouble to him, and maybe that's a good thing. At some point, I need to build a new life for myself and my brother.

I need to show him what he can expect from here on out.

Still, I can't help the irritation that gnaws at my nerves every time I think about the fact that all it took was one night with Jameson for him to turn into a complete asshole.

I shouldn't be surprised, knowing what I was walking into with a biker—the president, nonetheless. My mom usually dated guys lower on the totem pole, and they were terrible enough without having the ego and the admiration of an entire club fueling their actions.

At the end of the day, Jameson is a man looking out for his best interests. This is the perfect example of why I don't trust men.

Good job, Tempe.

He proved all my theories about bikers true, and then some. Which, I suppose, is the motivation I needed.

With Jameson avoiding the house these past few days, I've been focusing on my online classes. I'm almost done with my general studies, and so long as I get through this semester, I can start the physical therapy program in the fall.

Austin will be in kindergarten by then, so as long as I can time my classes for when he's at school, I can make it work. I'll need to set up a babysitter for late nights at the bar, which will be difficult but possible.

I've been apartment hunting with that in mind, trying to find something in a good school district that is a quick drive to Dirty Drakes. Someplace safe and secure. These are all logistics I didn't have to think about when I first started school, but now they're all that matters.

I'm going to be there for my brother.

It might take me longer to graduate, and I might have to work this terrible job longer than I wanted. But so long as I figure out how to balance the two, I'll build a better life for us. I'll show Austin an example of someone who works hard—someone he can look up to. I'll show him what Mom never represented to either of us—commitment.

The first step is putting down a deposit on an apartment I found. I need to tour it first, but that requires asking Jameson for a favor, which is the last thing I want to do after catching him at the bar with one of the patch bunnies.

I get it.

My father was a biker, so I know how things work between the men and women at the clubhouse. But seeing Jameson with her after he was with me made me feel like a jealous girlfriend.

I can't trust myself to face him until I get that in check. Not that I'll have much choice soon. Pearl had an appointment today, so Jameson offered to watch my brother. Once I'm done at work, I'll be forced to see him.

Marley giggles at the other end of the bar, and I look up to see her typing something into her phone.

It's a slow night, so I've been reorganizing the cocktail napkins and straws while she scrolls social media.

"Who's got you smiling so big?" I walk over as she tucks her phone in her back pocket.

"Remember that football player I was telling you about?"

"The quarterback?"

"That fucks with the stamina of a running back? Yeah." Marley bites her lip, barely holding back her grin. "He's taking me out tomorrow."

"A real date." I nudge her arm. "Look at you having an actual relationship."

"If that man keeps fucking me like he did last night, he can make an honest woman out of me."

I quirk an eyebrow. "That good?"

"That good." Marley smiles. "And don't try to pretend you don't know what I'm talking about. I've seen you walking around here the past few days. I'm not the only one with a guy on my mind."

"I do not."

"Oh yeah?" She glances over at Sonny and Reyes sitting at a table in the corner. "Then what's with the bodyguards?"

"They're just looking out for me."

"At who's request?" Marley grins, tapping her finger on her lower lip. "Could it be the knight in shining armor who came to your rescue a couple of weeks ago?"

I narrow my eyes.

"Thought so."

"He's no knight." I shake my head. "And his shining armor is actually a leather cut and a million red flags reminding me to stay away from him. Trust me. There's nothing going on there. He's helping me out of a bad situation."

"But how helpful is he, Tempe? Because you're awfully relaxed lately."

My cheeks heat with the reminder of Jameson's hands on my body. Hating what he did immediately after doesn't mean I can forget how it felt to be with him.

"Exactly." Marely starts walking away when a group of customers sits at her end of the bar. "Lie to yourself all you want, but you know I'm right."

Still, I wish she wasn't.

Grabbing a clean glass from the sink, I start drying it, hating that my thoughts are back on Jameson. It's impossible when Marley makes me face everything I'd rather not think about. Setting the glass down, I grab another as a body slides onto the barstool across from where I'm standing.

"What can I get you?"

"Whiskey neat." The familiar voice sends a shiver down my spine.

I look up into eyes that have haunted me since this man first forced his way into my house and killed my mother. Eyes that showed her no mercy as her body crumpled to the ground. Eyes that became a black hole while time froze.

His dark hair is slicked back, but it's long enough for him to tuck it behind his ears. His beard is trimmed but messy, and his eyes are pure evil.

"Hello, Tempe."

I take a step back, glancing behind him at Sonny and Reyes, who are drinking water and laughing about something.

"I wouldn't do that," he says when I open my mouth to yell for them. "You need to be a good girl if you want to protect your brother."

"Austin's already safe." My voice shakes as I glance back at the man.

He's with Jameson, and no matter what tension exists between Jameson and me right now, I don't think he'd let anyone hurt him.

The man grins. "Safe *for now*. But you'll wear your welcome out with the Twisted Kings soon enough. After all, Steel isn't known for keeping women very long."

My stomach sours, and it takes everything in me not to let it show.

"Who are you?"

"Someone who can help you if you cooperate." He skims me up and down. "You can call me Dimitri."

At least I've put a name to the monster, even if I don't believe a word he says.

"What makes you think you can help me? You're the one who set me up."

"You're still alive, aren't you?"

"No thanks to you."

Dimitri leans forward, glaring at me. "Did you think I sent you in there to die? Steel's too much of a cunt to hurt a woman. Everyone knows that."

"You say that like it's a bad thing."

He shrugs, shooting me a vile smile that tells me he isn't beyond putting his hands on a woman if he deems it necessary.

"What do you want?" I ask, setting the rag down on the bar. "They already found what you were looking for. I can't get you whatever you were hiding."

"It's interesting you still think that's what we were after. Either the Twisted Kings are as stupid as they look, or Steel isn't telling you everything."

"What's that supposed to mean?"

Dimitri tilts his head. "You'll figure it out soon enough. You already did what we needed."

"If you already got what you want, why are you here?"

"Can't a man just want a drink?"

"This isn't the only bar in town." I sneer at him.

Dimitri leans closer, pausing when his gaze dips to my cleavage before looking back up at me again. "Maybe I like the view at this one."

"You're sick."

"And you're feisty like your momma." He smirks. "Always liked that about her until I didn't."

My stomach spins. "How well did you know my mom?"

"Enough to know you got all her good parts." Dimitri wets his lips, watching me, and I step back.

I glance back over at Sonny and Reyes, and this time, I find Sonny looking at me. I start to lift my hand to signal for him, but a commotion from the other side of the bar catches his attention before I get the chance.

A guy yells, throwing his beer bottle against the wall.

I turn to see the scene play out, and Sonny and Reyes take notice, standing up and walking over as the guys begin to make a scene.

It all happens in a split second. One broken bottle and the room erupts. People are on their feet and cheering. The room swims with bodies moving around, and I get knocked by one of the bartenders rushing past me.

"Hey." I've barely gripped the bar to steady myself when Dimitri hops over it and grabs me.

"Well, isn't this convenient? Your bodyguards are too easily distracted." Dimitri's voice in my ear makes my stomach curdle.

I scan the crowd, but now multiple fights have broken out, and I can't find Sonny or Reyes in the mass of people.

"Get off me." I elbow Dimitri in the side, and he laughs, even as he grunts from the force of it.

"Is that how you like it, spitfire? Rough?" He grabs the back of my hair and tries to pull me toward a door that leads to the alley. "I don't mind if you want to put up a fight. It gets me all riled up."

"You're disgusting." I scratch his arm, drawing blood.

I can't let him get me outside. If he does, I might never escape him.

Grabbing his wrist, I dig my nails in, kicking him as hard as I can in the shin at the same time. It's enough to get him to release me, and I grab his wrist, spinning out of his grasp.

Dimitri lunges, aiming for my throat, but I dip in time, sinking low and punching him as hard as I can between the legs. He buckles over, grabbing himself.

"Bitch. You're going to pay for that." But his words come out choked as he grasps for air.

I expect him to grab at me the moment he recovers, but his gaze drifts over my shoulder, and he takes a step back instead.

"Another time, Tempe." He grits his teeth. "It's better you stay put right now anyway."

A group of men hurry out the side door, and Dimitri disappears with them, making his escape right as Sonny and Reyes come to my side.

"Who was that?" Sonny looks to where I'm rubbing my wrist.

"The guy who sent me to the compound."

Sonny tips his head at Reyes, who heads in the direction Dimitri disappeared, while Sonny stays with me.

"Are you hurt?"

I shake my head. "No, I'm okay."

"Come here." Sonny guides me to a barstool, forcing me to sit.

"I'm fine, really." But he's already pulling out his phone. "You don't need to call him."

Sonny doesn't bother responding because we both know he does. It's how the club works. Everything gets reported to Jameson Steel.

Just when I thought this was almost over.

Sonny dials Jameson while Dimitri's words revolve in my mind. He sent me to the Twisted Kings for a reason, but it's not the reason he told me in the first place.

I thought I had this figured out. I thought this was almost over.

I was wrong.

I assumed my role in this mess was done. Now, I'm worried it's only the beginning.

22

Steel

Soul stops at my side the moment I shut the door to my truck, eyeing Austin sitting in the passenger seat.

"Where's your girl today, Steel?" He knocks me on the shoulder as I walk around the front.

"Not my girl."

"So you don't care if I have a run at her then?" Soul grins when I freeze in place. "Cute little thing. Fiery, too, from what I've heard. I'm sure she'd—"

I grab the front of his shirt and pull him closer. "I'll strip you of your fucking cut if you finish that sentence."

"Mm-hmm." Soul smiles, fixing his shirt when I release him. "That's what I thought. Not your girl. Not your kid either, apparently."

He looks over at Austin sitting in my truck, grinning.

"Don't you have an engine to fix?" I push my hair off my forehead, circling the car to open Austin's door. "Go do that."

Soul stalks off, still grinning and seeing through all my shit. It's why he's pissing me off—to see what it will take to make me admit what Tempe is to me.

And now here I am, babysitting her brother instead of letting someone more qualified do it. All because Grandma had an appointment today, and Tempe was called into work.

She offered to call one of her friends from school, but the thought of anyone watching him but me pissed me off.

I'm fucking losing it.

Now I'm here at Kings Auto with a four-year-old.

I promised Havoc I'd help while Legacy meets with the contractor about the repairs at Sapphire Rise, and luckily, Austin doesn't seem to mind tagging along.

"This is the coolest." Austin hops out of his booster seat, his eyes widening as he looks around the auto body shop. "Is this where you make the bikes superfast?"

"Sometimes." I plant my hand on the top of his head and lead him into the garage. "Most of the time, we're just tuning them up."

"Hey, Steel. Brought us an extra set of hands?" Havoc looks up from the engine he's working on to wave at Austin.

"Jameson's gonna teach me how to oil his motorcycle," Austin answers proudly.

"Change the oil." I pat him on the top of the head.

"Got it." Havoc laughs, turning back to the engine he's rebuilding while I lead Austin to one of the far bays in the garage.

I brought my bike in earlier for maintenance and was halfway done when I got the call about Tempe not having a babysitter. Soul had a lot to say about how fast I jumped in the truck when I hung up, but I ignored him.

"You ever worked on a bike before, big man?" I ask Austin, leading him over to mine.

"No." He squats down, looking it over. "What's this?"

"The muffler."

He points above it.

"Footrest."

"Is this the engine?" He points to the gas tank.

"Nah, this is." I tap the engine.

"Cool." Austin smiles. "Havoc told me you'd show me all the parts."

He looks up, and the excitement in his eyes floods my chest.

I've worked at the garage on and off since I was sixteen and trained plenty of guys on the ins and outs of fixing a bike. But with Austin looking up at me like I've got the secrets to the universe in my back pocket, I want to sit here and teach him everything I know.

I want to show him how to take the bike apart piece by piece and put it back together, just like my father did.

"I'll show you anything you want, kid." I try to bury whatever that thought was that just rustled up inside me. "But let's start simple with changing the oil."

Austin hops up, following me around the garage while I gather everything I need. He asks me what everything is from the socket wrench to the oil pan. And he surprises me by memorizing each item the first time I tell him.

"Maybe you got a little mechanic in you, kid."

Austin smiles. "You think I could build a car when I grow up?"

"If you want to." I shrug, squatting down while Austin mirrors my exact movement. "I was just a little older than you the first time I helped rebuild a bike. My dad got a 1925 Harley Davidson JD motorcycle for us to work on. We spent a year taking it apart and putting it back together. We restored it until it was as good as new."

Working on that bike with my dad is still one of my favorite memories. He got it shortly after we lost Wyatt, and he used it to keep me busy while Mom slowly deteriorated.

We finished it after we'd already lost her, but to this day, that bike still reminds me of the in-between. The good in the middle. Before everything about my father got a little colder.

"Is this the bike?" He points to my motorcycle.

I shake my head. "No, that one's in the garage back at home. Maybe I can show you sometime."

Austin smiles so big it lights up his whole face.

"All right. First things first, we need to drain the oil."

I hand Austin a rag and get to work, explaining every step as I go. Austin holds the parts and hands them to me as I need them, asking questions about every step of the process. He's more observant than I expected, but I haven't spent much time around kids, so it's not like I know what to expect.

"You wanna pour?" I ask, positioning the funnel when we're ready to fill it back up again.

"Really?" His eyes widen.

"Sure thing." I hand him the oil, keeping hold of the bottom to balance it. "Pour slowly into here."

He tips up a little too quickly at first, so I have to slow it down.

"Patience." I steady it. "Nice and slow."

Austin chews his bottom lip as he focuses. His eyes squint like it's the most important task he's undertaken.

"Perfect." I stop the flow and take the oil from him.

We check the level a final time, and it's done.

"Now we just gotta run it." I stand up, swinging my leg over my bike. "Stand back for a second."

Austin presses his back to the wall of the bay, and I rev the engine, letting the oil run through it for a minute before cutting it off.

"That's loud." Austin's eyes are wide as he watches me climb off my bike.

"You get used to it." I shrug.

"I like it."

"Me too, kid. I always found the rumble of the motorcycle calming."

"Someday, I'm gonna learn to ride a bike." He swishes his cape around. "No training wheels."

"You got one back home?"

Austin shakes his head. "Bikes cost lots of monies. Tempe said maybe for my birthday."

A knot forms in my throat, and I get the sudden urge to drive him to the store to pick out a bike. Before he has a chance to notice, I turn, setting my rag aside and moving to the sink to wash my hands.

Austin follows, stepping up on a bucket to wash his hands beside me. "If I get a bike for my birthday, will you show me how to ride it?"

I should tell him I don't know if he'll still be here. And if he's not, I doubt his sister is going to want to be around me after what a dick I've been to her. But I don't have the heart when he blinks up at me with such innocence.

Planting a hand on his head, I shake his hair around. "For sure, kid."

"You're the best, Jameson." Austin smiles, jumping up and down beside me, landing in a different superhero pose each time he does. "What's next?"

"The most important part," I tell him. "Cleaning up."

Austin frowns, his shoulders deflating. "That's no fun."

"It's not all about fun, big man. But if you take pride in something, you take care of it. From the oil change to the cleanup. Isn't that right, Havoc?"

Havoc pops his head up in the adjoining bay. "That's right."

"I guess." Austin frowns, but he doesn't argue as we start cleaning up.

"He must be superstrong," Austin says, looking at Havoc, who is carrying a box of parts over to Soul.

"One of the strongest."

Austin looks up at me. "Does your cape make you strong?"

"Cape?"

He reaches up and touches my cut. "It's a cape, right? You're always wearing it."

I look down at where his fingers graze over the stitching. "I guess you could call it that."

"My cape makes me feel strong." He grabs it again and swishes it around. "Does your cape do that?"

Austin hugs the blue fabric around his body, curling into it as he watches me.

"Honestly? I've never thought about it like that." I squat down, bringing myself to his level. "I guess it makes me strong, even if not for the reasons you might think."

His eyebrows pinch.

"The cape isn't what gives you your superpowers, Austin." I brush my hands down the front of my cut. "It shows your loyalty. Your commitment. Your cape tells people what you represent and who you're willing to protect. But at the end of the day, the cape is just the symbol. What really matters is what you do when it comes down to it. The people at your side when you're fighting your way through. You're only as strong as the people you're willing to protect and the people who care about protecting you."

"Like family?"

"Yeah." I nod. "Like family."

After all, for me, that's the Twisted Kings.

"Maybe someday, I'll have a cape like yours."

"If that's what you want." I swallow hard, not sure why his comment stirs something up.

In my family, there's only one real tradition: passing down the cut.

I figured I'd skip that part. But with Austin looking up at me, he has me questioning what I might be missing out on.

"You ready for our final task?" I change the subject before I can think too much about it.

"Like a secret mission?"

"Sure."

"Then yes!" He cheers, and it's impossible to bite back my grin at his excitement.

"Here." I hand him a tire pressure gauge.

"What's this?"

"To check the tire pressure." I push the front tire. "This one should be good."

"How do you know?" His eyebrows scrunch.

"You get used to the feel of it after a while," I tell him. "But it's always better to double-check. Safety first."

I help him with the gauge as we check the pressure, confirming what I thought. "Perfect."

Austin hums, pushing the front tire.

"Whatcha doing?"

"Feeling it."

I grin, watching him press his whole hand on the tire, trying to figure out what I'm talking about.

"Ready to check the back?"

Austin nods, moving his hand to that one, doing the same thing he was in the front. He's not pushing hard enough to actually get a read, but I appreciate the attempt.

"What do you think?"

Austin pushes again, his whole face scrunching. "I think it's good."

"Let's double-check." I squat down and help him with the gauge. "You're right, it's perfect."

"It is?" His eyes widen as he looks at me.

I nod. "Yep, you've got a knack for this."

"I did it." He smiles so big, his blue eyes scrunch closed. "Maybe it's my superpower."

"Maybe. Either way, I think you've found your calling, kid." I hold up a hand for him to give me a high five, but he throws himself at me, wrapping me in the biggest hug.

Pure.

Unapologetic.

I'm frozen for a second, not sure how to respond.

Kids don't hug me. They barely talk to me. But as I place my hands on his back and pat it, he sinks into my hold and hugs me with his whole body. Like I've only seen him do with Tempe.

The protective urge that roars up in my chest has never felt as big as it does with Austin in my arms. He trusts me like I deserve it. Like he knows I'd never let anything happen to him.

I've thought a lot about family, deciding the club was the only one I needed. But with Austin in my arms, I can't help wondering if Legacy is right. Because whether I wanted it or not, Tempe and Austin are becoming something more than whatever I keep saying they are to me.

They're mine.

I've never felt as whole as I do with Tempe and Austin in my life, and I still can't decide what to do with that.

"Prez." Havoc stops beside us, and Austin pulls out of my grasp.

"What's up?" I stand, brushing off my chest as if it can erase whatever just shifted inside me.

Havoc turns, dropping his voice so Austin can't hear him. "It's Tempe."

"What about her?" My entire body is on alert the second he says her name.

Havoc glances at Austin once more, but he's distracted. "There's been an incident at the bar—"

I toss the tire pressure gauge in the toolbox and slam it shut before he can finish his sentence. "Austin, we gotta go."

"She's okay." Havoc follows. "Jameson, slow down, she's good. Sonny can bring her back here."

"No. Tell him I'll be there in fifteen minutes. She's not his responsibility." I open the door for Austin, slamming it shut behind him. "She's mine."

And it's damn time I start acting like it.

23

Tempe

I'VE ALWAYS FELT UNEASY around law enforcement because of my parents. Even without a record myself, they always assume I'm up to no good. Law enforcement wrote me off the moment I was born because of my blood, so I learned young not to trust them when I needed help.

Watching them now as I stand alone in the parking lot, my unease is confirmed. Cops circle the bar, arresting anyone who was fighting, while an officer has Sonny and Reyes cornered for interrogation, even though they were just trying to break it up.

Jameson pulls in just as the conversation between Sonny and the cop starts to escalate, and I cross the parking lot to meet him.

He climbs out, walking to me first.

"What happened?" He tucks my hair behind my ear, looking at me like he's searching for signs of battle.

I don't know why he's pretending to care when he's been ignoring me for days, but I don't need him worrying about me.

"Nothing I didn't take care of." I pull away from him.

"Tempe." My name is a threat, and as much as I'd like to stand here and argue with him, I feel Austin's eyes on us through the truck window.

"Dimitri showed up," I say reluctantly. "He's the guy who sent me to the clubhouse. He said his name was Dimitri."

Jameson's jaw tenses. "What else did he say?"

"Not much." I shrug, tucking my hands in my pockets. "He said he wanted me to stay put and that whatever reason he sent me to the clubhouse isn't what you think. That or you're keeping things from me."

Jameson scans my face, and I wonder if it makes any more sense to him than it does to me. Maybe Dimitri was right, and he knows the truth about why I was sent to him. If so, he hasn't said anything.

"What do you know, Jameson?"

He shakes his head. "Not a damn thing, apparently. What else?"

"That's it." I shrug. "He wasn't exactly forthcoming with information. And I was too busy fighting back to ask."

Jameson steps closer, tipping my chin up again, except this time, I don't pull away. I can barely breathe with him this close. His warm leather scent floods my nose, and my chest brushes against him with my inhale.

"Did he hurt you?" Jameson nudges my chin up so he can examine my face.

I swallow hard when he brushes his thumb over my jaw. "No. I didn't give him a chance before I punched him in the nuts."

Jameson's angry scowl cracks with a hint of amusement. "Good girl."

I didn't fight Dimitri off for Jameson's sake. It was to save myself. But something about his praise makes my insides flutter. So many men in my past have been intimidated by a woman who can stick up for herself, but Jameson isn't.

"Get in the truck, Tempe." Any amusement vanishes as he releases me and takes a step back, not saying another word as he reaches for the handle and opens the door. "I need to go check in with my men."

Once I climb in, he shuts the door behind me and heads over to where the cops are still talking to Sonny and Reyes.

"Are you off work?" Austin curls to my side the best he can in his booster seat.

"Yeah." I force a smile, squeezing his hand. "I am now."

He glances out the front window, his gaze landing on the cops. "Did someone break the law?"

"It was just a little mix-up." I angle his face so he's looking at me and not the men being dragged out of the bar in handcuffs. "There's nothing for you to worry about."

"I'm not worried. Jameson will take care of us."

Austin's faith in Jameson makes my heart ache because even if his trust is well-placed regarding our physical safety, it's a reminder that Jameson is one more man Austin is eventually going to watch walk away.

"Jameson said someday, maybe I can have a cape like his."

"His?" I glance over at where Jameson is talking to the cops.

"Yeah." Austin nods. "A black one."

That's when I realize he's talking about Jameson's cut.

I turn back to my brother. "You don't need one of those, Austin. You're already a superhero without it."

"Jameson said it's not about being a superhero. He said his cape is to show who his family is."

"You already have a family." Tears sting my eyes with my words because I know what he needs is so much more than I'll ever be able to offer him. "You have me."

Austin looks out the window at Jameson, his shoulders sinking.

"Hey." I squeeze his hand. "I've got you, okay? We're in this together. You and me. I promise."

Austin curls against my side, resting his head on my arm as he hugs me. And I hold him like I can give him all the things he deserves when I know I'm already failing.

One unstable environment after another.

One home after another.

Solving this problem will only mean more for both of us. And I'd like to think I'll figure this out like I always have. That I'll be able to build a life in which my brother can thrive. But there's always going to be that missing piece.

Austin settles into the silence of the truck, and I watch the scene unfold outside Dirty Drakes.

Marley waves goodbye after the cops finish taking her statement, and she climbs in her car to leave.

Jameson is still talking to the officers, and even if everyone is calm, I sense the tension from across the parking lot.

Not that Jameson seems to let it get to him.

There's something about how he commands a crowd that is undeniably intoxicating. He speaks to the cops with the full confidence of his patch, not caring that they'll immediately judge him for it.

Jameson demands respect no matter what they think of him.

At one point, he motions to me sitting in the truck, but I'm too far away to hear what he's saying. All I sense is the anger crashing out of him, no matter how calm he's being.

I can't figure out why he continues to fight for me, protect me, and stick up for me when he doesn't even act like he likes me. But there's security in watching him stick up for me in this moment.

After a few more tense words, the officers finally step back. They're letting Sonny and Reyes go but don't look happy about it. The cops watch them leave, and Jameson talks to them for a minute before they walk to where they're parked.

Jameson swings the door open, climbing in the truck.

"Everything all right?" I ask.

He grips the steering wheel, drops his chin, and is clearly thinking about something. It takes a moment before he starts the engine, his gaze moving to where Austin is holding my hand.

"Everything's fine."

We both know he's lying, but I don't question him in front of Austin. Today is just one more thing weighing Jameson down. One more reason he'll close himself off from me.

The drive back to the Twisted Kings compound is quiet, and I'm biting back everything I want to say for Austin's sake. Jameson stops briefly at a burger joint, but we eat without saying much to each other.

Austin, thankfully, fills the silence for us, telling me about changing the oil in Jameson's motorcycle and asking twenty questions about why pickle slices and relish don't taste the same even if they're both pickles.

Jameson surprises me by answering every single question. No matter how small or annoying. He keeps the mood up even when Austin refuses to concede his point. But between every half-hearted laugh, I sense the day weighing heavy on him.

At least he doesn't let Austin see it.

By the time we get back to the house, it's late, so I put Austin to bed. Pearl met up with her friends after the doctor so she's still not back. And when I walk downstairs, it's just Jameson and me again in the same awkward mess we've been in since we slept together.

"Thanks for picking us up, but you can go now if you need to." I walk over to the sink and grab some water. "I'm sure you have things to take care of back at the club."

"It's fine."

I tip my head back and let out an irritated chuckle. "Nothing's fine, and you know it."

"You're safe here."

I spin to face him, backing up to the counter and gripping it, trying not to scream when that's all I want to do right now.

Let it out.

But I can't.

Because there's a child looking up to me, and for him, I need to keep it together.

"Safe *here*," I repeat. "Safe *for now*."

"What's wrong with that?" Jameson grips the kitchen island, watching me.

"It's all temporary." I circle the island, meeting him where he is. "Being here is wearing on me, and just when I thought it was almost over, we've restarted the clock. When does it end? When is this over?"

"I don't know."

I roll my eyes. "Remember when I was the one with that answer and how you felt about it?"

"That was different." Jameson clenches his jaw.

"Is it?" I roll my shoulders back. "Because I'm starting to think this is all the same. You heard what Dimitri said. We don't even know the real reason he sent me here—unless you do, and you've just been keeping it from me."

"I don't." His tone tells me that's the truth, and he's not happy about it either.

"Well, there you have it. You keeping me here is apparently just giving him exactly what he wants. So what are we even doing anymore?"

"I'm keeping you safe. Why can't you see that?"

"At what cost? All I'm doing at this point is bringing heat on you and your club." The words catch in my throat. "You can't protect us forever, Jameson. We aren't your responsibility. But Austin is mine. I'm all he has left. At some point, Austin and I have to take this on ourselves, and I need to start getting ready for when that happens."

"Not yet."

"Then when?" I'm trying not to yell, but my chest is burning up.

I want to escape this man so I never have to think about him again, and at the same time, I don't want to let him go.

"I don't know, Tempe." He rakes his hair back, sounding as frustrated as I am. "You can go once I've figured this out."

"And how long is that going to take?"

"Don't you think I wish I had the answer to that question?" He stands up tall, taking a step closer. "Don't you wish I could just fix this fucking mess so we could all move on? So you and Austin could get out of here and get your lives back? I get it—more than you know. You two deserve so much more than you're getting behind these gates, but so long as you're in the middle of this, I refuse to have you out there unguarded. If I let you leave and something happens—"

He pauses, dropping his chin and shaking his head.

"You're my responsibility." He pins me with his gaze, so many emotions swimming in his ocean-gray eyes. "And tonight…"

I wait for him to finish his thought, but he sighs instead. "What about tonight?"

His gaze returns to mine, and he shakes his head. "You're a magnet for trouble."

"That's not my fault."

"I know it's not." He runs his palm down his face. "Fuck."

Jameson tips his head back and sighs. His eyes are closed, and so much stress radiates off him, filling the room around us. I should walk away but find myself stepping forward instead. Planting my hands on his chest and taking in some of the heat burning from his body.

No matter how irritating he is or how many days he's ignored me, he's been here for me and my brother. And sensing the waves of panic crashing, I can't help trying to comfort him.

Jameson looks down to where my hands rest on his chest.

"Are you okay?"

"Am I okay?" Jameson laughs, but it's unamused. "Fuck, Tempe. You're the one who was attacked tonight. Are *you* okay?"

"None of this is okay." I frown. "But I'll be fine. You don't have to pretend to care for my sake."

"I'm not pretending." He plants his hands over the back of mine. "*I'm not.*"

"You've barely been here." I fight back the burning in my throat. "You can hardly look at me."

His stare locks on mine. "And why the fuck do you think that is, wildfire?"

"Because you wish I'd leave."

He shakes his head once, slowly. "No. The opposite, Tempe. You're all that's keeping me together."

24

Steel

I SWORE I WOULDN'T kiss her again.

Once was bad enough when the electricity from her lips sparked like a brushfire ripping through my veins. But when my mouth lands on hers a second time, she incinerates my soul to ashes.

"Jameson." She pushes me away to break the kiss, but she's still holding on.

Her fingers grip my cut, and I wish more than anything my patch alone was enough to protect this girl I've tried not to care about.

"I hate you for ignoring me." She pulls me back in, waging the same battle with herself that I am. "I can't do this again."

"I know. I can't either." I catch the tear rolling down her cheek with my thumb. "But we both know we're going to anyway."

She blinks up at me, and her guard is down when it so rarely is. I'm getting a glimpse at the gentle side she seems terrified to show people.

I dip my mouth to hers and steal her arguments straight from her lips. She can fight me all she wants, but there's no denying this.

I'd know.

I've tried for days to get her out of my system. Gone cold turkey thinking that'd be enough.

But she's worse than any of my bad habits—than any addiction.

Tempe wraps her arms around the back of my neck, and I pick her up. Her pussy grinds against my cock with every step as I carry her to my bedroom and kick the door shut. Slamming her back into the wall, I grab her jaw again and tip her head back to kiss her deeper.

Her legs cling to me as the heat of her pussy presses against my cock.

If I were good, I'd let her go, but now that I've had her, I can't.

I plant a hand on the wall beside her head and try to hold on. But I'm slipping. The ground beneath my feet is unstable. The room vibrates with the hum in her chest when I shove my hips against her core.

Her nails dig into the back of my neck, and I want her to rip me limb from limb. Show me what she can do when the power of the universe lives inside her.

I dip my mouth to her throat and kiss a path to her collarbone before sinking my teeth into the smooth flesh of her shoulder. She tosses her head back with her scream, knocking her head against the wall.

"You're not supposed to let me do this, Tempe." I set her on her feet and spin her around, grabbing her by the hair and pinning her chest to the wall.

Snaking one hand down between her legs, I grab her pussy to pull her ass against my cock.

"Why not?" she shoots back. "You planning on loving me and leaving me again, Steel?"

"You're such a little brat sometimes." I grip her pussy so hard she screams; her nails scratch at the wall with the mix of pain and pleasure. "Call me by my road name again, and I'll teach you what happens when you fuck with the president."

She arches her back, grinding her ass against me. "You promise... *Steel*?"

This girl with all her sass thinks she can handle it. I'd shove her to her knees if I wasn't so desperate to be balls deep in her cunt.

"I warned you, wildfire." I unbutton her shorts and shove them down with her underwear.

Freeing my cock, I slide it between her legs, and she's soaking the inside of her thighs with her excitement.

With her shorts at her ankles, she can't widen her stance. And with how I'm holding her hair and pressing her cheek to the wall—she's at my mercy.

I push my cock between her thighs, rubbing against her pussy but refusing her the relief of having me inside her. The slick drip of her wet cunt soaks my cock, and I fuck her slowly between the thighs, teasing her until she's digging her nails against the wall.

Pulling her hips out further, I slam my hips forward to make her round ass jiggle.

"Jameson."

"You didn't ask for him, wildfire. You wanted Steel." I drive forward, still refusing her the pleasure she needs. "My club, my rules, remember? You don't get to feel good until I say so."

Tempe groans as I rub just shy of her pussy, the head of my cock teasing her with every stroke.

"You say you don't want this..." I reach around and rub her clit before smacking it with my fingers and making her scream. "But your greedy little cunt is begging for me."

I smack her pussy again, and she moans, tipping her forehead against the wall.

"I tried to stay away from you for your sake. But you couldn't help yourself, could you?" I circle her clit again before dragging my hand up and shoving my fingers into her mouth, forcing her to taste herself. "You ran this feisty little mouth until I had no choice but to put you in your place. Do you know what you're asking for, Tempe?"

I pull my fingers out and grab her throat, forcing her to stand so she's looking up over her shoulder at me.

"You." The word is a whisper on her lips.

A confession that comes with a flash of hesitation.

"You want me? You have me." I drag my thumb up and down the center column of her throat. "You've had me since the first time I saw you."

"You don't mean that." She blinks up at me, her chest heaving with every breath.

"I wouldn't say it if I didn't." I tilt her face so I can dip my mouth by her ear. "Why do you think I tried to stay away from you? Because if you let me fuck you again, I don't think I'll ever be able to let you go."

Her breath catches in the silence. My heart pounds in my chest.

I spin her around so I can look into her eyes, and I wait for her to fight me or fear me. For realization to flash in her gaze because she's too fucking sweet for a man who's done the things I have. But when her fingers find my wrist, she doesn't push me away. She stares into my eyes, and I swear the door opens to her soul.

"Stop me." I grip her throat.

Her teeth clench. "No."

I pull her off the wall, and her shorts fall from her feet as I lift her from the floor and carry her to the bed.

Setting her on it, I strip off the rest of her clothes before taking off my own. Her hazel eyes watch my cock as I stroke it in my fist, and I want to paint every inch of her skin until she realizes her mistake.

"Feet up," I command.

She spreads her knees and puts her feet on the base of the bed. Her wet cunt is spread and perfect. Tempe fights back in every aspect of her life. Except in my bed—she submits.

"Good girl." I grab her hips and pull her forward, leaning in to thrust my cock deep inside her.

Her pussy is a vice, gripping me. Welcoming me home.

I hold her knees wide while I pound into her sweet cunt, watching her body swallow every inch of me as I bottom out. She's almost too tight to take me, squeezing my cock until it hurts so fucking good, I can hardly stand it.

Taking her bare is the closest I've come to believing in heaven. Every slick inch of her pussy grips me as I drive into her.

Reaching down, I pinch her nipples and tug. Teasing them. Brushing the sensitive skin from the center of her breasts to her belly button then working my way back up again. I learn every inch until I find what makes her squeeze my cock like she's desperate for my cum.

"There you go again with that greedy little cunt." I drive in deep and pause, holding there.

Her pussy continues to squeeze me, needing the friction I'm refusing her.

"Please, Jameson." She scratches my arms, my chest; her body begging as much as her pretty mouth does.

"What do you need, Tempe? This?" I pull my cock out almost all the way.

So slow, she's not the only one I'm torturing.

"Yes," she pants.

"Then tell me who you belong to." I skate my fingers up the insides of her thighs, holding my cock deep inside her again. "No matter how much it pisses you off. Who owns this beautiful body of yours?"

"You do."

My fingers trace around her pussy, but I skip past her clit, making her moan.

"Tell me who's cum is going to fill you up."

"Yours." She tips her head back when I drift over her clit again.

"That's right, wildfire. *Mine.*" I pound in, and her tits bounce with every hard thrust. "I'm going to fuck this pussy so deep, you'll never forget it."

She rattles me up.

Claws me to pieces.

Tempe's carved my chest open and stolen things I didn't know existed.

I lean over her to fuck her deeper, and the weight of my body presses her back onto the bed. I need to seal our bodies together until I'm the man she deserves.

Her nails dig into my back as I settle between her legs and angle my hips to hit her where I know I'll light sparks. Her legs shake where they're hugging my hips, and her body vibrates with every hard thrust.

Her nipples graze my chest, and her smooth skin melts as our bodies press together. I claim her mouth and steal the sound coming out. Refusing to let one ounce of her escape.

"Jameson." She tips her head back.

"That's a good girl. Come for me." I thrust deeper. "I've got you."

Her heels dig into my ass as her pussy clamps my cock, and I can't hold back any longer when she falls over the edge, and her cunt squeezes. My cum fills her. I seal my mouth to hers and give her what her body demands with every pulse of her climax.

Tempe is shaking when I finally pull back.

Messy.

Sweaty.

Panting.

I brush her hair off her face to look down at her.

She's absolutely stunning.

"That was intense." She closes her eyes, taking a deep breath as I wipe her hair off her face.

"It was." My fingertips pause on the apple of her cheek.

"Don't worry." She smiles. "I won't hold you to the things you said."

"You better." I kiss her forehead. "Did you think I was lying?"

She shrugs.

"I'm a man of my word, Tempe." I tuck her hair behind her ear. "I don't say shit just to make you happy, especially when I'm fucking you. I meant what I said, and it's everything I've spent the past couple of days running from."

She looks down at where our bodies are still connected, smirking. "That'd almost be romantic if you weren't still inside me."

"There's nothing more romantic than me filling your pussy with my cum." I kiss her cheek when her hazel gaze flits to mine. "And I meant what I said. You have every right to hold me to it."

"You mean it?" She brushes her fingers over the scruff on my jaw.

"Every fucking word."

Confidence doesn't scare me. A strong woman doesn't make me want to run.

It's what drew me to this girl in the first place.

So when she smiles so big the sight is a sunrise in my dark room, my chest swells.

Pulling out, I widen her thighs, watching my cum drip out. I drag my fingers through her puffy cunt, collecting my release and shoving it back in.

"Jameson..." Tempe moans at the intrusion, tipping her head back. "You still haven't asked if I'm on birth control."

"Are you?"

She dips her chin to look at me, nodding once. "Yes."

I probably shouldn't be disappointed by that answer, but this girl makes me stupid.

I hum, tracing my hands up her thighs, over her stomach. "Guess we're going to have to do something about that."

It might scare her, but I don't care. She gave herself to me, and now she's planted all sorts of ideas in my head. Holding her offers me something I never saw myself having.

Peace I didn't think I deserved.

Happiness I'm terrified I'll destroy.

A life outside of the Twisted Kings.

Maybe we could water it. Maybe we could watch this grow.

Maybe I want more. If only she could want the same.

25

Tempe

My eyes flutter open to the feel of Jameson's fingertips grazing up and down my spine. I'm lying on my side, facing the glass door that leads out to the backyard.

The sun has yet to peek over the horizon, and the clock says it's only five in the morning, so Austin won't be awake for another couple of hours.

"Don't you ever sleep?" I close my eyes, sinking into the feel of Jameson's fingers roaming my skin.

"Not much."

I bury my nose into his pillow. It smells like cinnamon and detergent.

"Why not?"

"There's always too much to do or too much on my mind." His fingers pause, and I roll over to face him.

He props one hand behind the back of his neck and pulls me into the crook of his other arm. I relax against him, tracing his solid chest with my fingers. Our clothing is scattered, still sitting wherever we tossed it last night. Except his cut, which he carefully hung on the chair before he took me.

"You need sleep." I brush my finger along his jaw, tracing the stubble there and trying to soothe him. "You're going to wear yourself out if you're not careful."

He closes his eyes at my touch.

"I'll be fine. Besides, as long as I can continue to keep up with you, that's all that matters." He smiles, still not opening his eyes.

I laugh. "I definitely don't see that becoming a problem."

He glances down at me. "Not so long as I'm on this side of the dirt, wildfire."

"Why would you say that?" My eyebrows pinch, and my smile falls. "Don't tell me you have plans of dying."

"Not anytime soon." Jameson rests his hand over mine. "But men in my line of work don't have the longest lifespans. Especially ones with "President" stitched into their patch. My dad and grandad are two good examples."

"What happened to them?"

I'm still learning pieces of Jameson's history, and since he rarely talks about his family, I don't know much about them outside of the rumors. My dad mentioned once in passing that Jameson got his position when he was still really young, and because of that, he didn't think he deserved it.

"Well, my grandad went down in a bar fight. Or, at least, that's what the police report said. The lines between territories weren't as clear back then, and they stepped into rival territory without realizing it on a long ride back from Portland." Jameson scratches his jaw. "My dad, on the other hand... He was gunned down when a rival club tried to overthrow the Twisted Kings almost a decade ago. They got in a lucky shot he didn't see coming. One to the center of his forehead, and that was it."

Jameson rubs his hand over his forehead.

"I'm sorry."

He looks down at me, lifting my hand to kiss the back of it. "Nothing to be sorry for, wildfire. That's how this life is. And now here I am."

"Next in the line of fire?" I frown.

Jameson chuckles. "Well, I wouldn't put it that way..."

"I know. But I don't like thinking about you dying."

We might not have defined what we are to each other, but there's no more denying Jameson means something to me. The thought of leaving here rips my heart down the middle. And after his confession last night, I'm starting to think he feels the same.

"I appreciate you wanting me alive." Jameson cups my cheek. "And don't worry, I've no plans on going anytime soon."

"Does anyone ever plan to die?" I challenge, but when he frowns, a bad feeling stirs my gut. "What was that?"

"Nothing."

"That wasn't nothing. You clearly just thought something about what I said. Talk to me, Jameson."

Jameson takes a deep breath, scratching his jaw. "It just made me think about my mom. That's it. You're right. Most people don't plan to die, but she did."

"You mean she...?" But I can't finish the sentence as his nod confirms it. "I didn't realize."

"You couldn't have known. Half my men don't even know about it. My dad was really good at pretending it never happened."

"I'm sorry." I brush my hand over his chest. "How old were you?"

"Five."

"Young."

"Not young enough." He shakes his head. "I still remember it."

Jameson closes his eyes, and he's quiet for a moment. I rest my hand over his heart, and I swear it's beating harder than I've ever felt it.

"I remember the sagebrush more than anything. My allergies were going haywire. Mom made me take my medicine before Dad took me to the shop that day. It's the last thing she did for me." He lets out a heavy breath. "When we got home, all the windows were open. I walked into the living room behind Dad, and she was just hanging there—"

He cuts himself off, his jaw tensing.

"There was this beam above the staircase—" He swallows hard, and my heart hurts just picturing what he witnessed at such a young age. "Guess she couldn't handle the guilt."

"What did she have to feel guilty about?"

Jameson's eyes are filled with sadness, even if he doesn't shed a tear. "I had a brother—Wyatt. Mom was giving him a bath one day, and the phone rang. She got distracted. Dad said it was just for a minute, but by the time she got back, it was too late. *One minute* and everything changed. I was too young to remember any of that clearly. But Dad told me it was the one thing that'd always haunted him. Even after Mom left us, he said he barely felt what she did because nothing hurt like losing a child."

"That's a lot for a five-year-old to process."

And now it makes sense why Jameson resists any kind of connection outside his club. He's felt loss in ways most people never do.

It isn't his ego or his title that holds him back—it's his fear.

"My grandma moved in with us after that, and she's always been good to me. It was a big hole to fill, but she tried her best. I'll never be able to pay her back for that."

I plant a kiss on his shoulder. "From what I've seen, you try. You're good to her."

"I'm not good for anyone but my club, Tempe."

"You're good for me and Austin." I prop myself up to look down at him. "You took us in when you didn't have to. You make my brother laugh. You showed him how to change the oil on your bike. It's not always the big things that count. It's just being there for people. Austin sees that, and he appreciates it. We both do."

A small smile curls up in the corner of Jameson's mouth. "Kids are usually scared of me, but he sure takes after his sister. Always keeping me on my toes."

I laugh. "That's only because he looks up to you. And he trusts you enough to be himself around you."

Jameson's smile slowly drifts away as he stares at me, brushing my hair off my face. "Nothing's going to happen to you or him, Tempe. I won't let it."

"Promise?"

"On my life."

"Even when you get tired of us?"

Jameson grabs my jaw. "There's no such thing as getting tired of you."

His hand grazes my side, and he grabs my ass. He lifts me to him to steal a kiss. He nips my lower lip, and the mood in the room shifts.

Climbing up, I pull the sheet back and kneel between his legs. Wrapping my hand around his hard cock, I stroke it.

"What do you think you're doing, wildfire?"

"Thanking you for taking care of us." I run my thumb along his cock, teasing him. "And relaxing you before you start your long day."

"You want to relax me?" He laces his hands behind the back of his head and grins.

I nod.

"Then spit on it."

"Yes, President." I smirk, and his cock pulses at my words.

Leaning forward, I don't break our stare while I spit on his cock, stroking it up and down.

His chest vibrates with a growl when I do it again.

"What now?" I don't need direction, but I know he likes giving it.

And no matter how much I've resisted that in my life, I want to offer my submission to this man.

Stroking his cock again, his abs flex with every tight pull.

"Pinch your nipple for me, wildfire."

I reach up with my free hand and pinch my nipple, tugging and teasing it for him while he watches me. I toy with myself and stroke his cock. And he's patient, savoring every moment between us. Never rushing, even when I try to.

"You have such pretty tits." Jameson watches me grab my breast. "Let me get a taste."

I release my nipple and his cock, leaning forward to plant my hands on either side of his head so my breasts hang over his face. He tilts his chin up, looking me in the eyes but not moving his hands from where they're locked behind his head, as he darts his tongue out and teases one nipple and then the other.

My breasts are nothing special—a handful for him at most. But he worships them like he does every part of me. Like I'm his personal work of art.

"Are you going to do what I say, Tempe?" He flicks my nipple with his tongue. "Do you want to please me?"

More than anything.

"Yes," I breathe out as he draws my nipple into his mouth.

Jameson releases the peak, not breaking my gaze. "Then grab the headboard and let me taste that sweet pussy."

Nervously, I climb up the bed, facing the wall and grabbing the headboard. But when I try to hover over him, Jameson grabs my ass and pulls me down.

"Sit on my fucking face, wildfire. Ride my tongue, and let me fuck you with it."

"Holy shit." I tip my head back as he pulls my pussy to his mouth.

His tongue circles my clit before he drives it inside me. Grinding, losing myself in the soft circles of his tongue. In the rough scratch of his stubble on my thighs. He grips my ass and rocks my hips, kissing me between the legs like he's desperate for it.

"Jameson." I close my eyes and throw my head back.

He hums against my clit and picks up his pace, and that's all I need to see stars. My body shakes as I throw myself forward, grabbing the headboard. But he won't let me go, and he doesn't slow down. Fucking me with his tongue as I come hard for him.

"Perfect." He lifts me off him, licking the full length of me before shifting my hips back. "Now get down there and suck my cock."

I do as I'm told, slowly dragging my hands down the ripples of his chest as I move down between his legs. I grab the base of his cock and hold it upright, staring into his eyes as I circle the tip with my tongue.

"Fuck, Tempe. That feels so much better when I've still got the taste of you on my tongue." He strokes my cheek with the back of his knuckles. "You do such a good job pleasing me."

I close my lips around the head and tease him again before sinking my mouth over him.

Jameson grabs the back of my hair, digging his fingers into my scalp as I swallow him deeper. My hand strokes what I can't take, slipping up and down the base of his hard shaft as I swirl my tongue over his tip.

He's already leaking as I drag my tongue over the slit, and I savor the taste of him coating my lips.

Flattening my tongue, I run it along the vein on the underside of his cock then sink my mouth over him again. I hollow my cheeks, slowly dragging up and down, teasing him, staring up into his hooded gray eyes.

There's something so incredibly powerful about bringing him pleasure.

He's a man who commands a room. Who runs a club. Who is always in control.

Except right now, he's at my mercy.

A growl vibrates through his chest, and he watches me like I'm the only person worth looking at.

"Fuck." He drags his fingers down my back, and I draw this out as he watches the wet path I leave on his cock.

When I reach the tip, he holds the sides of my face still and juts his hips off the bed, forcing himself down my throat. I gag when he hits me deep and fast, tears springing to my eyes.

My hands squeeze the base of his cock as he pounds in.

The hard muscles of his stomach flex with every thrust, but right as I sense he's about to come, he pulls me off him.

"On your knees." He points to the floor, and I slide off the bed, sinking to the carpet as he stands over me.

Jameson grabs his cock and strokes with one hand, pushing my hair away from my face with the other.

"Tongue." His jaw clenches.

I stick my tongue out, and he places the head of his cock on it, sliding it over me slowly while stroking himself.

"You're so pretty, begging for my cum." He strokes again, still not thrusting in.

He rubs the head of his cock on my wet tongue, painting circles as he pleasures himself to the sight of it. With a final pull, his body stiffens, and the first warm rope of cum shoots into my mouth.

Jameson holds my jaw with one hand, stretching my mouth open, coating my tongue and lips with his release.

Cum leaks down my throat and drips down my chin as I stare up at him.

"Your tongue looks so much better painted in my cum than it does talking back to me, wildfire." He collects what's dripping with his thumb and shoves it into my mouth before pushing my chin to seal my lips around it. "Swallow."

I close my mouth and swallow him down.

"Good girl." He leans down to plant a kiss on my lips. "I'm going to fuck every hole. Fill every inch of you. You asked if I meant what I said to you last night, and I do. More than you realize. You're going to take me every way I want, Tempe. You're mine now."

26

Steel

Tempe holds Austin's ice cream in one hand while she unbuckles him with the other, and I watch them through the windshield as I circle the truck to open her door.

She says something that makes him laugh, and the giggle that bursts out of him has his whole body shaking. The scene is so domestic—sweet even. Something I'm terrified to get a glimpse of when I shouldn't entertain it.

But as I pop the car door open and Tempe takes my hand and climbs out, I consider going back to the emptiness I felt before them, and it has my stomach in knots.

Austin climbs out of the truck next. He jumps into my arms, and I fly him around in a circle before setting him down. He's still giggling, and his innocent laughter is something that's not usually heard at the clubhouse.

Slamming the car door shut, I think about the handful of times I've spent on four wheels in the past few years, when I'd rather be on two. But for them, I don't care.

"You coming to the party, Prez?" Soul puts out his joint, walking down the clubhouse steps.

Music is already echoing through the desert, while screams and hollers come from around back.

"In a minute."

"Can we go?" Austin jumps up and down.

I plant my hand on his head. "Not this time, big man. Adults only tonight."

Austin frowns, crossing his arms over his chest.

Tempe rests her hands on his shoulders. "Don't worry, we'll have our own fun."

"Why don't you go with Jameson, dear?" Grandma walks up with Sonny. "I'll watch Austin."

She went on our ice cream adventure today and rode with the prospects when I refused to let Tempe and Austin leave my side.

"I can't put that on you." Tempe frowns.

"It's fine, go. You're a twenty-two-year-old girl who deserves to live a little. Enjoy your night."

Grandma means well, but her words sink like lead. Tempe is only twenty-two. She has her whole life ahead of her, and she's holding herself back by getting involved with me.

Once she's safe, I should let her live the life she deserves. That was the plan from the beginning. But when I look at Tempe standing with her hands on Austin's shoulder, I have no idea how I'm supposed to do that.

"You promise you're okay watching him?" Tempe asks.

"Pearl has plans for us." Austin stands up tall, and I swear this kid is getting bigger by the day.

"Oh yeah? And what are those?"

Grandma leans down and whispers something in Austin's ear, and he smiles so big his whole face glows.

"It's a secret." Austin crosses his arms over his chest.

I pull Tempe to my side. "Ten bucks says it involves root beer floats."

My grandma winks at me because I know all her secrets, given she'd pull the same stuff with me when I was Austin's age and Dad was staying late at the clubhouse.

"Okay." Tempe relaxes. "But bedtime is eight."

"Of course." Pearl smiles, holding out her hand.

Austin takes it, and they hurry away, climbing in the truck so Sonny can drive them back to the house.

"There's no way he's going to be in bed by eight, is there?"

"Probably not." I shake my head. "But don't worry, she's good with routines, so if not then, soon after."

Tempe smiles, nudging me on the arm. "It's adorable how close you are with your grandma."

"Adorable?"

"That's what she said." Havoc walks past, smacking me on the back as he does. "You're adorable, Prez."

"Fuck off." I shake my head as he heads into the clubhouse, laughing.

Ghost hops off his bike next but doesn't look nearly as happy as Havoc.

"What's wrong?" I ask when he stops in front of me.

"No movement on the perimeter."

"They probably decided to cut their losses there. What about the bar?"

"Still no sight of him."

I tighten my hold around Tempe's shoulders. "Let me know if that changes."

"Will do, Prez." He heads into the clubhouse after Havoc.

"Who was he talking about?" Tempe spins in my arms to face me. "Dimitri?"

I tilt her chin up. "First off, I don't like hearing his fucking name from your pretty mouth."

She wets her lips, nodding.

"Second, that's club business; nothing for you to worry about."

"He's after *me*, Jameson. So don't use your *supersecret club business* excuse. I'm the one putting you in danger."

I smirk at her confidence because I'm going to have so much fun taming this girl's mouth if she continues to talk back to me in front of my men.

"That's fine, wildfire. He can come after me all he wants." I drag my thumb over her lower lip. "So long as he's not aiming for you or Austin, I can handle it."

Tempe opens her mouth to argue when Ghost pops back out of the clubhouse.

"Got something I need you to check out, Prez." His tone already has me on edge.

"Be right there."

Turning to Tempe, I brush her hair off her face. "You good to head out back yourself? I'll meet up with you as soon as I can."

"I'll be fine." She brushes her fingers over my cut, straightening it in the front. "Go take care of what you need to, President."

Every time she calls me that, I want to shove my cock inside her and never come out again. I've never wanted an old lady because I've got too many responsibilities that inevitably split my time, and no matter how understanding a person is, I'm well aware everyone has their limits.

But when Tempe runs her fingers over my patch, I let myself think for a minute that she could be strong enough to deal with a man like me. The same way she's been strong enough to step up for her brother.

I'd like to think she could handle it because she sees past the glamor of having the president's name on her back. She understands the downside. The pain. The disappointment. The hard parts of life that are bound to happen when you're with a biker.

But maybe she'd be willing to risk that if I was worth it to her.

Not that I am. And for the first time since I slipped on my cut, I'm disappointed I'll never be enough for someone.

"I'll be out there soon." I tip her chin up and kiss her, not missing that Soul is walking past me, chuckling as he walks over to Ghost.

I'm never publicly affectionate with women at the club. It gives a certain impression, and it sets expectations I'm not going to live up to. But with Tempe standing right in front of me, I can't help getting a taste of the comfort only she offers.

Tempe pulls back, planting her heels back on the ground. Her cheeks warm a shade, and I can't wait to do something about that later.

"Don't worry, Prez. I've got her." Luna pops up beside us and snakes her arm through Tempe's.

The purple in her hair is fading, showing off more of the blonde in the sun. She looks from me to the clubhouse doorway, and Ghost immediately stops staring.

"Come on, girl." Luna pulls Tempe away. "Looks like we have things to catch up on."

Luna winks at me over her shoulder, but it's not flirty. She's a sweet girl who had a rough go of it, so I took her in. And even if I know she's messed around with a couple of the guys, only one of my men really has her attention.

Walking up the steps to the clubhouse, I meet up with Ghost and don't miss that he's watching Luna and Tempe disappear down the hallway.

"You know she's gonna move on the second she's done with her classes if you don't fucking man up," I tell him.

"It's not like that, and you know it." Ghost shakes his head, turning his back on Luna.

"Lie to the guys all you want, but you can't lie to me, Marcus." I cross my arms over my chest. "It *is* like that, and I get what holds you back from doing anything about it, but it's a damn shame when she could be good for you."

"Doesn't matter what's good for me, Prez. I'm not good for her."

I shake my head, knowing arguing with him won't do any good. There's a reason Ghost is the way he is. Dark secrets only a couple of us know about. So while the patch bunnies treat it like a game, vying to be the one who breaks Ghost's celibacy streak, I know it's not going to happen until he works his shit out.

"All right. What do you have for me?" I change the subject, and Ghost pulls out his phone.

"Movement at your girl's house a few minutes ago."

"Dimitri?"

Ghost shakes his head. "Nah, a woman. Tempe's mom."

"What?" I snatch the phone from his hand and look at the screen.

It's an angle from the front porch, and it catches Tempe's mom climbing out the passenger side of a car idling at the curb. She hurries up the walkway, her eyes darting around like she's checking for anyone watching.

"How's she alive? That was a lot of fucking blood."

"No idea, but she is."

I wipe my hand down my face, trying to process what this means.

She's alive, and this is the first time she's showing her face. She hasn't tried to contact Tempe, and now she's acting suspiciously. It doesn't look good.

"What'd she do at the house?"

Ghost grabs his phone and changes cameras to one in the kitchen. "She went straight to this drawer and grabbed an envelope out of it."

"Any idea what was in there?"

"Silverware." Ghost shakes his head. "Looks like whatever she was after was hidden under the tray, but I have no idea what it is. You think she's in on all this?"

"I think it doesn't look good." I pat my pocket, itching for a cigarette but resisting when I know Tempe doesn't like me smoking.

Even if she'll eventually be smart and leave me, I can't help trying to be a better man while she's still around.

"That all?"

"Yeah. I'll let you know if she comes back."

"I'll talk to Tempe. She needs to know her mom's alive, but not tonight. She needs a break. We all do."

"Understood."

I follow Ghost into the clubhouse, wishing this weight wasn't sitting on my shoulders. Worse, wishing I didn't have to lay it on a girl already carrying so much around.

But Tempe needs to know for Austin's sake. If her mom is involved with the men who sent her to my clubhouse, the two of them are in more danger than I thought, and it's my job to protect them from whatever shit is about to rain down.

27

Tempe

LUNA LEADS THE WAY to the back of the clubhouse, and when we step outside, it's utter madness. Unlike the barbeque, the scene tonight is different, and more like the first night I came to the Twisted Kings compound.

A ring is set up in the center of the yard, and two guys are fighting. Blood spurts as one of them lands a hit on his opponent's nose. But they're both grinning, so I assume it's all in good fun.

There are no kids around. Booze and drugs are abundant. Coke, weed. A girl is lying across the bar topless while one of the guys licks whiskey off her breasts.

It's madness and a reminder why these men don't like strings or commitments.

This is Jameson's life.

Chasing what feels good when the pressures he faces are heavy. Finding ways to escape when reality weighs him down.

I understand it, no matter how much it hurts to think about it. But I don't let it fester. This is his world.

Just because I'm dipping a toe in doesn't mean I can judge. When I leave, he'll go back to whatever he was partaking in before I arrived, and I have no choice but to accept it.

Luna guides me through the crowd, not stopping until we reach the fire pit. A group of girls are huddled around talking, and all eyes land on me when we approach.

A redhead pops out of her seat and walks over to us, smiling. She's wearing shorts that show off the full length of her legs, and her flannel is tied up at her waist to show off her stomach.

"Hi, I'm Wren. Are you new here too?" She reaches her hand out to me.

Her long lashes flutter over her green eyes, and I try to bury my jealousy at how beautiful all these girls are when there's no room for jealousy here.

"Tempe." I shake her hand.

She clearly doesn't remember me from that day she was sitting at the bar talking to Jameson.

"Nice to meet you, Tempe." She smiles.

"Don't bother." Reina leans back in her seat, taking a sip of her drink. "She's not one of us, Wren. She's just the reason Steel's been antisocial lately. She'll be gone soon enough."

"Drop it, Reina." Luna rolls her eyes.

"It's fine." I release Wren's hand, turning my attention to Reina.

Just because jealousy won't do me any good doesn't mean I'm going to let her sit there and walk all over me.

I cross my arms over my chest, looking Reina up and down. She's pretty, especially tonight, with her makeup painted on perfectly. Her blonde hair is tied back, and she's a natural beauty, even if her breasts clearly aren't. The patch bunnies seem to flock to her, so I'd guess she's at least loyal to them.

If her interest in Jameson was genuine, I'd feel bad about the fact that she's hurt by him not showing her any attention. But one look in her devilish eyes, and I know there's only one thing she's after—his patch.

She probably sees nothing wrong with it, given the unapologetic way she chases after the men here. But if she knew Jameson like I do, she'd know he'd never put his name on the back of someone who only wanted him for that reason.

"What?" Reina snaps at me.

"You can be angry, or you can move on, Reina. But I'm not going anywhere so long as Steel wants me here, so you're going to have to deal with that." I glare, trying to ignore how his road name doesn't feel right on my tongue unless I'm using it to push his buttons.

"Well then..." Reina stands up, swaying her hips as she approaches. She's slightly shorter than me, and her curves are impressive in comparison. "In that case, I guess all I have to do is wait you out. And if I know my man, it won't take long for him to get bored of you."

My man.

Bored.

Every word burrows under my skin. I want more than anything to think that what Jameson and I share is special, but what if that's how he is with every girl, and that's why Reina's so heartbroken?

After all, he has the power to make a girl feel like the center of the galaxy all on his own.

He's attentive, patient, focused.

But that doesn't mean what he shows me is anything unique or special.

Reina grins like she knows she's getting in my head, and I hate it. My throat is on fire with all the things I want to say but don't. I can't claim him any more than she can, and I'm still not sure I want to. As safe as Jameson makes me feel, this life is dangerous.

It's unpredictable and messy.

Being with him means living in this environment twenty-four seven. Worse, inserting Austin into it. That's a commitment I don't think I'm prepared for.

"Hey, wildfire." An arm wraps around my shoulders, and I look up to see Jameson pulling me to his side. "Come sit with me."

Reina's smile falls as she looks up at him, and all the girls go quiet.

The way this man silences a group of people with his presence is something I've never witnessed before. And with how the girls around the fire pit are looking up at him like he's the moon shining in the sky, I don't know how any one person can be enough for him.

Jameson doesn't seem to notice as he pulls me to a different part of the yard. Luna follows, waving hello at almost everyone we pass.

"How are classes going?" Jameson asks Luna.

He stops at a chair that backs up to the clubhouse, pulling me onto his lap when he sinks into it.

"Good, this is my last semester for my associate's. Then who knows." She freezes when she sees the only other empty seat is directly next to Ghost.

"Sit." Jameson directs Luna to the chair, and even if she looks uneasy about it, she sits down.

I still can't figure out Ghost and Luna. She's one of the most outgoing people I've ever met, but around him, she gets nervous. They act like they've never spoken to each other when she's the one who helps him with surveillance.

"You want a drink?" Jameson brushes my hair off my cheek and tucks it behind my ear.

"I'm okay."

"Yes, you do." Luna perks up when one of the prospects comes by with a tray of shots. "We're supposed to be having fun tonight, remember? Here, drink this."

She grabs the whole tray and sets it on the table, passing them out to me, Jameson, and Ghost.

"To new friends." She smiles, lifting her glass.

It's been a long time since I've made a new friend, but as I smile back, I'm thankful for a friendly face around the club when most of the girls have been glaring at me.

"To new friends." I down the shot, and it goes straight to my head.

Jameson sets both our glasses to the side before planting a hand on my bare leg. I was feeling confident and wanted to look cute for our ice cream errand today, but now my dress is riding up and exposing my thighs. He brushes his thumb back and forth, teasing the hem with his fingertips.

"You cold?" His fingers drift over where my goosebumps prickle my legs.

"Yes."

I'm not really, but it's better for him to think that than to admit how easily my body reacts to him.

"Reyes." Jameson waves at the prospect as he walks by. "Grab a blanket for Tempe."

Luckily, there's a soft breeze tonight, so no one seems to think anything of it as Reyes goes and gets me a blanket.

Jameson lays it over my legs when Reyes comes back, and I turn sideways on his lap.

"Better?"

"Much."

He keeps his hand under the blanket, on my bare skin, tickling me with his touch.

"People keep looking at us," I say when another biker I don't recognize glances in our direction.

Jameson drops his chin to whisper in my ear. "You're hard not to look at."

"I don't think I'm the reason they're looking." I shake my head.

"Why not?"

"Because"—I glance around—"all the girls here are beautiful."

"No one's more beautiful than you." He squeezes my thigh.

"You don't mean that."

"Don't I?" His hand moves up my leg, dipping between them until his fingers graze over my underwear.

Luckily, everyone is too distracted by what they're doing to notice. Even Ghost and Luna disappeared after taking their shots, leaving me alone with Jameson.

His teeth graze my earlobe, and my body's on fire at his touch.

My eyes dart around, making sure no one is paying attention.

I'm not sure why I'm worried about that when there are people in corners of the clubhouse and yard fucking at any given moment. But something about Jameson touching me where anyone can see us feels borderline forbidden. Especially when everyone has been so vocal about how he doesn't claim women.

"Someone could see us." My eyes flutter as his fingers graze over me again.

"Good." He peppers kisses down my neck. "Then they'll know better than to fuck with you."

"I can handle myself."

"I know you can." He kisses my shoulder. "But you shouldn't have to at my club. They need to know where you stand."

"And where is that?"

"At *my* side." He pushes his thumb against my pussy, and I bite back a moan. "On *my* lap."

"For now."

I don't know what compelled me to say that. Either to remind him or myself. But it's dangerous to think this can become more, no matter how lost we are in it right now.

Jameson hums, not agreeing or arguing, and I don't know how to interpret his lack of reaction. But I'm distracted when my eyes flutter open, and I lock gazes with Reina from across the yard.

She glares at me, even though she's hanging on Havoc's arm.

"Don't let them get to you," Jameson says, likely noticing the direction I'm staring, so I turn my attention back to him.

"I'm not."

At least, I'm trying not to. After all, I'm the one in his lap right now. And from the negative reactions I'm getting, I'd guess that's not usual for him.

"Good." Jameson peels my underwear to the side. "Because you're all I'm thinking about."

"Is that so?"

He drives a finger into me, and my chest deflates with my exhale.

"Mm-hmm. Want me to show you?" He rolls his thumb over my clit.

"How?" The word nearly catches in my throat.

"Take my cock out, wildfire."

My eyes widen. "Here?"

Jameson kisses the spot behind my ear. "Yes. I need to teach you a little lesson."

"Is this really the time for it?"

Jameson pulls his hand out from under the blanket, dragging his wet thumb over my lower lip, coating me in the taste of myself. "You can either continue to question me, and I'll make you kneel at my feet while I fill your mouth with cum. Or you can take my cock out and sit on it under this blanket. Either way, I'll prove to you exactly what I'm thinking about in this moment."

Blood rushes to my cheeks. My core clenches at his filthy threat.

Jameson holds the blanket over me while I reach beneath it to unzip him. Thankfully, no one seems to be watching.

"Good girl." Jameson groans when I wrap my fingers around his hard cock. "Let me feel that wet cunt."

I spin so my back is to his chest, trying my best to be discreet as I lift and position him under me, but as I sink onto his cock, my head swims with the stretch. Once I'm fully seated, he circles an arm around me, holding me still against him.

"What are you doing?" I lean against his chest, resting my head back on his shoulder.

"Did you expect me to let you fuck me in front of all my men, wildfire?" He rolls a finger over my clit as he holds my body in place. "They don't get the pleasure of seeing you ride me like that. For all they know, we're just sitting here talking."

He toys with my clit, and my thighs clench.

"That's right." He does it again. "Have you ever heard of cock warming, Tempe? You think your pussy can make me come without you even moving?"

"Jameson—" I moan, but I'm cut off by him picking up speed on my clit.

It's torture, feeling him inside me and not being allowed to move.

"I want you to look around and remember something." He holds me tight as my body starts to build with his touch. "You're the one sitting on my cock right now. In the middle of my fucking club, where every damn one of them can look over and see who you belong to. Let them talk all they want. They don't get this—and they don't get me. Only you do."

He adds pressure to my clit, and when I try to shift, he holds me down over him. I swear I can feel his cock growing harder inside me as my pussy tightens with every flick of his finger.

"Make me come, Tempe," he whispers in my ear. "Squeeze my cock like a good girl. Claim me in front of all my people."

My nails dig into his thighs as I tip my head back.

I feel him in the deepest part of me, even if he refuses to fuck me like he usually does. Jameson touches me, and my chest burns with the pressure, begging to be released. And when my climax finally hits, I have to hold onto him to prevent from shaking for everyone to see. It sends every vibration to my core, and I'm squeezing him so hard with every pulse that he groans.

"Fuck." He buries his nose against my neck, and his cock twitches as he comes.

Just like he promised, without me having to move an inch.

He marks me in front of his whole club, even if we're the only two people here who know what we're doing.

That's all that matters. The point wasn't for them; it was for me.

He's mine—if even just for this moment.

28

Tempe

"What is this place?" I take Jameson's hand and accept his help off his motorcycle.

He swings his leg over his bike and climbs off. "Absolute nothingness."

"You're not wrong about that." I smile over my shoulder, and he snags my hand.

Jameson pulled his bike off the side of the road in the middle of nowhere, and there's nothing but empty desert around us.

"Well, it's pretty out here," I say as he helps me up onto a boulder, and I take a seat.

"It is." He stands between my legs. "It's one of my favorite spots to ride when I need to think."

I glance around the desert. It stretches for miles in every direction. Nothing but sagebrush and blue sky all the way to the horizon, and I get it. Jameson lives in a constant state of chaos and demand. If he's going to escape, it makes sense that it would be somewhere like here.

"It's beautiful." I wrap my arms around his shoulders, realizing he's not looking around at the desert like I am—he's staring at me. "Why did you bring me here?"

Pearl is watching Bea for the day, so she offered to watch Austin as well. Jameson said it was the perfect opportunity to go for a ride, but now that we're here, I get a sinking feeling there's more to it.

"Thought you might like getting out of the compound for a bit." Jameson tucks my hair behind my ear. "And we need to talk."

"Uh-oh," I tease, narrowing my eyes. "Jameson Steel's pulling the *we need to talk* card. That can't be good."

He chuckles. "Why do you say it like that?"

"You know, the classic breakup line that comes before *it's not you, it's me*. Not saying we're dating. I'm just messing with you."

"I guess I've never had to use that one." He shrugs. "Never had a girlfriend."

"Ever?"

"Nope." Jameson shakes his head. "Not that I'm a virgin."

"Shocker." I roll my eyes.

"Brat." He runs his thumb over my lower lip, teasing it. "What about you? I'm guessing you had to use those lines often, wildfire."

"Not even close." I kiss the pad of his thumb, and he drops his hand to my hip. "I don't really date either. Relationships and I don't mesh well."

"How so?"

"You mean besides the shining example of love I got from my parents?" I hitch an eyebrow.

He smirks. "Yeah, besides that."

I tip my head back, looking up at the sky and thinking. "I guess I've always just been a little too closed off for anything to work. And even when I tried, whatever I had to give was never quite enough."

"Why do you say that?"

For so many reasons he probably doesn't want to hear about. It's not sexy for a girl to carry around this emotional baggage. If Mom taught me anything, it's that men prefer their women compliant and their personalities easy to swallow. I'm none of those things.

But Jameson doesn't take his eyes off me, and I know he won't let this go without an answer.

"Technically, I have had one real boyfriend," I admit. "But I was barely eighteen at the time, so I'm not sure how serious you can consider it. He was a little older than me, and I could never seem to give him what he wanted... Saying I love you. Moving in. He was pushy about it, but I guess my heart's always been resistant."

"I don't like him already."

I smile. "You wouldn't. When I broke up with him, he got back at me by sleeping with my mom."

"You're kidding?" Jameson's back straightens.

"Wish I was. But it's not her fault. I wasn't living with her anymore, so she didn't know who he was. He played both of us. I stopped trying to date after that. Figured it was a better investment to just focus on myself."

"When are you gonna get me that list, Tempe?" Jameson brushes my hair off my face when a breeze kicks it around.

My eyebrows pinch. "What list?"

"Every fucker I need to kill for hurting you."

I almost laugh, thinking he's joking. But he draws a path over my cheek, up to the scar that cuts through my eyebrow, and I'm certain he means it.

"Never." I wrap my arms around Jameson's neck and pull him closer. "You're not getting into any more trouble for me. Besides, it's in the past. What do they say about that? It's what makes us who we are."

"So your past made you perfect then?"

I laugh. "More like… emotionally damaged and untrusting. But stronger, nonetheless."

Jameson leans in, brushing his lips over mine. "Strongest fucking woman I've ever met."

He claims me with his kiss, pulling my body to his, while the warm desert breeze flutters around us.

I never had a good example of what love is growing up. I didn't understand the point when it seemed to hurt so damn much. And after everything with my first boyfriend, I figured maybe I'd never get it.

But with Jameson holding me, I dare to think maybe it's possible. Maybe love can heal wounds instead of just slicing them open.

When Jameson breaks the kiss, I look up at him, framed by the bright blue sky. His gray eyes watch me as he traces his thumb over my lower lip. And I can't help wondering what he sees when he looks at me or how he makes sense of my mess. But I swear he looks past all the broken pieces my life left behind and understands what's beyond it.

"So, what did you want to talk about?" I ask, brushing my hands down the front of his cut. "You said we're out here to talk, right?"

He frowns, nodding. "We need to talk about your mom."

I press my lips together, and my heart constricts. "Did you find her body?"

"Not exactly." He grabs my hands and presses my palms to his chest. "Apparently, there's no body to find. She's not dead."

Not dead.

"What are you talking about?" My heart hammers. "I saw them kill her. The blood—"

"She survived it."

"How?"

"I don't know." He shakes his head. "But she did. Movement triggered a camera at your house, and Ghost got footage of her retrieving something."

"I don't get it." I shake my head, trying to make sense of what he's saying. "She was at my house? If she's alive, why hasn't she called? Why hasn't she checked on Austin? Why—"

"Tempe." Jameson pulls me in for a hug as tears sting my eyes.

He comforts me in his arms, not answering any of my questions. And as the first tear slips free, I hear what he's actually saying. Mom's alive, and she hasn't reached out to me. She disappeared with those men the night they sent me to the clubhouse. This was all a setup.

I bury my face against Jameson's chest, and my heart is racing. "What did she do?"

The question is more for me than him. And Jameson must sense that because he doesn't answer. He rubs my back and holds me to him.

"She really just left him." My heart aches for my brother.

"She probably was recovering at first." Jameson tries to excuse her, and I know it's for my sake because nothing about this situation could possibly look good from his end.

"But then she wasn't." I look up at him. "You said it yourself; she was at my house. She's clearly feeling better, and she hasn't even tried to come find us. Me, I get; I'm twenty-two and can take care of myself. But Austin... He deserves so much better than this."

I wrangle my hair back, shaking my head.

"And you'll give that to him." Jameson tips my chin up.

"What if that's not enough?" A tear slips free. "How am I supposed to explain that she just walked away? How do I fill that hole? I'm his sister, not his mom. How can I ever make this right for him?"

Tears streak my cheeks, and Jameson wipes them away with his thumb. "If there's one thing the club has taught me about family, it's that titles don't matter all that much. Actions define what we are to the people around us. You're there for Austin, and that's what matters. You're enough, Tempe. I've seen how that kid looks up to you. You're all he needs."

My chest expands as I soak in those words, knowing he understands it more than he admits in this moment.

"Thank you." I force a smile when he rubs his thumb over my cheek.

"Of course, wildfire." He cups my face in his hands, pulling me in for a gentle kiss.

The desert hums with the wind, and I let the peace of this empty land draw me in.

Resting my hands over Jameson's, I look up at him. "Where do you think she's been?"

"I don't know. The plates on the car that brought her to your house were stolen."

I don't like the sound of that. "What did she get when she was there?"

"An envelope in the kitchen. It was underneath the silverware. Do you know what it was?"

"I didn't know there was anything in there. Do you think—" I pause, dreading what I'm thinking. "Was she in on this?"

Since they shot her, I assumed she was just caught in the crosshairs. After all, I was the one Dimitri knew from the bar. He was there for me, not her.

Unless I was wrong.

Thinking back to what I saw in the kitchen, I remember how close they were standing. I remember the last words she said to him.

"Please don't."

Was there always more to this?

"We don't know anything for sure yet." Jameson frowns.

"But you think she was?"

"It's likely."

I close my eyes and fill my lungs like the air can be hope. But when I let it go, I'm as empty as I was when I thought she was dead.

Mom might be alive, but this isn't any better.

Whether she was in on this or not, she put Austin's life at risk for those men. The one person who has done nothing to deserve this.

"What do you need from me?" I ask. "I assume you're telling me because you need something."

"If you can watch the video to see if you recognize anything—"

"I can do that."

He nods. "I'm going to figure this out, Tempe. I'm not going to let anything happen to you or Austin. You have my word."

He tips his forehead to mine, and I close my eyes, holding my arms tight around his shoulders.

I never trusted words when lies are so easy to tell. But with Jameson, I believe him.

"Thank you, Jameson." I sigh, sinking against him.

"Anything for you, wildfire." He kisses me. "Anything."

29

Steel

EVERY TIME I TAKE a step forward lately, it feels like I'm going back five. Tonight, that needs to change.

Ghost hasn't been able to locate Tempe's mom or the car she arrived at Tempe's house in, but he was able to find an Iron Sinners safe house listed under the name Dimitri Stone. It's a break when we haven't had many of those in the past couple of weeks.

And right now, we need it.

After telling Tempe her mom's alive, things have been tense. She's still working through what to tell Austin, so for the time being, she's keeping it to herself, burdened by the full weight of the information. She doesn't want to give him hope when we don't know what it means yet, and it's weighing on her.

I need to get her answers.

I need to make this right.

Even if fixing this for them just means letting them go and carving a giant hole in my chest.

"How do we wanna approach this?" I hand Havoc the binoculars, and he lifts them to his eyes.

We've been staking out the safe house from a distance, and there are a couple of lights on, so I'm assuming someone is there.

Havoc reassesses the scene, humming as he scans the distance.

His special ops training comes in handy at times like this. Especially when there's nothing but empty desert between us and them and nothing to mask our approach.

The lack of cover is something that comes in handy when we're defending our own clubhouse. But out here, the open land is their advantage, not ours.

The moment we start in that direction, shit is going to hit the fan.

"Eastern entrance is our best shot." Havoc hands me the binoculars. "There's a turnoff past the main driveway that leads to a barn out back. The hill will keep us hidden on our approach, but either way, we're going to have to gun it and hope we outman them once we make the final turn."

At least this house is on the opposite end of Vegas from the Iron Sinners clubhouse. It gives us the upper hand when it comes to timing because even if the men inside call for help the second they hear our bikes, it will still take thirty minutes for backup to get here.

"You think Dimitri's there?"

"Doubt it." I shake my head.

As much as I wish Dimitri would be a sitting duck so I could rip him apart limb by limb, I doubt he'd be dumb enough to hide out at a house in his name. He has to know the first thing we'd do is search every database for him the second he offered his name to Tempe, and that thought alone means this could also be a trap.

Too bad we have no choice but to walk into it.

"We ready to roll out?" Soul asks, walking up behind me.

He and the second wave of men have arrived, and I look back to find them armed and ready. Whether we're at a disadvantage or not, it won't get better than this.

"It's now or never."

I climb back on my bike and rev the engine, knowing the men in the safe house might hear it, and we have no choice.

Tempe and Austin aren't safe until I neutralize Dimitri. And even if he's not here, I will burn every piece of property the Iron Sinners own to the ground, starting with this one.

My brothers follow me in formation on our bikes. We move in unison up the small hill that shields us momentarily from view. But the moment we turn around the other side, there's nothing but empty desert between us and the house, so we gun it, not slowing down.

My bike eats up the pavement as we rush ahead. At fifty yards out, the first gunshot echoes in the desert, and my men immediately split off and start to circle.

Just like we planned.

Hit them hard and without mercy.

There's no other option when they'll go down fighting just like we will. So long as I can keep a couple of them alive long enough to get some information, this will all be worth it.

I roll my bike to a stop and jump off, already reaching for my gun. Someone shoots through an upstairs window, and I duck behind a shed with Legacy to avoid getting hit.

He peeks his head out for a split second before another shot rings out.

It splinters the wood siding on the shed as the bullet barely misses him.

"I've got a clear line of sight if you can distract him." Legacy presses his back to the shed, holding his gun up.

He nods once, ready to move the second I take the heat off us.

We've been in this situation more times than I can count. At this point, battle is a choreographed routine.

I remember when Dad was in charge, and raids were more chaotic. We'd lose men every time, and there was no better plan than getting in and out to achieve our objective. I didn't realize back then why that was, but after Helix betrayed the club, it became clear to me.

Trust.

This only works if you know everyone has your back and you have theirs. It's the one good thing we have going for us after all the bad that happened.

There's a break in shots from the upstairs window when the shooter reloads, and I pop up, shooting rounds at the side of the house. He's out of view, so he won't get hit, but that's not the point. I'm just creating cover to give Legacy the perfect opening.

The second I pull back, the shooter does exactly what we expect, popping back up to take aim.

But Legacy is on it, and the moment his forehead comes into view, Legacy hits straight in the center of it.

He isn't ex-military like Havoc, but he's the best shot in the club.

"Nice." I grin at another Iron Sinner's soul going to hell where it belongs.

Soul and Ghost turn the corner of the house with a few others. "We're clear on the west side. Havoc and Sonny are clearing the house now."

It doesn't take long before Havoc waves us in, and I find three Iron Sinners tied up in the living room. A fourth lying in his own blood in the middle of the kitchen, and it's ironic, given Dimitri painted the same puddle of blood in Tempe's house.

Unfortunately, Dimitri isn't here.

Walking up to the men tied up in the living room, I assess them, searching for the weakest link and pointing to a kid who looks barely eighteen.

"Him first."

I make my way down the hallway that leads to the back of the house, and Havoc drags the kid with us, while the rest of the guys stay up front.

"In here." I point to a nearly empty bedroom, and Havoc drags him in.

There's nothing more than a mattress on the floor and a bag of clothes in the corner. The Iron Sinners treat their men as well as they do anything else—like shit.

"This your room, kid?"

He shakes his head, trembling.

He might not realize it yet, but he isn't cut out for this life. His eyes are too wide, and he's too damn scared when we've yet to do anything to him. Lucky for us, it makes him the perfect mark when I need someone to break.

I face the kid with my arms crossed over my chest. "I'm gonna make this real simple for you. Tell us where Dimitri is, and I'll let you walk out of here."

Just because I'm planning on burning Titan and his crew to the ground doesn't mean I'm starting with a damn teenager. Especially one who is bound to be weeded out of this life the moment he actually has to choose between himself and his club. If anything, I'm doing him a favor, testing his loyalty before Titan sniffs him out.

"I don't know where Dimitri is."

I plant the barrel of my gun on the center of his forehead, and his eyes slam shut. "Don't bullshit me. This is Dimitri's house. Where the fuck is he?"

"I swear." His voice shakes. "They don't tell us anything. We guard the guns out back, and Dimitri comes by once every few weeks to check in. But then he leaves again."

I lower my gun, and the kid blinks his eyes open.

"What does he do when he's here?"

"Not much." The kid shakes his head. "Checks inventory and lets Mastiff know about any new shipments. Most of the time, he's locked in the basement, but no one else is allowed down there, so I don't know what he's doing."

"All right." I nod at Havoc. "Keep him here while I check it out."

Making my way back down the hall, I head to the door that I assume leads to a basement.

"Ghost, Soul, you're with me. Legacy, keep an eye on things."

Legacy nods while Ghost and Soul head downstairs. At the bottom of the steps is a separate door that takes a pair of bolt cutters to get through. The room is mostly empty and hot. There's no air circulating, and every surface is covered in dust.

I make my way to the table at the other side and find stacks of pictures and plans. The blueprint for our tattoo parlor. Printouts of codes and building regulations.

It confirms what Ghost found on the drive. They've been using our own secrets to shut down our businesses on the Strip.

Flipping through the stack of photos and building plans, a folder at the bottom catches my attention, and my gut plummets when I open it.

The picture on top is one of Tempe walking out of Dirty Drakes. Beneath it is one of her getting in Sonny's truck.

One after another, the pictures follow her every movement. Some of her working, some of her getting home. A few of her and Austin in the backyard from before she started staying at my club.

Dimitri has been watching her and Austin's every move for longer than I realized.

My fists clench as I stare down at the photos.

"What'd you find over—" Soul doesn't finish his sentence as he sees what's in my hand.

It's a picture of Tempe sitting on my lap outside at the clubhouse. Her eyes are closed, her head is tipped back, and I know exactly what moment this is. It's a picture that could only have been taken by someone on the inside.

"Fuck." Soul drags his hand through his hair. "What do you wanna do, Steel?"

I crinkle the photo and toss it to the ground. Every bone in my body feels like it's grinding together. They're watching my girl. They're watching Austin. And worse, one of my own men is doing it.

"I want to send a message." I look Soul in the eyes. "We're going to remind these traitors what happens when they fuck with what's mine. And then we're going to burn everything Titan owns to the ground."

30

Tempe

I PARK THE TRUCK while Sonny and Reyes roll to a stop beside it. Usually, one of them drives, but since Pearl is with me and Austin, they rode ahead and behind us.

Jameson still won't let me leave the compound without an escort, and as much as I complained about it at first, I'm thankful after everything that's happened.

Dimitri tried to get to me at work.

My mom is alive.

I don't know who to trust lately, but the only person who has lived up to his promises is the man I showed up here fearing in the first place.

Climbing out, I glance back at Sonny. "Give me a second."

"I'm coming." Austin tugs at his seatbelt.

I reach in to squeeze his hand. "I need to see if he's busy first, okay?"

Austin stays put, and I shut the door behind me, walking up to the open bays at the garage. Jameson said the guys were short-staffed at Kings Auto today, so he woke up early to help out.

I respect how he shows up for his club and their businesses in every way. No matter how big or small the task, he's there for his men.

Havoc spots me first, leaning against the truck he's working on and smiling. "Steel, you've got company."

He yells for Steel, who pops out from underneath the truck.

I didn't think anything could be sexier than Jameson in his cut, commanding a room at the clubhouse. But when he climbs to his feet wearing a simple white T-shirt and jeans, streaked in oil and grease, my chest flutters. His cut hangs on a hook at the side of the bay, and I guess it's so he doesn't ruin it because his T-shirt is stained and messy.

Jameson smiles as he wipes his hands clean with a rag. It's so sincere it steals my heart.

"Wildfire, what brings you here?" He walks over to me, tossing the rag to the side. "Or, should I say, what brings *both of you* here?"

He waves at where Austin is sitting in the truck.

"Austin wanted to come see you at work, and I told him he could, but only if you weren't busy." I dip my thumbs in my pockets, suddenly nervous about showing up here unannounced. "Is that weird? That's weird, isn't it? Sorry, I should have called you first."

"Tempe." Jameson reaches his hand behind my head, tangling it in my hair when I try to take a step back. "You never need to call first. If you or Austin want to see me, come see me. If I'm busy or out on a run, you'll know about it. Otherwise, interrupt me whenever you want."

Jameson dips his mouth to mine, claiming me in a kiss.

Soft but deep.

Intimate but quick.

And when he pulls back, I know this isn't one-sided. That as unexpected as this is, he feels it too.

A life I didn't see myself having with a man I would never have trusted if I hadn't seen with my own two eyes that I could. Jameson's world might terrify me at times, but I never feel anything but safe with him.

More than that—*seen*.

Good, bad, and broken; he worships every piece.

It's like I've spent my life running, but with him, I take a moment to just be still. Whether it be evenings sitting on the couch with Austin between us, watching episodes of superhero shows, or mornings sipping coffee quietly with Jameson on the back porch before the sun has a chance to heat the day. I settle in those moments.

I crave *more*.

More smiles on my brother's face.

More excitement in my life.

More reasons to get out of bed than the monotony of schoolwork or a shift at Dirty Drakes.

Jameson stares into my eyes, and as Austin hops out of the truck and runs over to us, I want all of this for as long as I can have it.

Austin grabs onto Jameson's leg the second he reaches us, getting grease on his shirt. He smiles up at Jameson and sees the same man I do. Not a patch or a club leader—but a man. Someone who has survived more grief than I have.

Someone who's been broken by love and life as much as me and my brother. And somehow, the three of us found what we didn't know we needed in each other.

"Hey, big man." Jameson releases my face to plant a hand on Austin's head, tossing his hair around. "No cape today?"

Jameson glances at me; his eyebrows knit.

"He said he didn't need it."

"Oh yeah?" Jameson looks down at Austin.

"I'm still strong, though, right?" Austin asks him.

"You know it. Remember what I said? It's not the cape that makes you a superhero. It's the people around you. You still feel strong without it, don't you?"

"The strongest." Austin grins, planting his hands on his hips and posing like a superhero.

"Then I guess you're all set."

Jameson winks at me, and it flutters to my core.

Gentleness from a man who rarely shows it. A man who gave my brother the confidence to take his cape off, even in these unsettling circumstances.

I've been resistant, scared to let anyone help me in life. But what if Jameson's help makes me stronger, not weak? What if nothing else felt right because nothing before this was meant to be?

"Looks like you brought the whole crew." Jameson waves at his grandma, who's still sitting in the truck.

"Tempe and Pearl need dresses." Austin's shoulders deflate.

"Dresses, huh?" Jameson skims my bare legs in my shorts, and my skin prickles at what I'm sure he's imagining before his attention returns to Austin. "You don't look too thrilled about that."

"He's not." I brush Austin's cheek with the back of my hand. "Hence why I promised we'd come to see you before shopping to cheer him up."

"Why don't you leave him with me while you guys run your errands?"

My eyebrows pinch as I look up at Jameson. "You're busy."

"Exactly." He squats down and looks at Austin. "I could use another set of hands. You up for it?"

Austin smiles, nodding his head with excitement. "Yes!"

"Excellent. Hop on." Jameson has Austin spin around, and he lifts him onto his shoulders.

Austin giggles as he grips the sides of Jameson's face, steadying himself when Jameson stands back up.

"You really don't have to do this."

Jameson leans in, kissing the top of my head. "And let you torture this poor kid by taking him dress shopping with you? No way. Besides, we've got an engine to rebuild."

I look up at Jameson, and tears sting my eyes. With the two of them looking down on me, my heart might as well collapse in on itself. I'm so overwhelmed with the rush of warmth bursting in my chest.

"Have fun, wildfire." Jameson kisses me on the forehead before turning to walk away. "Try to stay out of trouble."

Jameson grips Austin's legs, carrying him back into the bay, and all the guys' heads pop up to welcome their new helper.

How am I ever going to rip Austin away from this? It'll break his heart as much as mine.

All I can do is grip my stomach and hope I'm not the only one feeling this way.

Climbing back into the truck, I start the engine, and Pearl glances over at me.

"Looks like we lost one to the garage."

"It's more exciting than dress shopping, apparently."

She nods, smiling.

The drive to the Strip is quiet, and I appreciate how easy it is to be around Pearl. She never judges and has a calming presence. I can understand why Jameson is so close with her, and I'm thankful she was there for him after his mother's death.

I'm pretty sure if anyone is responsible for the heart he buries beneath his cut, it's her.

"Looking for anything in particular?" Pearl asks, climbing out of the truck and following me inside the store when we get there.

Sonny and Reyes find a spot in the corner of the shop to stand and talk while we browse the racks.

"I need a dress that'll look good over a bathing suit." I lift one off the rack and hold it up. "Jameson said he's moving tomorrow's barbeque to Lake Mead, so I thought I'd find something nice for the beach. You'll be there, right?"

"Of course. Austin has big plans for sandcastles."

I smile at Pearl, appreciating how she's let us into her life.

"I should probably grab another pair of black shorts while I'm here. I need to pick up a few more shifts at the bar to afford the down payment on this apartment I've been looking at."

Pearl chuckles, shaking her head as she searches the rack. "You still planning on leaving?"

I shrug. "We can't stay forever. Besides, I'm sure Jameson is looking forward to getting his space back."

"I can promise you that's the last thing he wants." Pearl quirks an eyebrow.

"What makes you say that?"

"Because I know my grandson. There are very few things that he'll protect with his whole heart when it's easier for him to pretend he doesn't have one. But he'll do anything for his brothers, his club, and his family."

"I know."

"Then you should see that's what you and Austin are to him now."

I shake my head, trading one dress for another. "He's just worried about our safety."

"Not just your safety, Tempe. I see how he looks at you. How he looks at Austin. My grandson has never let anyone into his life the way he's opened himself up for you two."

I pull a dress off the rack, holding it up to me in the mirror. "I don't know why."

"Because you see him for who he really is, and you accept that about him." Pearl walks beside me and grabs my shoulder, meeting my gaze in the mirror. "Have I ever told you about when I met his grandad?"

I shake my head.

"Well, he tried to scare me away with the club just like Jameson did with you at first. He thought I couldn't handle all that comes with it. But I proved him wrong really quick." She smiles, and I don't doubt it. "It takes a woman with a backbone to be with one of those guys. Especially when he's got the president patch on his cut. But you've got a spine if I've ever seen one, Tempe. One that can handle his club. It takes a strong man to do what they do. But it takes an even stronger woman to love them."

I swallow hard. "You really think I'm that strong?"

"I know you are." She squeezes my arm. "What his momma did nearly ripped our family apart, and not for the reasons you might think. We all do bad things. We all make mistakes that we can't take back. But a family heals together—fights together. She was too heartbroken to do that, and Jameson still hasn't recovered."

Pearl takes the dress from my hand, holding it to me and brushing her fingers over it.

"But we can't let pain be all we are. We have to live for those we lose. Jameson doesn't deserve to suffer his whole life because of his parents. This punishment he inflicts on himself because of what happened isn't fair to him. You help him see that. You show him life outside the club and love greater than he grew up with. And I get the feeling he does the same for you. After all, you're not your father, are you, Tempe?"

I shake my head, pressing my lips together and fighting back tears.

"I didn't think so." Pearl squeezes my hand. "Believe in yourself. All three of you deserve happiness, and you bring that out in each other."

Pearl pats my shoulder, walking away to search the racks while I stand frozen.

Jameson and I have both spent so much time fearing the sins of our bloodlines that we've cut ourselves off from what we could be if we let ourselves see past them. And I'm terrified to admit I want more, but I do.

For Jameson, I want to be everything Pearl thinks I am.

I want to be his.

31

Steel

I'm never the last one to church, but the weight of today sits on my shoulders, and when I take my seat at the head of the table, it's no lighter.

"Where are we at with the Iron Sinners?" I ask, leaning back in my chair.

"Titan got our message." Ghost smirks. "Went over as well as we'd expect."

"Good."

After storming Dimitri's house, we burned it to the ground. The kid who cooperated walked free to hopefully make better choices moving forward, but the others weren't so lucky. It's not my preference to leave bodies the cops could trace back to the club, but Titan's going for the jugular, and I refuse to sit around and take it.

No matter what happens moving forward, we're fighting back. I'll skin the entire Iron Sinners population until I get the answers I'm looking for.

Until Tempe and Austin are safe.

"When do you think he's going to retaliate?" Legacy asks, tapping his boot on the ground because he can never sit still.

"Sooner than later," Ghost answers. "He and his men have been seen scoping out a few of our businesses across town. They're anxious and looking for an opening."

"Anxious is good. Means Titan's about to make a mistake."

My men give me shit sometimes because I don't make big decisions for the club without thoroughly analyzing what I'm getting us into. But it's better to be right than impulsive. I'd rather strike hard when I know it'll hurt than throw darts and wait for something to stick.

It doesn't matter if we're thirsting for blood. It's my responsibility to make sure the club is prepared in every situation.

Titan isn't known for doing the same.

He's impulsive. Antsy.

Sometimes it works in his favor. Like when he caused a scene outside the compound and got us to thin our crew around town to reinforce our border. But right now, I'm hoping to use it against him.

I look over at Ghost. "Any leads on who's working us from the inside? I need to know who took those pictures."

Ghost shakes his head. "Everyone checks out on paper, even the prospects. Which means Titan probably had someone with skill wipe their public records. I'm starting to think he has someone besides Richter running security after it took me so long to hack the flash drive. Whoever encrypted it is good."

"As good as you?"

Ghost smirks. "I cracked it, didn't I?"

I nod, thankful Ghost is on our side because if there's something to find, he will. No matter how long it takes.

It's a blessing and a curse when time isn't on our side right now.

"No one outside this room knows we have a traitor in the club, and it needs to stay that way until we weed them out." I look around the room. "Soul and I are going to sit down with every member until we figure out who is working against us. Someone is going to crack."

"And when we find out who the traitor is?" Havoc grins.

"Then we'll have a little party."

All my men look happy about that, even if nothing about this situation is settling. There's something satisfying about painting the Shack in a traitor's blood. And it's something we're all too familiar with after Helix and his accomplices turned against us.

"If that's all we have on the traitor, let's move on to the next order of business." I cross my arms. "The appeal went through, so it's official. Chaos is getting out."

"Fuck yes." Havoc pounds the table with his fist. "How did Monroe manage that?"

"Looks like the prosecution's secret witness backed out." I glance over at Soul, and he grins, knowing exactly why that is.

Soul is my VP for a reason, and the lengths he'll go to for the club outrival everyone's but mine. He might seem like a carefree guy, but beneath what he shows the world are depths that lead to his twisted, dark side. A side that teases the line between immoral and sick if it means the Twisted Kings will benefit.

Havoc grins. "Well, isn't that convenient?"

"When's he coming home?" Legacy asks.

"Friday. They're processing the paperwork now, but they're also being dicks about it, so it'll take an extra few days. I told Chaos to sit tight and not piss anyone off until he's on this side of the gate. We don't want him giving them any excuse to keep him in there."

I glance over at his empty chair at the table, ready to have all my brothers back in their seats.

"We needed that good news." Legacy brushes his hair back. "If shit keeps going how it is with the Iron Sinners, we're going to need another set of hands."

I nod. "Soul already filled Chaos in. He's ready to get to work."

"But first…" Soul laces his hands behind the back of his head. "The man deserves a proper welcome home."

I chuckle, nodding my head. "The prospects are already on it. The Reno and LA chapters are coming out for the celebration."

Our enemies might fear Chaos for his borderline sadistic methods of torture, but he's revered by his brothers in the club for his loyalty. It's why he has the respect of the club, regardless of how much he lives up to his road name.

"It'll be good to have him back." Soul rests his elbows on the table. "And who doesn't love an excuse for a party?"

"Especially a chapter mixer." Havoc grins.

Whenever more than one chapter converges, shit gets wild. Last time our Reno brothers were in town, we had to rebuild part of the bar after someone lit a match to the spilled booze, thinking it would turn out like it does in movies.

My men might be smart in battle, but they're reckless drunks when we're celebrating.

"Better hide your girl if the Reno crew is coming, Steel." Soul winks at me. "Reaper might respect ya, but without your name on her back, he's gonna shoot his shot no matter how much it pisses you off."

"Maybe even to see *how much* it'll piss you off," Legacy points out, ticking an eyebrow in a challenge.

They aren't wrong. Reaper and I have been friends since we were kids, and that's exactly why he'd do it. The second he catches wind of something between me and Tempe, he'll test just how deep my loyalty to her is. And the thought of another guy making a play on her has me seeing red.

"About that—"

"Oh shit." Soul's eyes widen. "Are you about to say something stupid like I think you are?"

I scratch my jaw, knowing I'm about to break every rule I thought was absolute before I met this girl. "Yeah, I am."

"Are you claiming her, Prez?" Legacy plants his elbows on the table, and the entire focus of the room is on me.

I look around at my brothers, knowing that for the past thirty years, nothing has ever been more important to me than them. But Tempe and Austin changed that. I'd give everything up, from my soul to my cut, if it meant keeping them whole.

When I moved them into my house, it was supposed to be temporary. A safe place to store them since I never slept there anyway. But from the moment Tempe and Austin walked inside, I knew I never wanted them to leave. A sentiment that's growing with every passing day.

I need them in my life like I need air in my lungs.

If they leave, I'll never recover. And it's about time I do something about it.

"Tempe's mine," I say, looking around the room. "I want to ask her to be my old lady."

My patch gives me a lot of power in the club, but the reason we're a brotherhood is that the most important decisions made between these walls aren't made by one man. They're put to a vote. And nothing is more important than inviting someone to become one of us in any capacity.

Claiming an old lady included.

When that happens, she becomes part of the club. The club vows to support and protect her from there on out. Even in the event of a brother's death, she'll always be taken care of.

She'll always be family.

"I know her loyalty has been in question—"

"Mostly by you," Ghost points out.

"Right." I nod. "Helix being her father didn't help win over trust."

"Or her trying to kick your ass when she met you," Ghost pipes up again, smirking.

"All true." I glare at him. "She's got fire."

Havoc leans forward, grinning. "Gonna need it if she's going to put up with you, Prez."

"That's for sure." Legacy chuckles.

"Damn." Soul shakes his head. "I'm gonna owe Chaos two grand. I swore it wasn't going to get this far."

"Does that mean you're offering your support?"

Soul straightens up, planting a hand on my shoulder. "I can't pretend to understand it, but she makes you better, Jameson. Of course I fucking support it. I want what's best for you, brother. And apparently, that's her and the kid."

"Thanks." I nod.

"Besides..." Soul pulls back, grinning. "Less competition means more pussy for the rest of us."

"Beautifully said." Havoc laughs, and I just shake my head. "Congratulations, Prez."

He smacks me on the shoulder, and Ghost nods, offering as much of a smile as he ever does, which isn't much.

"When you gonna ask her?" Legacy tips his chin up.

"This afternoon."

"Hence the sudden change of plans, moving the barbeque to Lake Mead? Getting all romantic on us, huh?" Legacy grins, and I nod. "Let's hope she says yes then."

The guys laugh, and I shake my head. "She fucking better."

"She will." Havoc nods. "You know she will."

I think she will.

But I also understand this life is hard, especially being with the man sitting at the head of this table. Tempe is a strong woman, but I'm asking for all her faith. All her trust. I'm asking her to not just believe in my club, but in *me*.

Either way, I'm willing to put my pride on the line and see this through if she'll give me a chance. Because when I consider not claiming her—of not living up to the promises I've made Austin—I can't fucking breathe. If they walk out of my life, I might not recover. The three of us aren't the family we saw ourselves having, but that's what we became anyway.

Hopefully, she feels the same.

"If we're done here, I'd say this calls for a drink." Soul stands up, and the rest of the guys follow.

They slowly filter out of the room, and when the doorway clears, I spot Tempe through it, standing in the center of the clubhouse.

She's wearing a dress I've never seen before, and the sight of her nearly stops my heart.

It's maroon on the top, and it hugs her chest. The waist is a thick band of black fabric that molds to her, flowing out at her hips. The full length of her smooth legs is on display. And when her eyes meet mine, she steals what's left of my desiccated heart.

She's it for me.

I'm a goner for this girl.

32

Tempe

STEEL MEETS ME AT the threshold of the room where they hold church.

It should be illegal for him to look like he does. His forearm is propped against the doorframe, tugging his T-shirt up just enough for me to get a hint of his solid stomach. Showing off a trail of perfectly cut muscle that is pure temptation.

"Hey, wildfire." He tips my chin up and plants a gentle kiss on my lips when I reach him.

The nickname he's given me, paired with how he teases my lower lip with a kiss, has my insides melting. I slip my hands beneath his cut and plant my hands on his hard chest.

"That dress is beautiful on you."

"It's a pretty dress." I smile up at him.

He brushes his thumb over the apple of my cheek. "Only because you're in it. Come here."

He slips his hand into mine, pulling me into the room and shutting the door.

It's dark since the only windows in here face inside the clubhouse, and right now, the blinds are closed. There's a single bulb overhead, but it's not bright.

Looking around, I see that one wall is covered in photographs. There are no people in them, just the open road. Some are black and white, others color. And the varying landscapes make it clear they were taken all over the country.

"What are those?" I ask.

"A tradition my grandad started when he formed the club. On your first run as a ranking member, you take a shot of the open road to mark the first miles of many spent as a Twisted King."

"Which one's yours?"

Jameson smiles, pointing to a photo on the far left. "Maryland."

"That's a long trip," I say, admiring the beautiful forest road in Jameson's picture.

Jameson's smile falls. "That was right after the former leader of the Iron Sinners took my dad out. We chased him all the way across the country after we made our way through the members of his club, trying to figure out where he'd gone."

"Did you find him?"

Jameson nods, and I don't need to ask what happened to know what Jameson most likely did.

I glance at the images on the wall. The history of the club. The traditions they hold on to, and the things that they value. A bond I've never experienced when everything in my life has always felt temporary.

Glancing around the room, I take in the space the members consider sacred.

Their *church*.

"Am I allowed to be in here?" My gaze moves to the large wooden table in the center.

The Twisted Kings logo is carved into it, and someone must have taken a torch to add extra dimension because there are char marks on some of the edges. The chairs surrounding it are large and sturdy, with one that must be Jameson's at the head of the table.

"You're allowed to be anywhere you want, wildfire. So long as we're not in the middle of church."

"I figured you guys had more rules than letting everyone at the compound run wild." I smile, walking around the table slowly and brushing my fingers over the smooth wood. "This is beautiful."

"My grandad carved it."

"Really? It's gorgeous."

Jameson nods. "Yes. And for the record, *people* aren't allowed to run wild around here. But *people* aren't *you*."

"Oh yeah?" I smile when he meets me at the head of the table, reaching for my chin. "What makes me so special?"

"Generally speaking… everything." He grins, and I can't help but laugh.

"Someone woke up in a good mood this morning. Not that I'm complaining; keep the flattery coming, President."

Jameson shakes his head, dipping his chin and laughing, but there's a nervous edge to it, and I don't know why.

He rests his hands on my hips while he towers over me, and his eyes are serious when they lock onto mine. I'm still learning all his little ticks, but the intensity in his gaze tells me whatever he's about to say is either really good or really bad.

"Did something happen?" My eyebrows pinch, and I bite the inside of my cheek to settle my nerves.

"Nothing bad… I hope." He tucks my hair behind my ear. "I don't want you and Austin to leave."

"I know. Not until this is over."

He shakes his head. "Not just then. I don't want you to leave in general. *Ever*."

I blink up at him, swallowing hard. "What are you saying, Jameson?"

My heart races as I look into his gray eyes. As I'm swept out to sea in the middle of the desert. As he lifts his hands to my face and looks down at me like he's torn himself completely open.

"Tempe, I'm not a good man." He sighs. "This life is hard, and the club will always have more attention than you'll like. I'm loyal to my men, and because of that, I'll always stand with my brothers. Before you and Austin, that was enough for me. All that mattered was my club."

He drifts his thumbs over my cheeks, and I feel the tears already welling behind my eyes.

"But then you came in and stole a hell of a lot more than you ever intended. You found something beating in my cold chest, and you made me see what life could be like if I stopped trying so damn hard to run from it."

Jameson leans in to kiss my forehead, pausing with his lips brushing my skin.

"I know it's selfish to ask you this—to ask you to bring Austin into this life. But I swear, I'll do everything to give you both what you need. To treat you right and make sure Austin has the support and family he deserves. You two give me purpose. You help me breathe. You see the man, not the patch. You see me. I want to love you for it. To thank you for it. I want us to be a family."

"Jameson—"

"Just think about it." He pulls back, dragging his thumb over my lower lip. "I never wanted a family, knowing what it feels like if you lose it. But now I realize that's just because my family hadn't come into my life yet. But you and your brother—that's what you are. My family. Promise me you'll at least think about it."

"Jameson." I reach up and grab the sides of his face, smiling up at him. "I don't have to think about it. The answer is already a yes."

He swallows hard. "Are you sure? I know I'm not an easy man to get along with."

"I can handle you just fine, President."

"That so?" He grins, and I nod.

Jameson sinks back into his chair, pulling me with him so I'm straddling his lap. But he hasn't released my face, so I'm hovering with my mouth just over his.

"You understand what it means being my old lady?"

"I've been briefed on the matter."

His eyebrows pinch.

"Pearl," I explain.

"Of course." Jameson chuckles before relaxing his smile and staring into my eyes. "I know it's not an easy decision or an easy role in the club, given... everything. So I want to make sure you've thought it through."

He could be referring to the danger of being with a biker. Or he could be referring to the women who still refuse to accept that he's moved me into his life. Either way, in my heart, I accept the struggle to be by his side.

"Outside forces don't determine what we are to each other, Jameson. Not our pasts, not your enemies. You'll always be their president, and I understand that role comes with responsibility. But when it comes to you and me, all that matters is what we choose together—what we build together. And who we are to each other. Will you be loyal to me?"

"With all I am." He cups my face, and when I look into his eyes, I genuinely believe him.

"Will you protect us?"

"To my grave."

"Then that's all that matters." I lean in for a quick kiss. "Family."

Jameson drags my hair back and kisses me deeper. His tongue tangles with mine, and I rock in his lap. The back of the hard chair digs into my knees, even as my shins sink against the leather seat cushion.

My chest brushes against Jameson's leather cut, and I hand myself over to the man who helped me understand what it really means to be there for someone. What it means to really care about a person who isn't my blood.

Who showed me what honor and loyalty really are.

"I love you," he whispers.

"I love you too." So much I didn't think it was possible.

His hands drift down to my hips, and he cups my ass before tugging at my skirt to slip his hand under it.

"No bathing suit under this dress?" He growls against my mouth. "I told you we were headed to the beach this afternoon, and if you strip down to nothing in front of my brothers, I'm gonna be the one betraying my club when they look at you."

"Figured you'd prefer the easy access," I tease.

He drags his nose along my throat, nipping at the side of my neck. "When it's just you and me... yes."

I rock in his lap, tipping my head back when he moves to kiss the path down to my breasts.

"But all my men are going to be at the lake, looking at how pretty you are in this dress. The last thing I need is the wind giving them a show when I'm the only one who sees you like that. They can wish all they want that it could be their name on your back. But it never will be. Why is that, Tempe?"

"Because I'm yours."

"Mm-hmm." Jameson hums. "And I'm yours right back. It's an honor that you want to claim me like that, wildfire. Something so fucking hot, I can't resist needing to thank you for it."

"Oh yeah?" I tip my forehead to his. "And how do you plan on doing that?"

"By filling you with my cum."

"About that..." I graze the sides of his neck with my fingers. "My pill pack just ran out, so we might want to use something until I get to the doctor."

"No." He shakes his head, pulling my mouth to his.

"What do you mean, no?" I murmur against his lips.

"If it's up to me, you're staying off the fucking pill from now on anyway."

I pull back, smiling. "Did Jameson Steel just admit he wants to knock me up?"

I've never really thought about having my own kids when I could barely picture myself having a relationship. But the love and security this man brings into my life has the thought ballooning my heart.

"Fuck yes, I did. The more of you, the better. Little miniature Tempe's running around the compound."

My eyebrow hitches. "You realize they could also turn out just like you."

"Then good luck with that."

I laugh, and he catches my mouth in a kiss. He holds my jaw and connects me to him. With his free hand, he works the buttons on his jeans, and I shift so he can pull out his hard cock.

My fingers grip it, and the growl that vibrates through his chest has my body aching.

Shifting away, I try to pull myself from his lap to sink to the floor, but he stops me.

"Why won't you let me please you?" I lean in, teasing the shell of his ear.

"I don't want you on your knees in here. I want to take you on my throne like the queen you are." He lifts my hips. "Sit on my cock, wildfire. Let me worship you where you belong."

I stare into his eyes as I slowly sink onto his hard shaft. He stretches me, filling me in the way only he can. His hands on my hips shove me the final inch until I'm fully seated. And I don't take my gaze off him as I start to circle my hips.

"You feel like the paradise I don't deserve." He kisses the center of my throat.

His fingers on my arm make the strap of my dress flutter down as he kisses up my neck. I chase the feeling of him all over me, riding him in desperation for my release.

"That's it. Ride my cock like a good girl. It's yours. Only yours."

I wrap my arms around his shoulders and pull Jameson in for a kiss. We melt together as I claim a man who was so out of reach when I met him.

We were wandering alone at two ends of a desolate desert. And somehow, we managed to find each other.

I've spent my whole life fighting, but in Jameson's arms, I don't feel the need to anymore. I've found my safe space—my partner. I hand myself to him because that's what he does to me, unapologetically.

When he comes, he marks me deeper than any stitches securing a patch to a vest.

He marks me as his.

And he's mine.

33

Tempe

Luna stops beside me, wearing neon-purple sunglasses. She smiles, tipping her face up to the sky.

"I love Nevada." She waves her arms out.

"That's because it's April, and the weather is bearable." I laugh.

"True." She drops her arms.

I look across the beach to where Austin is helping Jameson set up a grill. A few prospects are carrying chairs down the hill to the beach from where the motorcycles and trucks are parked up at the overlook.

We're the only ones in this particular stretch of the lake, and even if it's more rocks than sand, it's a nice, secluded space for the club to relax.

Jameson gives Austin a one-armed hug for helping him with a folding table, and my heart expands watching them.

It's strange to think this is going to be our life now. I never would have imagined it, given my resistance to everything Helix represented. But Jameson changed my perspective. This isn't just a club; it's a family. For him, I'm thankful to be part of it.

"I should probably go to find the sunscreen." Luna examines her arms, glancing up to where a few of the patch bunnies are applying lotion to each other in an attempt to get the guys' attention.

"Maybe if you ask nicely, Ghost will help you rub it on."

"You're terrible." Luna smiles, a blush painting her cheeks.

"And you're in denial."

Luna follows my gaze to where Ghost is watching her. But the second their gazes meet, his stare drops to his phone.

"What is it about a man covered in tattoos that's impossible to resist?" Luna sighs. "Not that you're on the hunt anymore now that Steel locked you down. The first of the ranked members to take an old lady. Honestly, I did *not* see that one coming."

"Thanks?" I laugh.

"You know I don't mean it like that." Luna threads her arm through mine. "But those guys are better known for riding bikes and shooting guns than relationships."

"Honestly, I'm just as surprised as you are. I wasn't planning on any of this when I came here. I never wanted a relationship either. But something just… I don't know. Something just makes sense when I'm with him."

"You deserve it, Tempe. You both do." A genuine smile creeps up Luna's cheeks. "And who knows, maybe it'll rub off on the rest of them now."

"Maybe if you do something about it, it will." I poke her arm.

"Yeah, yeah." She releases me, pulling a hair tie off her wrist to wind her freshly dyed purple hair into a ponytail. "The second you have proof Ghost is pining after me, you let me know, and I'll lock him down. Until then, I'm convinced he's the *least* interested in me out of all of them. So I refuse to sit around waiting."

I shake my head because she doesn't see that he's already pining after her, but there's no use trying to convince her until they're both willing to admit it.

"Let's go get our feet wet," Luna changes the subject.

"You have fun. I need to check in on Austin. Looks like he's digging a moat around Pearl, so I should probably make sure she doesn't need saving."

Luna laughs, walking toward the water. "Good luck."

I make my way across the beach. There's a slight breeze cooling the air, making it the perfect temperature to be outside. A gust rustles my skirt, and luckily Jameson made sure I put my bathing suit on before leaving so I don't give everyone a show.

Nearly half the club is here, patch bunnies included. Reina still glares at me every time we make eye contact, but she hasn't approached me or said a word since Jameson stood in the center of the clubhouse and announced me as his old lady earlier.

Hopefully, we learn to coexist because I'm not going anywhere, and as much as I wish she would, I understand she's as much a part of this club as any of the girls are.

Besides, just because Jameson's past is staring me in the face in the form of a beautiful blonde doesn't mean I don't have my own history. What's in the past is exactly that. If I'm going to accept this life, I need to embrace what I've signed up for.

There's no being half-in with a man like Jameson Steel. I either need to trust him or leave. And when I look up to find him watching me walk toward the group, the smile on his face confirms I have nothing to worry about.

Ghost pulls Jameson's attention with something on his phone, so I head over to Austin.

There's not much sand on this side of the lake, but Pearl found a decent patch to set her chair up in. Austin and Bea carved a moat around her, and now they're filling it with water.

"Safe in your castle?" I stop at the edge of the moat.

"Of course. So long as I have my little knight in shining armor." Pearl smiles, watching Austin dump another bucket of water into the moat.

"Faster," Bea says to Austin as the sand drinks up what they just poured.

Her blonde hair is in a ponytail that bounces around as they run back toward the lake. I'm thankful Austin has a friend through this transition, and I hope that makes it easier. Someone for him to share movie nights and playdates with at our house.

Our house.

I don't know when I started thinking of it like that, but that's what it is now. A home when I've never really had one.

"I hear my grandson wised up." Pearl smiles. "Congratulations."

"Hope you don't mind us sticking around. I know there's not much peace and quiet with a four-year-old stampeding through the house."

"Not at all." Pearl shakes her head. "It's been far too quiet for far too long. I love having Jameson back home again. And the two of you are an added bonus."

"Thanks, Pearl."

She nods, and Austin adds another bucket of water to the moat. He's been quick about it, and it's now overflowing.

"I think that's enough."

Pearl laughs when it splashes her feet, and I snatch the bucket up from him.

"You like it?" Bea and Austin look up at me, smiling proudly.

"It's perfect."

"Honey Bea," Legacy calls for his daughter, holding up a bottle of sunscreen. "Come here."

Bea's shoulders sink, but she reluctantly makes her way over to her dad while Austin runs back to the water. I follow him, crouching down to help him dig a rock out of the ground.

"What are you up to now?"

"Jameson said if I get a flat one, it skips." He grabs a flat stone and throws it into the water like he's pitching a baseball, so it immediately sinks.

"You've gotta toss it like this." I dig another flat stone out of the dirt and stand up. "Like a frisbee. Try to keep it flat when you throw it."

I show him how it's done, and my rock skips twice before sinking. Something Austin doesn't seem impressed by.

He scours the ground around us, and when I spot a flat stone peeking out of the water, I hand it to him.

"That one should work." I stand behind him, setting his hand in the right position with the stone. "Like this."

I move his arm back and forth slowly so he can adjust to the movement before letting him go.

Austin's entire face scrunches as he focuses on the water. He reels his arm back, and then, mirroring the movement I just showed him, he tosses the rock in. It skips once before disappearing under the water.

"I did it!" He jumps up, landing in his signature superhero pose, even if he's no longer wearing his cape. "It skipped."

"It did." I smile when he immediately starts running around, looking for another stone.

I'm still figuring out what experiences Austin had when he was gone with Mom and what I need to make up to him.

I watch him toss rock after rock into the water, and I want him to have all of them. He deserves the childhood she never gave me. One where he could just be a kid, not worrying about the responsibility that eventually comes from growing up.

Bea gets distracted by a kite while Austin runs up and down the water. His feet splash with every step. After a few laps, he finally slows down, pausing beside me and resting his head on my leg.

I brush the side of his cheek with my hand and look out at the water with him.

"Does this mean we're leaving?" Austin tosses a rock into the water, and it immediately sinks.

"Why would you think that?" My eyebrows pinch.

"Mom let me do fun things when she told me bad stuff." Austin digs his toe into the sand. "But I don't want to go."

"Then good thing you're not, big man." Jameson comes up behind us, sweeping Austin up into his arms, and Austin starts laughing when Jameson tickles him.

Jameson holds my brother, turning to face me, and the smiles on their faces are so big, my heart snaps in two. One piece for each of them.

"You mean it?" Austin asks, looking from me to Jameson. "We're not leaving ever?"

"Ever." Jameson ruffles the hair on top of Austin's head. "You and your sister aren't going anywhere. You're mine now."

Austin's eyes well with tears as he pulls Jameson in for a hug. "You can be mine too, then."

"I can?" He pats Austin on the back.

Austin nods, hugging Jameson tight.

Family.

I always thought it had to look a certain way, and because mine didn't, it meant I'd never have one. But watching Jameson hold my brother, knowing he'll protect and love us with his whole heart—with his whole club—I find the family I never expected.

Jameson winds his free arm around my shoulders and pulls me in to kiss the top of my head. The soft waves of the lake lap at the shore after being kicked up by a boat passing at a distance. And I lose myself in that steady sound.

I pause.

I stop fighting.

And I stop running.

For them, I just want to be here.

"Ice cream!" Austin shoots upright in Jameson's arms, looking over at where Legacy is pulling ice cream out of a cooler.

"You want some?" Jameson sets Austin down, and he immediately starts bouncing.

"Bathroom first." I hitch an eyebrow at my brother, who can barely stand still.

"I don't have to go."

"Let's just try, and then you can have all the ice cream you want."

"Fine." He skulks.

"I'm gonna help Havoc set up the sunshade." Jameson glances over at where Havoc's struggling to balance both sides.

"Okay, we'll be right back." I motion to the overlook, where a bathroom is hidden behind the cars and motorcycles in the parking lot up above.

I lift onto my toes and give Jameson a quick kiss before glancing down at Austin's feet. "Grab your shoes. No bare feet in the bathroom."

He's so excited at the promise of ice cream that he can barely get them on his feet before he's grabbing my hand to pull me up the hill.

"Sonny. Reyes," Jameson yells for them, pointing at me and Austin.

"It's just a bathroom break." I smile.

"Sorry, wildfire. The two of you are never going anywhere alone again."

I shake my head, laughing, even if I do understand it. Being my father's daughter was dangerous, and we didn't speak. But Jameson being the club's president puts me at even more risk, whether I'm around him or not.

Austin tugs me up the hill to the overlook, and we make our way to the bathroom. It's getting late in the day and the road is empty.

Sonny and Reyes stand outside while I take my brother in, and I'm glad they have soap because it's clear no one has cleaned the bathroom in a while.

The smell is still lodged in my nose when we make our way back out, and I almost trip over something.

"What—" I look down to see Sonny lying on the ground with blood pouring out of his neck. "Sonny."

But before I can drop down to put pressure on his wound, a hand slaps over my mouth, and someone grabs me. I look over at Austin as Reyes snatches him off the ground and covers his mouth with a cloth.

"No." The word is muffled with the hand over my mouth, and I only get in one good kick when something pricks my neck.

It all happens so fast that I can't scream or fight.

My vision starts to blur, and the last thing I see is a clear blue sky before the world turns black.

34

Steel

Havoc hands me a beer, and I walk over to where my grandma is still sitting in her chair on the beach, holding an ice cream for Austin for when he and Tempe are done in the bathroom.

That kid's excitement for the smallest things has me feeling some kind of way. It doesn't take much to brighten his day, and I wish that was something easier to hold on to the older a person gets.

"Come sit," Grandma says, shielding her eyes with her hand as she looks up at me.

I drop into a beach chair beside her. "I see Austin took it upon himself to protect you from intruding armies."

She looks down at the moat, smiling. The water is already gone, but she still hasn't moved her chair.

"He did. And I hear you did something smart." Grandma reaches for my hand and squeezes it. "It's good seeing you happy, Jameson."

"They make me happy." I take a sip of my beer, mulling over that word.

Happy.

It's not something I've really strived for. My men need me diligent, attentive, present.

But happy?

My mood's never mattered, so long as I can protect my club.

With Tempe and Austin, it's different.

Yes, I need to protect them. But my vigilance isn't what gets me smiles from them first thing in the morning. They aren't solely concerned with what I do for them. They just want me around. My purpose when I walk through the door to my house has nothing to do with the patch on my cut. They just need me—Jameson.

A better man than I've been in the past, and I want to be that for them.

"This is the best decision I've made in a while." I stare out at the water. "I hear I should thank you for talking to Tempe. Bringing her up to speed on what it means to be an old lady."

Grandma laughs. "Someone had to. You boys have all been runnin' wild for far too long, so there's no one else to support her through this. She'll need that, no matter how tough the girl is."

I glance over at my grandma. "Thank you for being there for both of us."

"All I did was point out what we both already knew: that she can handle this so long as she can handle you. She's a strong girl. One with the backbone needed to stand at your side and the good sense to challenge your ego if you're acting up."

"She will." I chuckle. "She's a lot like you. Not scared of shit. Sticks up for herself—"

"Makes you a better man."

I rake my hair back, taking a sip of my beer. "I'm trying."

"You put too much pressure on yourself, Jameson. You do a lot of good for these men." She glances back at the guys laughing around the barbeque. "Your grandad and your father would be proud of you. Our boy growing up. Living up to the legacy they left. I know you haven't always wanted the pressure that cut places on you, but you've embraced it in ways even they couldn't have thought possible."

I look down at my president patch, remembering slipping this on for the first time the night my dad was gunned down. There was still blood staining the white stitching at the time, and I wore it as a badge of honor until I got revenge for his death. It was a reminder of what I was expected to give to my club if it came to it.

My blood.

My life.

I was young and thought I knew so much more than I did back then. It was a baptism by fire while I was on a path of vengeance. I had a lot to learn, and looking back, it took me far too long to do it.

I grew up with this club. Around these men. And in the process of being what they needed, I somehow found and *lost* who I was. I forgot what we were really fighting for until Tempe stormed in and reminded me.

She had the blood of a traitor running through her veins, but she wasn't him. She was fate trying to tell me something.

"I'm gonna ask her to marry me," I admit, looking over at Grandma. "I haven't said anything to the guys yet, but tonight, I'm going to ask her."

Grandma smiles, and it's the only approval I need. This part doesn't require a vote from my men, and it doesn't technically need Grandma's either, but I want it.

She's been here through my best and worst times.

Through my mom's death.

My grandad's.

Through my dad's—*her son's*.

She's been here for me as much as the men in the club.

"Good." Grandma squeezes my hand and sits back in her chair, smiling as she looks out at the water.

A slow breeze ripples the surface, and it tickles the back of my neck.

I glance back over my shoulder at the overlook above, but I can't see the bathroom from here, and something about how they still haven't returned feels wrong.

They should have been back by now.

"Everything all right?" Grandma asks, her gaze moving to where I'm scanning the hill.

"I don't know. It shouldn't take this long." I climb out of my chair and set my beer down as I pull out my phone and dial Sonny.

It rings until it goes to voicemail, so I dial Reyes.

Same thing.

I start making my way across the beach with a sour feeling settling in my gut. "Havoc, why aren't the prospects answering?"

He looks up from where he's grilling burgers, immediately handing the spatula to one of the prospects milling around. "Where are they?"

"Austin had to go to the bathroom, so Sonny and Reyes took him and Tempe." I point to the overlook as I start up the path up the hill.

Havoc meets my pace, pulling his hair back and reaching for his phone. He must not get an answer either because he just as quickly tucks it away.

"I swear to God if something's wrong—" I shake my head and move faster.

"Steel?" I hear Ghost yell from a distance, but I don't slow down.

I'm already up the hill and crossing the parking lot. It's filled with our trucks and bikes, and the bathroom is on the opposite side.

There's no sound. No movement.

I know before turning the corner something's not right, and when I see Sonny bloody on the ground, my fears are confirmed.

"Fuck." Havoc drops to Sonny's side, feeling for a pulse.

I've got my phone out, and I'm dialing Patch, but when Havoc shakes his head, I know it's already too late.

"Never mind." I hang up when Patch answers and dial Ghost instead. "Get to the bathrooms."

Hanging up, I storm into the bathrooms, only to find them empty. There's no sign of Tempe, Austin, or Reyes.

By the time I walk out, Ghost is crossing the parking lot toward us with an ice-cold glare.

"This is not happening." I grit my teeth, heading toward Ghost.

"We'll find 'em, Steel. I swear on my fucking life." Havoc pulls out his phone and calls Mayhem, who's still back at the clubhouse.

I vaguely hear him giving orders to organize the men there, but I'm too focused on Ghost to pay attention.

"We have a problem." Ghost stops in front of us.

"No fucking shit. Tempe and Austin are gone."

Every ounce of sanity I have left is being tested, and those words cause something in my brain to snap.

I close my eyes and tip my head back, taking a deep breath. No good comes from me losing it right now. All it'll do is put Tempe and Austin at risk. They need the man I swore I'd be for them. The man who runs this club and protects what's his.

Exhaling, I look back at Ghost. "What is it?"

"It's about Tempe and Austin." He flips his phone around so I can see the screen; it's a text message from an unknown number.

Unknown: How does it feel to lose, Steel? First your business. Now your girl. Your club is next. We're coming for you.

Ghost opens the picture attached to the text, and it's an image of Tempe and Austin in the back of a van. Both of them have their eyes closed, so I'm guessing they've been knocked out with something. Dimitri is holding Tempe's head up so he can show her off to the camera, and his lips are so close to her cheek that it makes my skin crawl.

"They don't mention a trade," Havoc says, looking over my shoulder and reading the message.

"I noticed."

And no trade is more concerning than if Dimitri was asking for something.

No trade means he already has what he was looking for.

What he said to Tempe at the bar rattles around in my head. He didn't send her to the club for the flash drive.

He wanted her here.

But for what?

Havoc hangs up with Mayhem, and the rest of the guys have made their way up the hill toward us, either because Havoc waved for them or they sensed something was off.

I turn to Ghost. "Is there any way to tell where the picture was taken?"

"I need to get it back to my computer at the clubhouse to see if I can trace it, but if I had to guess, it's a burner phone. And there's no geotag on the image."

"So, nothing?"

Ghost shakes his head, not looking any happier about it than I am.

We've been tracking Dimitri for weeks. And even when we found the house in his name, he wasn't there. Now he has Tempe and Austin, and we're still no closer to finding where he's hiding out.

I take a deep breath, smoothing my hands down my cut and finding my center.

Focusing my rage.

Honing my clarity.

They don't need me falling apart. For them, I have to keep it together.

"Everyone back to the clubhouse; we need to regroup." I look around at my men. "Find my family. And if they touch so much as a hair on either of their heads, we're going to burn this city to the fucking ground."

35

Tempe

My ears are ringing.

It rattles me awake, and I fight to blink my eyes open. My head hurts, and my body aches from lying on a hard, cold surface.

I plant my palm on the ground and search for my center of gravity when it feels like I'm spinning.

I'm in a basement, or at least somewhere underground. It's cool, and the only light in the concrete room comes from the far corner.

Pushing myself up, my head spins, and my stomach heaves as I struggle not to vomit. Whatever they stuck in my neck has my head woozy, and it's definitely not all the way out of my system.

I feel around me as I try to place myself in the room. My hands are free, and from what I can tell, I'm not chained down. But that's not comforting when I know they'd only do that if they didn't think they were at risk of me breaking out.

My vision clears, and I look around, searching for my brother.

"Austin." I try to lift, but everything feels heavy, and when I search the room, I don't see him.

"Don't worry, he's taken care of." Dimitri's voice comes from the staircase, and he stands up as I blink him into focus. "He's going to take longer to come to from the sedatives. Being little and all."

I'd almost think he's saying it because he cares, but I know better.

"Where is my brother?"

"That's not something you need to worry about." Dimitri steps forward, and my hands shake.

His gaze moves to my bare legs, sending a cool chill up my spine. I smooth the bottom of my skirt, uneasy with how he's watching me.

"Why are we here? Why are you doing this?" My throat is scratchy, so the words come out rough. "I already told you I don't have whatever it is you sent me to the clubhouse for."

"And I already told you that didn't matter." Dimitri laughs. "You're still not getting it, are you? We never needed the flash drive to make it out."

"Flash drive?" My eyebrows pinch.

"Cute." Dimitri squats down in front of me. "They didn't even tell you what they found, did they? You just cooperated while they kept you in the dark, doing anything and everything Steel wanted. I heard you were nice and compliant."

My teeth grit. "You don't know what you're talking about."

"The pictures say otherwise." His dark eyes gleam.

"Pictures?"

"Let me guess, Steel didn't tell you about those either. Wouldn't want you worried someone was watching while he fucked you all over his clubhouse. Turns out you're a whore just like your mother."

"Don't talk about my mother," I snap.

"Why not? She's the one who got you into this mess in the first place."

"What are you talking about?" My throat burns as I stare into the eyes of the devil. "Where is she?"

"Where she belongs. Burning in hell for lying to me." Dimitri glances to a dark corner of the basement where there's a lump underneath a blanket.

He stands up, walking over to it, grabs the edge, and pulls back. Bile rises in my throat at the sight of my mom's mutilated face. Her skin is gray, and her eyes are empty. But her face is battered from whatever they did before slitting her throat.

Even after seeing the video of her at the house, I held out an ounce of hope. That someday, she'd explain everything, and it would all make sense again. Now, she'll never get the chance.

This isn't like before when her death was an illusion. It's the cold truth staring at me. She's gone. She isn't coming back. I really am the only family Austin has now.

My fingers tremble as I brush my hands over my legs. Goosebumps prickle my skin as a tear rolls down my cheek. I'm fighting to hold them back, but it's useless.

"Why?" I shake my head; tears stream down my face. "I just saw her—she was alive."

"She was." Dimitri tosses the blanket back over her body, turning to face me. "Made an awful fucking mess when she changed her mind that night and tried to stop us. But the doc managed to patch her up long enough for her to get me what I needed."

My head is spinning, and it's taking everything in me to hold back the vomit. "What could she possibly have that you needed?"

Dimitri tilts his head to the side, watching me.

"The envelope?" I answer my own question.

"A birth certificate," he snaps. "Proof."

I shake my head, trying to process what he's talking about. "Proof of what?"

But even as I ask the question, a sour feeling settles in my gut.

"She never told you, did she, Tempe?" He grins, and it's filled with malice. "Why do you think Austin isn't down here with you? Who do you think she was trying to protect?"

My heart races as I put the pieces together.

Mom refused to talk about Austin's dad, and the few times she did, I got the impression she was scared, but I didn't know why. Now I do.

"You're his father."

For the first time, I see it. The shape of his nose—a little sharp at the end. The thick eyebrows and the strong cheekbones. As much as I hate to think it, Austin looks just like him, and I don't know how I didn't put it together before now.

Once more, Dimitri squats down, his eyes gleaming. "You're not as stupid as your pretty face makes you appear. But you're as blind as she was."

I pull away when he reaches for me, but he doesn't let me get away. His hand grips my jaw so hard it hurts.

"Where is my brother?" I ask again, even if he refused me an answer the first time.

"Don't worry. My son is safe now that he's free of you and your fucking Twisted Kings. He'll be raised with the right colors on his back now that he's home... You, on the other hand, have served your purpose."

"So you're going to kill me?" I swallow hard. "If that was the plan all along, why didn't you just shoot me in the kitchen and take Austin when you had the chance?"

"That was the plan until you decided to be a little bitch and hid him from me." Dimitri's teeth clench. "Besides, Titan needed something done, and with your mother being a defiant whore, you were the next best option. Lucky for us, it worked out for the best."

"But they caught me." I shake my head.

"That was the fucking point, Tempe." He stands up, pacing the room, watching me. "They were always going to catch you."

I swallow hard, processing what he's saying. "What did you do?"

"The real rot always starts from the inside." Dimitri sneers. "Steel should have learned that lesson after his vice president turned his back on his club, but lucky for us, he didn't. It's one thing to attack from the outside, but to make it really hurt—to destroy someone—you have to rot them from the inside out."

"I don't understand."

"We never needed you to get the flash drive out of the club. We just needed them to find it. We needed them to wonder why a traitor's daughter would be looking for it. We needed them to doubt you. It's the only way Ghost would trust it."

Dimitri walks up to me, grabbing my jaw and forcing me to look at him when I try to pull away.

"The harder it was to hack, the less they'd suspect what we were doing. And the more Steel focused on you, the more distracted he was to what he'd just let in." Dimitri pinches my cheeks with his hold, and tears sting my eyes. "You think you were there to take something, but you weren't. You were there to deliver the package. The moment Ghost hacked that drive, we got everything we were looking for."

A tear rolls down my cheek. "You planted a virus."

"Something like that." Dimitri grins. "All thanks to *you*."

"I didn't do anything for you."

"But you did do *something for us*, didn't you?" Dimitri drags his thumb over my mouth, and the feeling like I'm going to vomit returns. "You kept Steel's attention. You were the perfect little distraction, being Helix's daughter and all. He was too busy focusing on your pretty face to see us coming."

"And what if he had decided I was a traitor like my father instead of keeping me around?" I glare.

Dimitri drags his hand down my throat, and I push him away, but he just chuckles.

"Steel isn't blind, and he's not known for killin' women." He stands up, pacing the room again. "You've got a pretty face and a traitor's blood in your veins. Everything we needed to keep Steel's attention while Ghost let us in."

"You can't—"

"We already did." Dimitri grins down at me. "And now my son gets to watch and learn while I make your boyfriend's club suffer for everything they've done to the Iron Sinners over the years."

"Don't do this," I plead, hating that I have no other choice. "You can't take Austin."

"He's mine."

"He doesn't even know you." I shake my head.

"And whose fault is that?" Dimitri yells.

A shiver runs down my spine, and I get a glimpse of the man my mother spent Austin's life running from. The real reason she probably avoided Vegas for the past four years. If Austin was here, Dimitri could have gotten to him sooner.

"Please." I climb to my knees, trying everything I can for my brother. "Austin is only four. He's not going to trust you. He'll be scared. Please let me see him. He needs a familiar face."

I think of anything—say anything—to try and talk my way out of this.

"He already has a familiar face." Dimitri smirks. "One Steel made sure he was nice and comfortable around from what I can tell."

My eyebrows pinch as the memory of being dragged into the van floods back to me. "Reyes."

The last thing I remember before the world faded out was Reyes grabbing Austin. In my haze, I wanted to think he was trying to save him. But he wasn't.

Steel trusted him to protect us, and now they're going to use that familiarity against my brother.

Dimitri nods. "Steel should blame himself, honestly. He's the one who gave a prospect full access to his life. Who do you think planted the flash drive in Helix's room in the first place? It's not like he could walk up to Ghost and hand it to him. They'd be too suspicious."

"Reyes is an Iron Sinner?"

"Born and raised."

"But how...?" Jameson would have looked into a new prospect, and Ghost seems like someone who doesn't let things like that get past him.

"Let's just say Steel's not the only one with resources now. It doesn't matter how deep Ghost digs, he'll never be able to discover who Reyes really is."

Who he really is?

A traitor.

A merciless killer.

It won't matter once Jameson finds out what the two of them have done. I'm not a killer myself, but I hope

Jameson makes them pay, whether I'm around for it or not.

I take a deep breath, gathering my composure. "Steel is going to find us, and when he does, he'll make you pay for what you've done. Your whole club is going to suffer for this."

"You're awfully confident for a biker slut."

I glare up at him. "And you're awfully confident for a murderous piece of shit."

Dimitri storms across the basement at my comment, winding his arm back and striking me across the cheek. His knuckles hit so hard I see spots, and my back slams into the wall behind me.

He grabs my hair, forcing me to look into his sick, devilish eyes.

"I've changed my mind. Death would be too easy for you after all. You want to know what the Iron Sinners do to bitches who don't know how to keep their mouths shut? I'll show you." He tosses my head away, and the back of it hits a wall. "Steel won't find you out here. No one will. And when I bring my men back downstairs, you're going to wish I'd slit your fucking throat."

The darkness in Dimitri's gaze sends a shiver up my spine as he glares at me, and with a final dark chuckle, he walks up the stairs, slamming the door behind him. Something clicks, and I assume that must be a lock.

Steel will find me.

He has to.

But until then, I can't sit around and wait. I have to get out of this basement before Dimitri and his men come back. I have to find Austin.

If I don't, I'm not sure either of us will survive.

36

Steel

THE CLUBHOUSE IS BUZZING. My men tear apart the bunkhouse searching our prospects' things for any clues that will help us find Tempe and Austin.

"No bugs," Ghost confirms. "And from what I can tell, Sonny is clean."

"Reyes?"

"Burner cell inside his mattress, but the contacts have been wiped. I'll dig into it now to see if I can get anything off it."

I nod, and Ghost heads toward a room in the back of the clubhouse where he hides away to take care of business.

Soul walks over, hanging up the phone as he stops in front of me.

"I don't like that look."

"You're going to like what I have to say even less." Soul drags his hand down his face. "The Iron Sinners hit two of our businesses at the same time as they snatched Tempe and Austin. They're trying to split our resources."

"Which ones?"

"Kings Auto and Sapphire Rise. They tossed both and stripped anything they could from the offices. No real damage, so it could just be a distraction, but they were definitely looking for something. I've got a few men checking it out now."

"There's nothing in either of the offices for them to find." I scratch my jaw, relieved Legacy was paranoid and suggested we keep all records secure at the clubhouse for the time being. "As far as the damage is concerned, Chaos will have to deal with it when he gets out. It's not a priority tonight. Who did you send?"

"Mayhem and Boone."

"Tell 'em to just keep it under control. We'll deal with it tomorrow."

Soul nods, shooting off a text. "Any word on your old lady?"

My old lady.

My chest seizes at the reminder that I just got her, and I'm already failing her. I knew the risk of bringing her into this, and still, I did it anyway. It should be a lesson, but even after I find them, I'm not letting them go.

I shake my head. "No, but Ghost is trying to scrape data off a burner phone he found in Reyes's room."

"I still can't fucking believe it." Soul's jaw clenches. "I had a bad feeling about him, and I should have listened to my gut."

"Same. But he came back clean." I shake my head. "We still need to figure out how that happened."

Soul nods in agreement.

"Prez." Havoc waves me over to the pool table, where he has a map of Vegas stretched across one side of it. A pile of guns is stacked on the other.

He's slipping into battle mode, and I'm glad because we've been toeing this line with the Iron Sinners for too long. They took my family—started war.

No prisoners.

No mercy.

I don't care if Rick Zane is the one funding the Iron Sinners operation, or if they have access to all the money, resources, and dirty cops in Vegas. I'm going to rip their club apart, starting with the man who took Tempe and Austin.

Havoc points to a spot on the map just past the city line. "Ghost was able to trace a call made on the burner phone to a landline here."

"That's a long shot." Soul shakes his head. "One phone call."

"It's better than nothing." I pull out my gun. "Get everyone loaded up in the next ten minutes. I want a bullet in Dimitri's head before the sun rises. And the second my family is back, we're going to send Titan a message. Judgment day is coming."

I look around the table, and my men nod their heads in agreement. We've been putting off war with the Iron Sinners for too long because it's expensive, messy, and clubs waging war brings nothing but attention from law enforcement.

But Titan made this personal when he put a hit on *my* woman.

My kid.

He's not getting away with it.

Nine minutes and seventeen seconds is all it takes to get everyone loaded up. We're lucky it's the middle of the night, or our caravan would draw a lot of attention. But so long as we keep outside the city limits, we can handle any cops we run into this far outside of Vegas.

The house Ghost traced the call to is located halfway between the Twisted Kings compound and the Iron Sinners clubhouses. Close enough that if we don't move quickly, the Iron Sinners will easily be able to call for reinforcements.

At least it's in the middle of nowhere. Nothing gets police on speed dial like the entire club rolling into the suburbs fully loaded.

Patch is driving the van I'm riding in, but he'll stay behind when we get to the house. He's only riding along to triage anyone who goes down when this inevitably turns into a shoot-out. If one of my men gets hurt, we can't exactly bring them to a hospital. Bullet wounds raise questions, and I don't have any answers the cops will like.

When we hit the final turn toward the Iron Sinners' safe house, it's a straight shot to our target. Patch cuts the headlights so no one will see us coming. It's eerily quiet inside the van, and I sense my brothers mentally preparing for battle.

Ghost's phone chimes, cutting through the silence.

"Any news?"

He pulls out his phone. "Something from an unknown number."

"Don't like the sound of that."

"Shit." Ghost's eyes widen with whatever is on his screen, and when Legacy leans in to see what he's looking at, his eyes immediately dart up to me.

"What is it?" I reach forward, and Ghost passes me his phone.

It takes me a moment to process what I'm looking at. It's a video feed, but it's grainy and dark. Looking closer, I spot Tempe curled up in the corner of some sort of basement, and Dimitri is pacing back and forth talking to her.

"How the fuck are we seeing this?"

"They sent me a link to the feed." Ghost rests his elbows on his knees, leaning forward.

"Is there any sound?"

Ghost shakes his head.

"Can you track where this is coming from?"

"If I were back at the clubhouse, maybe."

"Fuck." We could be headed in the wrong direction. "How far out are we?"

Havoc checks his watch. "Five minutes max."

We're too close to turn around just to hack a feed. With any luck, it's coming from the house we're heading for. If not, I'll save that regret for later.

Turning my attention back to the screen, I watch Tempe.

It's hard to see her face clearly with the quality of the video, but her shoulders are rolled back, and her chin is tipped up. Her mouth is moving with whatever she's saying, and I can tell she's spitting out all that fire I love about her.

She's a fighter. She'll do whatever it takes to survive, and all I can do is hope she hangs on until I can get there.

I search the room for Austin, but he isn't there, and it has me on edge. I swore I'd protect them, and I failed. Now, they could be on opposite sides of Vegas—maybe even different states.

I can't let myself think that.

"Do we know if this is live footage?"

Ghost shakes his head. "No, but if I had to guess, it is."

I hope he's right because it means that, as of this moment, Tempe is still alive.

"Three minutes," Havoc announces, and my men start readying their weapons.

Instead of pulling out my gun, I focus on the screen.

Dimitri is pacing still, droning on about something that has Tempe's shoulders sinking. Whatever he just said rattled her, and it's one more reason I'm going to make him suffer.

He pauses, and what he says has Tempe's back stiffening. She tilts her chin up and says something to Dimitri that has him crossing the room.

One step.

Two.

Three.

And when he stops in front of her and winds his hand back, my heart cracks.

He hits her.

He fucking *hits her*.

In a split second, Dimitri moves to the top of my list.

He hit what's *mine*.

Hurt what's mine.

Mine to love.

Mine to protect.

Soul flinches beside me, so I know he saw it too, even if he's smart enough not to say shit.

"One minute," Havoc announces.

I pass Ghost the phone and pull out my gun. While I assumed being this close would set me on edge, Dimitri just gave me my reason to stay calm. To stay focused in a way I've only been once before—on that empty road in Maryland, the day before I put a bullet between the eyes of the man who killed my dad.

Closing my eyes, I listen to the hum of the road. The tires rumble against the pavement. The van licks up the miles like I do on my bike when I'm driving that stretch between the city and the clubhouse.

I set my mind on that length of concrete in the empty desert at night. Moon in the sky and sagebrush in the air.

Vegas heat seeping through like hell knows this city is built on sin.

We'll all burn here.

The van rolls to a stop, but I keep my mind on that road as I open my eyes and say a final prayer. I'm not religious, but for the two of them, I'll try anything.

"No lights outside, but someone's definitely in there." Havoc assesses the scene.

I look through the front windshield to see what he's talking about. The house is dark except for a light coming through the blinds in one of the rooms. If they're here, they're cocky enough to think we'll never find them because they don't have so much as a lookout.

Ghost pops the back door of the van open, and we climb out one by one.

"Legacy and Ghost, you're with me. We're going through the front." I tip my chin to the right. "Havoc and Soul go around the back. Everyone else needs to split up. I want every inch of the perimeter covered."

The rest of our crew is pulling to a stop behind us. All vehicles have their lights off, so they don't see or hear us coming.

One by one, the vans empty, and everyone grabs their guns.

"You sure you don't want me knocking on the front door first?" Havoc asks.

Usually he would, given it's his job to protect the club during operations like this.

But when I shake my head, he doesn't argue as I make my way past him. He doesn't try to protect me for the sake of the title on my patch. My brothers know there's no one stepping into that house before me if Tempe and Austin might be inside it.

Legacy and Ghost follow me to the front with a solid show of force. My men are quiet as we slowly circle.

Given how dark it is, there's a good chance Tempe and Austin aren't here, but I can't let myself think about that. Doubt does nothing but get people hurt in these kinds of situations.

We quietly make our way to the front door, and I stand on one side, with Legacy on the other. There's movement in the house, but without a clear view, I can't tell how many people are inside.

Legacy pulls out a flash grenade and holds it ready.

The second I nod, Ghost kicks the door in, and Legacy tosses it.

A blinding flash of light accompanies the loud bang from inside the house, followed by a chorus of men shouting. We flood from both sides before they have a chance to figure out what's going on.

For Tempe.

For Austin.

Bullets rain in the name of my family, and I feel it in my bones that they're here.

I'm coming.

37

Tempe

I PULL MYSELF TO standing, still feeling a little woozy as I find my balance.

The drugs are still running through my system, but I'm pushing through, knowing I can't stay here and wait for Dimitri to make good on his threats. If I don't get out of this basement and find Austin now, I might not get another chance.

But first, I walk over to my mom, crouching down and resting my hand on the blanket. A tear slips from my eyes, and I wish this was like when she was in the kitchen—when she wasn't really gone. If she could just wake up and tell me they didn't use and discard her all over again.

She doesn't.

"I'm sorry, Mom." Another tear slips out. "I'll take care of him. I promise."

I rub my eyes with the heel of my hands and pull myself together. I don't like leaving her body here, but I don't have a choice.

Slowly making my way to the staircase, my flip-flops slap against my heels, so I pause. I'm still wearing my sandals from the beach, and the sound is going to give me away if anyone is up there.

Reaching down, I slip them off and toss them to the side. They won't help me hide, and they're terrible for running, so even if it might hurt, I'm going to have to do this barefoot.

Making my way to the staircase, I take the first splintery step and wince. Small slivers of wood dig into the balls of my feet, but I don't let it slow me down.

When I reach the top step, I press my ear to the door and listen. It's quiet on the other side, and any voices sound far enough away that I might have a chance as long as no one is guarding the door. Reaching for the handle, I try to turn it, but it's locked.

It was too much to think it would be that easy.

I crouch down and examine the door handle from this side. There's a hole in the center that reminds me of the locks that used to be on the doors at an apartment Mom rented when I was in middle school.

I've picked this particular lock before, and I say a silent thank you to Mom's magician ex for teaching me random things I never thought I'd need to know.

I hurry back down the stairs, looking for anything that might fit inside the small hole.

A safety pin, a stick.

Scanning the room, something on the ground catches my attention, and I walk over to find a bobby pin. There are very few reasons the guys would need this, which makes me think I'm not the first female they've kept down here.

I pick it up and try to ignore that thought.

Hurrying back up the staircase, I squat down to get another look at the lock. There's still no sound coming from the other side as I bend the bobby pin and slip the long side into the hole. I can't see what I'm doing, so I feel around with the pin, searching for a latching mechanism.

The bobby pin catches on something, and I try to tug, but it sticks, which means I've found the right spot. Pushing in and down, I twist, and the snapping of metal is followed by a light clicking sound.

It's either broken or unlocked, so I close my eyes and take a deep breath as I try to turn the handle, hoping for the best. And when it turns, I exhale.

The door creaks as I slowly push it open, and I freeze, listening for movement. I wait for signs of footsteps from the other side, and when I don't hear any, I push it open more.

Stepping out of the basement, I'm met with a dark hallway. There's a dim light coming from one end, and from what I can tell, I think it's the front of the house. The other direction is dark and quiet, with doors on either side.

I quietly close the basement door behind me, and with the final creak of the hinges, I hold my breath and wait until I'm certain no one heard me.

Making my way down the dark end of the hallway, I peek inside each room as I pass. There are mattresses and clothes on the floor. It's messy, and the entire house reeks of body odor and cat urine.

Glancing in the room at the end, a small body on the mattress catches my attention, and I hurry inside when I realize who it is.

"Austin," I whisper, dropping my knees to the mattress as I crouch over him.

I brush his sandy-brown hair off his forehead and run my fingers over his cheek.

"Austin, I need you to wake up for me. Please."

Austin's blue eyes blink open slowly. "Tempe?"

He rubs his hands over his eyes.

"Careful." I brush the side of his face when he tries to sit up.

The drugs they used to knock us out kept him asleep longer than me, but his body is fighting it off faster now that he's awake.

Austin pushes himself to sit but stays right at my side. "Where are we? Where's the bathroom?"

I'm relieved that's the last thing he remembers.

He has no idea what's going on—what his father has done or what's happened to our mother. And even if I'm not looking forward to explaining this to him later, I'm thankful I can be the one to tell him rather than have him hear these truths from Dimitri's mouth.

"We aren't at the bathroom anymore." I squeeze his hand. "Can you stand?"

I'm still a little wobbly myself as I lift off the mattress and stand over him, reaching out a hand. He laces his fingers in mine, using me as leverage to pull himself up.

"I feel funny." He grabs onto my arm.

"I know, me too."

He looks around again, and his eyebrows pinch. "Where's the beach? Where's Jameson?"

"Jameson's coming to get us right now."

That might not be true, but even if Jameson doesn't know where we are, I'm positive he's doing everything he can to find us. He won't let us get hurt. I'm sure of it.

"Why isn't he here?" Austin's voice cracks. "Is the bad man back?"

I press my lips together and inhale through my nose. I don't want to scare him, but with all he's seen, he's smart enough to be worried.

"Yes, the bad man's back." I angle his face up. "But nothing is going to happen to you, okay? We're going to get out of here, and Jameson will come get us. I won't let anyone hurt you. I promise."

"I won't let anyone hurt you either." Austin gives me a hug.

He believes it with all his heart, and it makes my eyes sting as I fight back the tears. No child should have to be this strong. I'm the one who's supposed to be there for him. And that's what I'm going to do.

Voices start getting louder as footsteps move down the hall. The men are either coming for me or him, so we need to move.

"Can you walk?" I whisper.

He nods.

"Let me see." I hold his hand so he doesn't fall, and I'm happy he doesn't lose balance when he takes a step, even if it's slow.

"Good." I brace against the wall when my head spins, fighting the haze that's still fogging my senses.

Glancing around the room, I eye the door, knowing we can't go back the way I came with the men making their way through the house. I look around the room, searching for another way out, and spot a window.

I squeeze Austin's hand and look down at him. "I need you to be as quiet as you can, okay?"

"I can be super quiet," he whisper-yells, which isn't as helpful as he thinks, but I can't blame him.

"Good." I pat the back of his hand. "Follow me, and don't say a word."

I guide him to the window. Quickly but quietly unlatching it and pulling it up. Luckily, it doesn't creak like the basement door, and I manage to get Austin through it quickly.

Outside is nothing but a wide stretch of empty desert, meaning we're in the middle of nowhere.

I don't know if Jameson will find us out here or if we can survive walking once the sun rises, but we have to try. At least we can put some distance between us and them as long as it's dark out.

"Wait there." I set Austin on his feet outside and climb through the window next.

Dropping to the ground, a stone digs into my foot, but I can't let myself think about that right now.

Pulling Austin out of view from the window, I hold him against the house and look out at the desert. There's nothing for miles except an empty shed in the distance, and I decide we can head in that direction first to at least provide some cover for us. Past that is the slightest change in elevation and what appears to be a road winding around the property. I don't know how far away civilization is or where the road leads, but our only chance is to make a run for it.

"You ready?" I grip Austin's hand.

He bites his lip, nodding.

"We've got this." I force a smile. "Don't turn back and don't stop for anything, you understand?"

My temples throb, and my eyes burn. I want to cry or scream, but I can't. For Austin, I need to be strong.

"Let's go."

We hurry across the empty yard, and the ground is rough on my feet, but I try to ignore it. It wouldn't have been any easier running in flip-flops.

"This way." I point toward the shed at the back of the property as voices inside the house get louder, and I assume Dimitri figured out we're gone.

We reach the shed, and I freeze, pulling Austin against the side of the building, when a set of headlights flashes on the road. They turn off before getting to the house, and I can't tell whether it's more of Dimitri's men or someone else.

Austin's chest heaves with every breath as I hold him against me. Panic swells in my chest no matter how much

I fight it off. And just as I'm about to take another step, a bang rings out in the desert.

Men start shouting, and gunfire sounds.

"Jameson." Austin looks up at me.

I plant my finger over my lips. "Shh. We don't know."

We can only hope.

I hold Austin against the side of the shed as more screams are followed by gunshots. It could be Jameson, but it could also be any other rival club.

Pulling Austin's back to the building, I motion for him to be quiet so I can peek around the corner.

"Where do you think you're running off to?"

Dimitri's voice comes from behind me as fingers tangle in the back of my hair. He yanks so hard my scalp burns, and tears sting my eyes. He pulls me back, and just as he does, I get a look at a man running in the distance.

He's too far away to see who he is, but I spot the skull and wings. I clearly make out the crown and Twisted Kings lettering.

Jameson and his men found us.

I fight with everything I have. Scratching Dimitri and kicking him with my heels. He won't let go, but I'm no longer scared to fight and yell now that I know Jameson is here. As long as I can keep Dimitri distracted, I can save my brother.

Jameson will find him.

He'll keep him safe.

"Austin, run!"

38

Steel

Gunshots sound as Iron Sinners spill out of the house, trying to make a run for it. They're taken down one by one by my men guarding the perimeter.

Inside, Havoc and Ghost sweep the rooms, putting down anyone who points a gun at us. A few are restrained with zip ties to see if we can get any information out of them, but overall, it's a bloodbath.

"Clear."

"Clear."

My men work through the rooms one by one.

The house is larger than it looks from the outside. A long hallway stretches all the way to the back with bedrooms on either side. Dirty mattresses and clothes scatter the floor, and handcuffs hang from the metal bed frames, telling me exactly what the Iron Sinners use this house for.

Another mess to clean up for another day.

Havoc and Soul clear half of the rooms while I clear the others. And Ghost sets up a perimeter with Legacy.

"A few men made it to their bikes before we could clear the garage. I think one was Reyes." Havoc pops his knuckles.

"Fuck." I wipe my hand down my face. "Is anyone tailing him?"

"Yeah, but we were too slow. He's gone." Havoc shakes his head. "Any luck in here?"

"It's clear."

No Tempe or Austin.

No Dimitri.

Gunshots ring out from the side yard, and I rush outside to see what's happening.

Legacy's standing at the corner of the house, firing at a few men hiding behind a truck in the distance. One pops up, and Legacy aims for his forehead, painting the desert with brain matter.

I press my back to the side of the house and take two more out as they try to rush Legacy from behind.

"Jameson!"

At first, I think I'm imagining Austin's voice. But when he calls my name again, his cry splices my heart down the middle.

I search the yard to see where his voice is coming from, and that's when I spot little legs running as fast as they can toward me.

"Jameson!" Austin screams again.

An Iron Sinner catches sight of him at the same time as I do, but the moment he makes a move, I plant a bullet in his chest and run toward Austin.

"Cover us," I yell for Legacy, who shoots anyone in an Iron Sinners cut.

My legs burn as I run to Austin. Tears spill from his eyes when I reach him. I scoop him up, pulling him back toward the cover of the house. His little arms hold me so tight they're cutting off air.

Or maybe he's not that strong, but either way, I can't breathe.

I can hardly think.

Nothing matters outside of keeping him safe.

Some families are born, but some families are built—like my club. Like Austin and Tempe coming into my life. The kind of family I never wanted because I'm not a good enough man to deserve this kind of love.

But as Austin shakes in my arms and a sob rips from his chest, I'm that man for him. It doesn't matter that I'm not his father; he's my kid. My responsibility. My ray of sunshine in a desert where I didn't think I could stand any more heat.

"I've got you. You're safe. You're safe." I rub his back, holding him close, wishing I could erase the pain that's filled his life to the brim.

I hug him tighter, trying to absorb what he's going through.

"Austin." I rub my hand down his back. "Where's your sister?"

I scan the yard, but there's no sign of her.

Austin lifts his head, and his cheeks are stained in tears as he looks to the left. I follow his gaze to a large shed that stands at a distance.

"The bad man got her. She told me to run." His voice cracks. "She said I had to run."

A tear slips out, and I crouch down to set him on his feet, looking him in the eyes. "You did the right thing, Austin. You did good. I'm proud of you."

"You are?" He wipes his eyes.

"Of course." I brush his hair off his forehead. "You came and got me. That's exactly what we needed you to do."

He nods, chewing the inside of his cheek.

I look up at my men making their way over. They're quiet, even if their eyes move from me to Austin, making it clear they're thinking what I am—Tempe's not here.

"I need you to go with Ghost for me."

Austin jumps into my arms again, wrapping himself around me and holding tightly. "Please don't go."

"Listen to me, big man." I pat his back, and he pulls away just enough to look at me. "I've gotta go get your sister, okay? This is important."

"I'll go with you."

"I need you here." I rub his back. "Think of it as your mission."

"A secret mission?"

"Exactly, and very important. Will you help Ghost keep a lookout while I go find your sister?"

Austin looks over at Ghost, who nods.

I squeeze his shoulder. "Can I rely on you to help me with this, Austin?"

"Will you get Tempe?"

"Yes." I almost choke on the word as it comes out, and again Austin flies into my arms.

"I'll keep the lookout." He squeezes tight. "I'll keep you safe."

Ghost takes my spot by the house, squatting down by Austin. "Want to help me check the cameras?"

Austin nods, distracted by Ghost's phone while I slip away.

Legacy doesn't leave his perch, keeping a lookout for stragglers as I make my way to where Havoc is stepping off the porch.

"Austin said Tempe is that way." I point to the shed.

Havoc nods, grabbing another gun as we pass the vans.

When we reach the building, Havoc winds left, while I keep to the right, sticking as close to the building as I can to maintain cover. There's a muffled scream on the other side and a scuffle in the dirt, so I pick up my pace.

"Bitch." Dimitri's voice is sharp and out of breath.

I turn the corner with my gun aimed straight ahead and find Dimitri holding Tempe from behind.

She's wrestling him. Clawing at his arms and tucking her chin so he can't cut off her airway. She kicks him in the shin, and he folds over, grunting. Grabbing his arm, she bends forward and flips him to the ground.

My chest swells at the sight of her fighting back with all she has. Even when I notice she's barefoot and a cut on her forehead is bleeding. Her chest heaves as she fights Dimitri, and as I move forward, I'm not quick enough.

Dimitri is back on his feet before I can get in a clear shot, grabbing Tempe by the hair and holding her in front of him.

"Dimitri," I shout his name and his gaze snaps to mine.

He looks from me to Havoc as he holds Tempe by the hair. With his free hand, he brings a gun up to the side of her head, and she stops fighting when the barrel presses to her temple.

Her eyes widen as she meets my gaze across the yard.

"Jameson—" She's cut off when Dimitri pulls her hair harder.

"Let her go, Dimitri."

"And then what?" He laughs. "You'll just put a bullet in my head."

"If you're lucky."

I'd like to drag him back to the Shack and tear him apart from his fingernails to his teeth. Better yet, I could give Ghost a few hours to let out his demons. But right now, all that matters is making sure Tempe is safe.

"Always knew you Iron Sinners were pathetic fuckers," I taunt him. "Too scared to fight your own battles."

Havoc slowly circles, but he doesn't get any closer as we both keep our distance. He's looking for any shot he can take, and I'm hoping he gets one while I keep Dimitri distracted.

"Your men are dead. You will be too in a second. There's nothing left for you to fight for."

"That's where you're wrong." Dimitri narrows his eyes.

"Am I?" I take a step closer, watching him shift each time I do. "Reyes left you here. Everyone back at the house is dead. This battle is over. You're the only one left."

Dimitri's jaw clenches, and even if he hates me, it's clear he's not happy to hear that. "It doesn't matter. I'd do anything for my club."

"I'm sure you would. But what would they do for you?"

Most outsiders view all motorcycle clubs the same, but that's only because they don't look closely enough. There are a lot of differences—from what we traffic to who we protect.

But the biggest difference between the Twisted Kings and the Iron Sinners comes from within.

There's nothing I ask of my men that I won't do myself. There's nothing I won't sacrifice that I don't also expect them to. We have each other's backs to the end. No one runs from a fight, and no one backs down.

"You think you've won this?" Dimitri sneers. "We already got what we needed. Why do you think Reyes blew his cover?"

"You want to talk about winning right now? You're not walking out of here."

Dimitri laughs, spitting a wad of blood on the ground. "Like that matters. Do what you want. This doesn't end with me. Your club is going to burn around you, Steel. Titan made sure of it. Reyes made sure of it. This is far from over."

With a cocky step, he creates just enough of an opening for Havoc to shoot him in the shoulder, forcing him to release Tempe.

She runs from his grasp the second he lets her go, and I close in before he can try to make a run for it.

Havoc grabs the arm with the bullet wound, driving his thumb in and forcing Dimitri to his knees. When he cries out in pain, I grab his jaw and force his mouth open further, shoving my gun between his teeth.

He tries to wiggle away but can't.

I could draw this out; I could torture him for information. But one look in his eyes tells me I won't get what I'm looking for. Dimitri was a pawn—a distraction.

They left him here because they no longer have use for him.

"Do me a favor." I look Dimitri dead in the eyes. "Give your boss a message from me."

I press the gun deep enough for it to click against his teeth. Havoc releases Dimitri to make room, stepping back. And before Dimitri can blink or try to fight me off, I send a bullet down his throat.

For Tempe.

For Austin.

Dimitri slumps to the ground, and I plant three more rounds in his chest just to make a point.

The last shot echoes and then there's just silence.

"Jameson." Tempe's hand lands on my shoulder, and I turn to face her.

She's looking down at Dimitri, and I wait for something to register. *Fear. Anger*. But her face is blank as she stares down at his body.

"Look at me, wildfire." I tuck my gun away, gripping her chin so she'll face me.

Tears swell in her eyes. "Austin..."

"I've got him. He's back at the van with Ghost."

"You came for us."

"Of course I did." I brush a tear from her cheek. "I'll always come for you. Come here."

I pick her up, and she winces at my touch. I don't know the full extent of what Dimitri did to her yet, but it makes me wish I could kill him all over again.

"I can walk."

"Just let me take care of you."

For once, she doesn't fight as I hold her to my chest. She simply stares up at me—my spark in the wind. My wildfire that's always ripping through the brush, carving her own path because she doesn't trust anyone else to do it.

Except right now, she hands herself to me. We're no longer alone, and she finally allows me to just be here.

Tempe curls against my chest, and I kiss the top of her head. Her hand weaves around the back of my neck, and warmth returns to my bones.

"Thank you, Jameson."

"Nothing to thank me for, wildfire. I'll always find you. Remember what I said? To my grave." I kiss her again. "I love you."

She looks up at me with a smile cracking her face. "I love you too."

We walk back over to the house, and it's crawling with Twisted Kings now. If the Iron Sinners were going to send more men, they would have already.

Soul and a few other men are carrying bodies through the front door, and I angle Tempe away because even if I know she can handle it, she shouldn't have to.

Walking around the vans, I stop where Ghost and Austin are sitting inside one of them, watching something on Ghost's phone.

"Tempe." Austin smiles when he sees her, and I set her down inside the van so she can hug him.

Austin clings to her, resting his head on her shoulder and reaching a hand out to pull me to them.

"I knew it. That is a cape." Austin curls against us, squeezing before looking up at me. "You are a superhero."

Before tonight I might have argued that I'm just a bad man who does bad things and uses good excuses to justify them. But with my family in my arms, Tempe looking up into my eyes, I let myself believe it.

What is a superhero anyway?

Someone willing to sacrifice themselves for the people they care about? Because I'd do anything to hold onto this forever.

Epilogue
Tempe

Three Weeks Later

Austin bounces up and down as much as he can for being strapped into his booster seat. He's bursting with excitement while Havoc drives us to the clubhouse.

"What are you so excited about?" I squeeze Austin's knee.

He smiles at me. "It's a secret."

I glance over at Havoc, who's holding back a grin at Austin's comment. "Why do I feel like the two of you know something I don't?"

Havoc winks at Austin, both refusing to answer my question, which only confirms something is going on.

Austin turns back to me, smiling and pretending to lock his lips.

He's as tight-lipped as Jameson was this morning about why he needed us at the clubhouse, and I'm curious what they're planning.

Whatever it is, I'm not complaining about the excuse to get out of the neighborhood. It feels good to be doing something.

After everything that happened with Dimitri, Austin and I have been spending a lot of time inside the compound gates. I always knew the Twisted Kings attracted danger, but now I realize it's more complicated than I thought—especially finding out Austin has blood ties to a rival club.

Dimitri might be dead, but the threat will always be there. All I can do is try to protect Austin, hoping he chooses a path that follows the missions of a club like Jameson's and not that of a club that aims to destroy and hurt women.

I now realize my mom had many secrets and that not all the bad things she did were because she was being hurtful or selfish. Some of her choices were to protect my brother, knowing his father was after him.

She loved a bad man once, and what Dimitri forced her to do wasn't her fault. She tried to stop him that night, and it changed the course of everything. Her fighting back is the reason I was the one sent to Jameson's clubhouse.

Mom made a lot of bad decisions, but I'll always be grateful she unknowingly brought Jameson into my and my brother's lives. She drove us to a man who will protect us with all he has.

I should probably fear Jameson for what I saw him do to Dimitri at the Iron Sinners' house. Every violent rumor about his blind vengeance played out in front of me as he made Dimitri pay for what he did to me and Austin. But at the end of the day, Jameson only did it to protect us—*his family.*

Dimitri might have been Austin's dad, but he also sacrificed me and my mother—the only people Austin cared about—to get what he needed. Whatever he felt for Austin wasn't love. The only thing he was loyal to was his club.

He's as much family as Helix was, maybe even less so. I have no regrets about Austin having to live his life without him.

Someday, I'll need to talk to Austin about what really happened that night. I'll have to tell him about his father and the terrible things he wanted to do. For now, Austin needs to heal, especially with his nightmares getting worse. Just because he doesn't know the truth doesn't mean he isn't battling the memories.

Jameson found a therapist to come to the compound and meet with Austin a couple of times a week. Now all we can do is be here to support him and love him while he heals.

While we all heal.

I've been quietly battling my own trauma from that night. Overwhelmed with guilt about the fact that I'm the one who led Jameson into his enemy's trap. Jameson swears it's not my fault, but I played a part, nonetheless.

I've tried keeping busy to take my mind off it, but it hasn't worked out well.

My first shift back at Dirty Drakes ended with me hiding behind the bar when someone dropped a glass on the floor, and I haven't been back since.

For now, I'm going to focus on my degree. And when I'm in a better place mentally, I might find a quiet job at a physical therapy office. A place I can help people.

In the meantime, I'm helping my brother adjust to this new life. We're reestablishing a routine while we grieve our losses and move forward. And when Jameson isn't with his club, he's there with us, helping us see it through.

Havoc rolls the truck to a stop, and Austin jumps out of his seat the moment I undo the buckle. He climbs over me and hops out, jumping up and down with excitement. Soul gives him a high five when he reaches the top of the steps to the clubhouse, and I have to rush to catch up to him.

"Hand." I slip mine into his when I come to a stop beside him.

Jameson has enforced stricter rules for the clubhouse during the day, so Austin and Bea can come and go freely without the risk of walking in on anything. But I still don't like Austin wandering the clubhouse unattended. In the event someone decides to rebel, I'd rather not have to explain it to a four-year-old.

Austin holds my hand as we make our way inside.

It's late April and already warm. A week ago, the club switched from fans in the clubhouse to air conditioners.

I can only imagine how expensive that is, given the size of this place.

Havoc leads us to a back room at the clubhouse. It's a lot like the bar up front but smaller, and not open to outsiders when they throw parties. There are three pool tables in the center and four dartboards along one wall. A small bar sits off to one side, and a few of the guys are milling around.

"Steel, your old lady's here," Havoc calls out to him when we walk into the room.

Jameson turns around, and Austin immediately runs across the space to jump into his arms.

"Big man." Jameson lifts him up, setting him on his knee.

He's sitting at the bar talking to Chaos. And when he catches sight of me, he winks.

Chaos doesn't offer as friendly of a welcome. He has his back to the bar, and Wren, one of the patch bunnies, is standing between his legs, whispering something to him. She giggles, licking the side of his neck as he takes a sip of his drink, watching me walk over.

Unlike the rest of the Twisted Kings members, he hasn't been as welcoming.

He rarely acknowledges my presence, and even if he's not rude, his glares prove he's only holding his tongue out of respect for Jameson. It's clear he's not as supportive as the rest of the men that Jameson claimed me as his old lady.

Jameson says it's because Chaos was behind bars when it all happened and that he's still adjusting to being out.

But as Chaos's dark gaze narrows, I get a feeling there's more to it.

"You look beautiful, wildfire." Jameson catches me when I stop beside him, pulling me in for a kiss.

"Eww." Austin wiggles out of Jameson's lap, skulking toward Havoc to get away from us, and Jameson laughs.

He slides off his barstool and snags my hand. "Come with me for a second?"

"Okay..." Once more, that tension I've felt all morning stirs, and I wonder what they're all up to.

Jameson glances at Havoc.

"I've got him." Havoc pats Austin on the head. "We're gonna shoot some darts."

"Please be safe. Aim at the dartboard."

The guys chuckle, and I know I'm being overprotective. But I can't help it after everything that's happened.

Jameson tugs my hand, guiding me toward his room at the clubhouse. It's rare that we stay here, but sometimes, it's our getaway when Pearl offers to take Austin for the night.

"Didn't get enough of that this morning?" I smile as he guides me into the room and kicks the door shut.

"I could never get enough of you." He grabs my ass and tugs my body to his, planting a kiss on my lips. "But that's not what we're doing here."

I pull back, and that's when I take in the room around me. The shades are pulled shut to keep out the heat, but the darkness is warmed with a candlelit glow. Rose petals scatter the floor and bed.

"What is this?" My smile grows as I look around.

Jameson steps back, holding both my hands in his. "It's where we met."

"You mean where I tried to kick your ass?" I correct him, and he laughs.

"Exactly. And that's why you're my wildfire." He grins. "So, this felt fitting."

"For what?"

Jameson leans in and plants a kiss on the center of my forehead. "To ask you a question."

He looks down, and I'm lost in his gaze. In the intensity of his focus on me. It's like he hasn't taken his eyes off me since the first time we locked gazes across the bar.

My stormy ocean I'll forever be lost in.

"I was going to do this weeks ago, but with everything that happened, I wanted to make sure you knew what you were signing up for when I asked you this." Jameson cups my jaw. "I'd like to say that's the last time we'll ever see anything like we did, but I can't. And I hate it, but it's the truth. If I were smart, I'd let you go, but I'm too selfish to do that."

"I wouldn't want you to." I rest my hand on his jaw, brushing my fingers over the scruff. "Besides, that would be too simple. If you did that, you wouldn't be the man I fell in love with."

He smirks. "I don't make this easy, do I?"

"I don't need this to be easy. *Hard* I can handle if it means having this. All I need is you." I cup his jaw. "All *we* need is you."

"Good." Jameson sinks to his knee in front of me, pulling a ring out of his back pocket. "In that case, you need to know you're all I need to. You and Austin are my whole world. The air in my lungs. My heart learned to beat when I met you, and losing you would stop it. Tempe Madeline Evans, please say you'll marry me."

My hands fly to my mouth as I look down at him. Tears spring to my eyes as my fingers shake.

"You want me to marry you?"

It's one thing for him to claim me as his old lady, but this would be on paper. *Legal.* Something I know most of the guys in the club resist for that very reason.

Jameson nods. "I want you to be mine in every sense of the word. As my old lady. As my wife. I want you to be mine without question."

"Well... when the president gets on his knees, how can a girl say no?" I smile, and he kisses the back of my hand. "Of course I'll marry you, Jameson."

He stands up and pulls me in for a kiss before even placing the ring on my finger. My body melts to his. I grab his cut and hold him close.

Leather. Cinnamon.

A man strong enough to fight the beasts I had guarding my heart.

"How long can Havoc keep Austin busy?" I skate my hands down and grab onto his belt, but Jameson grabs my wrists, stopping me.

"Sorry, wildfire. We've got one more surprise."

"This is more than enough," I say, wiggling my fingers to show off the ring.

Jameson shakes his head. "This one's not for you."

I groan but don't argue as he leads me back out of the room toward the bar, where Austin and Havoc are shooting darts. Havoc is clearly winning, but Austin is smiling, not caring.

"Hey, Havoc," Jameson shouts. "I think I promised someone something if they helped me change the oil on the bike last week, didn't I?"

Havoc grins, looking from Jameson to Austin. "I think you did."

Austin's attention snaps in Jameson's direction. "A bike?"

Jameson chuckles. "Come on, big man. Let's take a trip out back."

Austin nearly runs to the back slider as Jameson follows him into the backyard.

Jameson presses a kiss to my forehead, letting go of my hand to walk over to a bike sitting in the center. It's painted black and silver, just like Jameson's motorcycle. But thankfully, this one doesn't have an engine.

"It looks fast." Austin runs circles around it, inspecting every detail. "How fast is it?"

"Guess we'll have to find out." Jameson holds it up so Austin can climb onto the seat.

His toes rest on either side, and he's grinning.

"Not too fast," I remind them, and Austin frowns.

"Don't worry, I've got him." Jameson winks at me, and it flutters to my core.

To my heart.

Because I know in my soul he's telling the truth. He's got him—he's got us. We're safe, and we're home.

Epilogue
Steel

Two Weeks Later

The desert is quiet this far away from anything. We're parked up on a hill so we can look out and watch the sunset.

Heat from the day radiates, but it's nothing like the fire Tempe lights in my chest when her fingers brush up and down my cut.

Something about this girl in leather, straddling me where she sits on the front of my bike, is a peace I never thought I'd find.

A place I never thought I'd belong.

"It's beautiful out here." Tempe sits up, her fingers grazing the skin on the back of my neck.

I've been showing her all my favorite getaway spots. Places I used to ride when I needed some peace and quiet. And now I want to mark them with her.

I push her honey-brown waves off her face, and she smiles.

"Nothing is as beautiful as you, wildfire."

She brushes her lips against mine, and my body ignites. I need this girl like I've never needed anything.

Tempe winds her legs up over my thighs, holding on tight while my feet are planted firmly on the ground. Her chest presses to mine as she runs her tongue over my lower lip.

Reaching up, I grip her throat and deepen the kiss. She sucks my tongue into her mouth, and her moan vibrates through her chest. She teases the line of my belt with her fingers, toying with me.

"Careful, Tempe." I nip at her lip. "I'm not above fucking you on this bike."

She rolls her hips against my straining cock, tempting me. "Promise?"

I skate a hand down her chest, over her stomach, and grab her cunt. "I warned you, wildfire."

Leaning in, I sink my teeth into her lower lip, and she moans.

"Jameson." She tips her head back as I kiss a path down the center of her throat.

"That's not what you call me when you're sitting on my bike, Tempe. You know better than that."

She smiles, biting her lip. "Sorry, *President*."

"Such a good girl." I grind the heel of my hand over her pussy, and she moans. "But now I'd like you to be bad and strip for me."

"Out here?" Her eyes take in the empty desert.

The sun has just dipped below the horizon, lighting her cheeks with a warm glow.

I release Tempe and sit upright on my bike, not saying anything, which is her answer.

Tempe runs her teeth over her lower lip, scanning my face, likely realizing I'm not joking, as she grips my shoulders and hops off my bike.

Her fingers find the button on her jeans, and she slowly undoes the zipper, stripping them down her beautiful legs.

I can't blink as I watch her. I can't breathe.

She loses her shoes, her pants. And when I think she'll try to stop there, she reaches for the hem of her shirt and slips it off until she's in absolutely nothing, standing like a naked goddess in the Vegas desert. So beautiful, it's possible she's a mirage, and I'm hallucinating.

"Are you going to climb off and fuck me now?" She smiles sweetly, even if we both know she's anything but.

I shake my head, reaching for my belt and undoing it. Her eyes burn as she watches me pull my cock out.

"No, but you're going to hop on and ride this."

Tempe takes my free hand as I help her back onto my bike. She's careful like she's expecting it to wobble because she's still not that familiar with motorcycles.

Her naked body slides onto the leather, but I just watch as she climbs to straddle me, not touching her. Admiring her tits as they bounce when she takes her seat.

"This is how I'd always like you riding my bike."

She pulls me close and draws her mouth to my ear. "You sure you'd be okay with your club seeing me like this?"

No fucking way. Just the thought has a growl burning in my chest.

"That's what I thought," she whispers.

I reach for her pussy and shove two fingers in. She's already slick and drenching my hand. She rolls her hips to drive my fingers deeper, her cunt squeezing me when I curl them inside her.

"You don't belong to my club, Tempe. Who do you belong to?" I roll my thumb over her clit, and her lashes flutter.

"You."

Pulling my fingers out, I lift my hand and suck them into my mouth, tasting her. I'm tempted to climb off my bike and spread her wide so I can spend all night eating her dripping pussy, but she's feeling feisty, and I'm inclined to fuck that sass out of her instead.

"Lift." I grab the base of my cock and hold it up.

The moment she lifts, I take her hip and shove her down on me. Hard enough to kick the air from her lungs. She digs her fingers into my shoulders, and the sweetest little gasp falls from her lips when I bottom out.

"Good girl." I draw my palm up between her tits, teasing one nipple and then the other.

They bead under my touch, and she grinds her hips on my cock, searching for the pressure. She writhes in my lap, framed by the sunset. Her body slides up and down, slicking across the leather seat of my bike. Her pussy grips me, and her chest rolls in waves as her body moves.

Her tits beg for my teeth, so I dip down to bite the soft flesh. Kissing the spot to soothe the pain and then teasing her nipple with my tongue.

She needs balance. Pleasure with a hint of pain and resistance. She likes the challenge.

Tempe tilts her hips, and it sends me so deep that the desert darkens around me. The earth stills.

But instead of moving, she holds there, with me buried deep inside her. Pausing, she squeezes my cock and teases me.

"What do you think you're doing?" I grab her hips.

"You mean this?" She squeezes my cock again, still not moving. "Don't like it?"

Her pussy tightens. She constricts in slow pulses that have me desperate to flip her over and pound into her.

"Are you trying to torture me, wildfire?" I grab her throat and pull her face to mine.

"Maybe."

"You won't win that game. You know that."

She narrows her eyes, staring at me while she squeezes my cock with her pussy in slow pulses. But she can only last so long because as I tighten my grip on her neck, she starts to rock with desperation.

With my free hand, I grab her hip and hold her still, stopping her.

"No moving now, Tempe. You're the one who started this."

She clenches my cock, but this time, I don't think it's on purpose.

It's the anticipation.

The fact that I've taken control away from her.

"Please." She tries to wiggle her hips, but I don't let her.

"Thought you wanted to drag this out?" I graze my mouth over her jaw, nipping at the shell of her ear. "Thought you wanted to tease me with your pussy."

"I did." Her chest heaves with every breath as I kiss the sensitive flesh behind her ear. "But I need you too badly to be patient."

"You do?" I shift my hips back just slightly, driving them in at the same time as I use my grip on her throat to pull her to me.

Her cunt soaks my cock, dripping and making a mess from her desperation.

"Yes." She moans when I do it again.

"You know better than to play games with me, wildfire. You can't win them. And do you know what happens when you're bad?" I pull back and, in a swift move, hop off my bike and spin her so she's bent over it. "You get taught a lesson."

I drive my cock in so hard her ass wiggles for me. Threading my fingers into her hair, I tug, forcing her back to arch. Her ass jiggles with every hard thrust, and I dig my fingers into it.

"You want to feel good, wildfire?" I ask her, spitting on her ass and watching it drip down her tight hole. "Are you going to obey your president?"

"Yes." She grips the bike when I skate my thumb over her ass.

I spit again before pushing in. Working her until she relaxes. The deeper my thumb drives, the louder her screams and the tighter her pussy gets. I push, and I can feel the pressure on my cock as she drips down my thighs while I claim her.

"I'm going to take this ass soon," I tell her, hitting her deeper with my cock and thumb at the same time. "You're going to beg me to."

"Yes. Please." She screams, and it's eaten up in the empty desert.

"You're so tight, Tempe." I thrust my hips forward. "So eager for my cock in every hole."

She submits to the feeling, and I'm tempted to shove my cock in her ass right now, but with how tight she is, we're going to have to work her up to it.

I tilt my hips, and her cunt grips me. She loses her scream as I pound into her harder, angling for the spot that has her legs shaking. I bottom out as she comes, pulling my release with her. Watching my wet cock slide in and out of her beautiful cunt as I paint her insides with my cum.

Only once her body stops quivering do I pull my hand away, but I stay buried where I belong inside her. I push my hips forward, forcing her pussy to take every last drop.

She glances over her shoulder, smiling at me. "What are you doing?"

"You think I've knocked you up yet?" I plant a hand on the globe of her ass.

Her pussy throbs at my question. A vice around me like the thought of it makes her beg for more of my cum.

Tempe smirks, watching me. "Not yet. But we can keep trying."

"Oh, we will." I lean down to kiss the back of her head, keeping my cock as deep inside her as it can get to make sure every drop stays in. "And I'm going to enjoy it."

***

By the time we make it home, it's dark, and dinner is ready, but I have to drop Tempe off and head to the clubhouse after Ghost texts that he needs something.

Ever since Tempe told us what the Iron Sinners' real plans were with the flash drive, he's been on edge. It's not his fault we let them into our system. I gave the order for him to hack the drive. But he still blames himself for not seeing through their plans.

At least he was paranoid enough to use a computer that wasn't hooked up to our main network when he did it. They were able to access the cloud using our Wi-Fi connection, but they couldn't hack Ghost's private server.

From what he can tell, the Iron Sinners stripped financial records and our business plans for a new strip club, but they weren't able to access bank accounts, or anything that will cause immediate damage.

It's given us time to decide how to go after Titan and his men. We're being careful knowing Rick Zane is bankrolling them, so they have access to more resources. But an attack is coming.

The war never ends; it just evolves.

My father was right about that.

Walking into the clubhouse, I see a few of the patch bunnies stocking the bar for the chapter mixer tomorrow night. We had to push back Chaos's welcome home party after the Iron Sinners took Tempe and Austin hostage, but things have finally settled enough to celebrate our brother being home.

A few of the guys are milling around as I make my way through the clubhouse. They're drinking, playing pool, and having a relaxing night. Still, I can't shake the uneasy feeling that's been stirring inside me all day.

"Everything good, Prez?" Soul yells from across the bar when he spots me. "Thought you were gone for the day."

"I was." I tip my chin up. "You seen Ghost?"

"Out back."

I walk through the clubhouse.

Something's wrong; I just can't put my finger on it.

When I step outside, I spot Ghost sitting by himself on one of the chairs at the fire pit. It's dark, and his face is only lit by the glow of his phone.

"You needed to see me?"

Ghost looks up, setting his phone in his lap and taking a sip of his beer.

He's been quieter than usual. Keeping to himself. He says it's because he's focused on rebuilding our firewalls after the Iron Sinners broke in, but I sense there's more to it.

"What's the problem?" I walk up and drop into the chair next to him.

Ghost tips his head back, closing his eyes. "Remember the coding on the flash drive? It was too complex to be Richter, and I had this feeling Titan was working with a new tech guy."

"I remember."

Between the virus they planted and the fact that they were able to wipe Reyes's real identity from every public record, we knew someone with more skill than Richter had to be involved.

Ghost looks over at me. "I figured out who it is."

"Who?" I rest my elbows on my knees, leaning forward.

He picks up his phone and flips through it. His expression is tense as he hands it over, showing me a text on the screen.

Unknown: Been a while, Ghost. Did you think I'd forget about Albuquerque? Or about the girl? I warned you not to go digging. You should have listened.

My eyebrows pinch as I try to piece together what I'm reading. The club stopped running product through Albuquerque a little over a year ago when things went south with the Merciless Skulls. What started as a misunderstanding turned into a war we quickly squashed because the club was so small. Any remaining members fled or joined other clubs. But there weren't enough to keep track of them.

We haven't been back since.

I look up at Ghost. "Who's the girl they're talking about?"

Ghost looks over his shoulder through the glass doors that lead into the clubhouse. His gaze sets on Luna, who's sitting reading a book, and realization hits me like a ton of bricks.

One year ago.

Albuquerque.

Merciless Skulls trophies aren't the only thing we brought back.

"You said she was living out of a car on campus. You brought her in. You vouched for her." I grit my teeth. "Where did you really meet Luna?"

He glances back at me, not answering my question. He doesn't need to. I already know I'm not going to like whatever he has to say.

Ghost lied to his club—lied to me. And we're all about to pay for it.

Extended Epilogue
Tempe

Two Years Later

My fist lands on the punching bag, and the beam creaks as it swings. It's early in the day, so the sun is just now peeking over the horizon, but the gym is already warming up.

I grab the bag and slow its swing, steadying it as I catch my breath.

"Tempe!" Austin calls my name from the barn door, and I turn to see him bolting toward me.

Jameson's following him into the barn, grinning, with Ember on his hip. She's wearing my favorite sunflower jumper and is tugging at his patch like she thinks she can peel it off his cut.

"There you are." Jameson winks at me as Austin grabs onto my leg. "The kids were looking for you."

"*The kids* were looking for me, or you were?"

He pulls me in when he reaches me and kisses me on the forehead. "All three of us."

"I'm sweaty," I say as I pull back.

But Jameson just shrugs. "I like you all sweaty."

I roll my eyes, and luckily, the kids are still too young to notice the innuendo. "I know you do. But this is a different kind of sweaty."

The way his eyes light up when he drags his gaze over me says he doesn't see the difference.

Jameson can barely keep his hands off me, and it gets worse when I'm pregnant. He says there's something about knowing I'm growing our family that makes me impossible to resist.

"I thought the doctor said to take it easy." He plants his hand on my stomach, holding it over the bump that is still barely showing.

"The doctor said to take it easy with this wild little girl." I tickle Ember, and she giggles, clutching onto Jameson. "She said nothing about this pregnancy. Everything's been fine so far, and it's going to stay that way."

Jameson frowns.

"I promise the second I'm told to sit still, I will. But I'll go stir-crazy if I slow down this early. So let me have this as long as I can."

"Don't worry, Tempe's tough. She's got it." Austin smiles up at Jameson. "Come here, little spark."

Austin calls Ember by the nickname Jameson gave her, and Jameson sets her down. They clutch hands, and

Austin guides her over to the large mat in the center of the room, teaching her how to roll around on it.

She giggles at Austin every time he flips over.

"Just promise me you'll take care of yourself." Jameson spins me so I'm standing with my back to his chest, and he wraps his arms around me, caressing my stomach.

"I promise."

Jameson plants a soft kiss on the side of my head. "You done working out yet?"

"Why? Do you need me to take the kids? They're good here if the guys need you for something."

"Nah, not that. Soul has things under control today. I was hoping to take you, actually."

"Me?" I glance up over my shoulder at him, biting my lip. "What did you have in mind?"

"A ride. Some alone time." He pulls my ass to his body.

"Alone time, huh?"

"Mm-hmm." He peppers kisses down my neck. "Grandma's gonna watch the kids for us."

"Can I shower first?"

He brings his mouth to my ear. "We're just gonna get dirty again."

"Still." I spin in his arms, wrapping mine over his shoulders. "I'd rather be clean so when I get dirty, it's all because of you."

Jameson's smirk grows. "Can't argue with that."

Giggling comes from over my shoulder, and I turn to see Ember tackling Austin. He says he's teaching her how to be a superhero, and right now, they're reenacting one of his favorite scenes as he pretends to be the villain, and she takes him down.

While Austin is more like Jameson—careful and patient. Ember is wild and feisty like me.

"We got lucky." I smile, watching the kids.

"I got lucky." Jameson turns my chin so I'm facing him, planting a kiss on my lips. "I'm still not sure what I did right to get all this. I'm so amazed by you, wildfire. The things you've given me. The love you share. What did I do to deserve you?"

"You did everything, Jameson. You take care of us. You protect us. We aren't a family without you."

I kiss him—claim him.

I hand my heart over to him, and he does the same.

For as much doubt as I had when we started, Jameson has proved his unwavering loyalty every single day. His devotion knows no bounds, and I can't imagine my life without him.

Jameson angles my face to kiss me deeper, and I melt into it. I sink against this man who is endless for me. Who is everything for our children. Who built this club and our family with the entirety of his heart.

And when he pulls back and looks down at me, I wouldn't want to live my life any other way.

"Time to drop the kids off so we don't scar them for life," he says. "I've only got so much patience when it comes to you."

Ember squeals from behind us, catching our attention before I can respond. And when I turn, I see she pinned

Austin to the mat. There are five years between them, so he could win, but he's being a good brother to her.

"Save me." Austin laughs, looking at Jameson.

Jameson kisses me on the top of the head. "Looks like I've got a battle to fight first."

He grins, winking at me as he makes his way over to the kids.

Sweeping Ember up off Austin, she giggles as Jameson swoops her through the air like she's flying.

Jameson might have once thought there was only one role meant for him—president. But seeing him with Austin and Ember, I know that doesn't come close to the role he was born to hold. Because as a father, he's more fearless than I've ever seen him.

He protects our family. But more importantly, he nurtures it.

Whoever he is for his club, he's more than that for his children.

For me.

He took in me and my brother without hesitation, and he loves us regardless of the blood running through our veins. We've built a home. An unbreakable safe space. And that's all that matters.

Jameson rolls over, and Austin and Ember tackle him at the same time. He pulls them in for a bear hug, and they all laugh.

Placing my hand on my stomach, I know that soon, there will be another one added to the pile, and my heart warms at that thought.

I didn't know if I would ever truly experience what it means to have a family. And anything I imagined paled in comparison to this.

Jameson gave me more than a home. He gave me love. He gave me life. And as he tips his head back and meets my gaze, with our family climbing all over him, my chest expands.

It's everything I could have wished for and more. All because I found him.

Acknowledgements

Thank you for reading Jameson and Tempe's story. These two stormed into my heart and broke it into a million pieces before putting it back together. I still get choked up when I read certain scenes with Austin. This was my first "parent" romance of any kind, and I didn't realize how much I would love that trope until I wrote it.

I hope you enjoyed reading their story as much as I enjoyed writing it.

To my readers, I'm so excited to start a new series with you. The love and excitement you show my books means everything to me. I couldn't do this without you. Thank you for following me down the many paths I've taken on this journey. You are the best!

Chris, thank you for being my sounding board when I'm struggling with a plot hole. For believing in me during the tough times and supporting me always. I love sharing this life with you!

My boys, I love you with my whole heart. Watching you grow up will forever be my greatest blessing.

Mikki, I don't know how I'd survive this roller coaster without you. Thank you for the long, silent facetime calls where we just sit and work, keeping each other company. Thank you for always putting things in perspective. And thank you for being the most amazing sister.

Mom, I'm never going to let you live down the first time you saw this book cover. Thank you for confirming I made the right call in changing everything. Thank you for always being the most supportive and incredible mother. I love you.

Alba, thank you for an incredible friendship. You have the biggest heart, and I'm thankful for every moment we've had together.

Sam, you always say what I need to hear, whether I want to hear it or not. In this case, it was much needed. I appreciate that you always push me to do the story justice.

Kat, I can't believe we're working on yet another series together. It's a blessing that I found you when I did. I can't imagine this journey without you.

Vanessa, thank you for always making me smile. Your messages and comments while you edit breathe life back into me when I am feeling worn out and done with a book.

Maggie, your messages kept me going on this one. Thank you for listening when I just need to vent. And for being there to cheer on every little accomplishment. I'm so thankful for our friendship. This is a lonely profession sometimes, and I am so grateful for you.

To my ARC Team, thank you for being on this journey with me as we enter my MC romance era. I appreciate you shouting about my books from the rooftops and showering them in love. It fills my heart up.

Books By Eva Simmons

Seattle Singles

Match Make Him (*Matchmaker meets Billionaire*)

Write Him Off (*Second Chance, Friends to Lovers*)

His Daring Vow (*Enemies to Lovers, Fake Relationship*)

Enemy Muse (Rock Star Romance)

Heart Break Her (*Celebrity Crush*)

Forever and Ever (*Opposites Attract*)

Heart of a Rebel (*Second Chance*)

Worth the Trouble (*Forbidden Love*)

Twisted Roses (Dark, Taboo Romance)

Lies Like Love (*Stepsiblings*)

Heart Sick Hate (*Boyfriend's Brother*)

Cold Hard Truth (*Her father's enforcer*)

Word to the Wise (*Her brother's apprentice*)

Twisted Kings (Dark MC Romance)

Steel (*MC President and his traitor's daughter*)

Ghost (*MC Tech Genius, Gamer Girl with Secrets*)

Reckless (Kinky, Dark, Billionaire Romance)

Reckless Games (*Hot, Holiday with a Billionaire*)

Reckless Promises (*Mafia heir, forced marriage*)

Reckless Possession *(Ex-Boyfriend's Father and his friends)*

Sigma Sin (Dark College Romance)

Saint *(Stalker)*

Eternal

About Eva Simmons

Eva Simmons writes dark and dreamy romance with complex heroines and morally twisted bad boys who fall hard for them.

When Eva isn't dreaming up new worlds or devouring every book she can get her hands on, she can be found spending time with her family, painting a fresh canvas, or playing an elf in World of Warcraft.

Eva is currently living out her own happily ever after in Nevada with her family.

Printed in Great Britain
by Amazon